Z-BURBIA

JAKE BIBLE

Foreword

Zombies, man. Zombies.

What can I say? I dig them. I've written many different types of zombies stories from military scifi in the Apex Trilogy (zombies in mechs!) to religious satire in Bethany and the Zombie Jesus (satire, yes, but not blasphemous) to young adult different in Little Dead Man (conjoined twins where one is alive and one is undead). But the Z-Burbia series is my first time tackling straight up, Romero-esque zombie fiction. And I had a blast doing it!

As many of you zombie aficionados know, Romero was all about the social satire. So I figured why not go all out and make my setting a suburban subdivision? I had one hell of a good time taking my own personal experiences in a subdivision and adding in some undead and post-apocalyptic flavor. I hope y'all like the result.

I do have plans to keep this series going so I'm looking forward to the feedback from my fans and readers. This series will have plenty of gore and violence, but also plenty of tongue in cheek humor. I think y'all will like the balance I strike between those.

And just a big thanks to all you zombie lovers out there! You're why I write this crazy stuff!

Cheers,
Jake

CHAPTER ONE

People that move to a subdivision do so for only a couple of reasons. Ours were price and location. Great price for the size of the house and great location since it was just on the edge of Asheville, NC, down by the French Broad River. Once the dead began to walk the earth, the price didn't matter so much anymore. It was all about location.

The Blue Ridge Mountains are part of the Appalachian Mountain range, a range that stretches from Georgia up to Maine. Our neck of the range is in Western North Carolina, specifically Asheville, known as the Paris of the South because of its eclectic mix of arts, music, and vacation possibilities. A long time destination for those that think outside the box, Asheville is surrounded by hollows (hollers), coves, gaps, and valleys, filled with generations of hard working North Carolinians that, while free thinking and independent, aren't known for their outside the boxedness. Conservative through and through, most are used to making it on their own in the best of times. Come the apocalypse? That conservative pragmatism kicks into overdrive and sure comes in handy.

This makes for an interesting dynamic in the region. You see, when the dead began to rise from their graves, morgues, funeral homes, and other places, urban dead are supposed to stay dead, they pretty nearly wiped out the progressive, freethinking population of Asheville. Well, wiped out the living population; the undead population is growing and thriving. Let's hear it for undead progress! This left a few urban survivor pockets (Whispering Pines being one), surrounded not only by a sea of undead, but by

1

multiple groups, families, factions of rural survivor pockets hell bent on getting, taking, and scavenging what they can from the ruins of Asheville.

Good times for all.

So, I stand in front of my bathroom mirror, razor in hand, wondering what will become of my family, as I hear a stray gunshot here and there from outside our two-story, 2700 square feet, cookie cutter house. The image in the mirror is of a forty-year old man, blond-red beard, soon to be bald head (okay, *balder* head since growing hair hasn't been my forte for years), six feet, 200 pounds, exhausted, and semi-malnourished. Yeah, I'm a peach.

Another gunshot goes off and I set the razor down. Normally, I'd yell from the bathroom at the kids to find out what is going on, but that was pre-Z (pre-zombies). In today's world, you keep your mouth shut and stay quiet. Noise attracts the undead. We take the whispering part of Whispering Pines, very seriously nowadays.

So I'm a little more than alarmed as to why I hear gunshots. Guns are noisy. We're an arrows, spears, slingshots, and other quiet projectiles kind of subdivision. This was signed into the covenants by the HOA (Home Owners' Association) Board and ratified at one of our first post-Z HOA meetings.

"Jace?" Stella asks from the bedroom door. "Have you heard anything?"

Stella Stanford, my beautiful wife and mother of my two children (boy: Charlie, sixteen, and girl: Greta, thirteen), the rock that I rely on, and asker of the obvious.

"You mean other than the gunshots?" I ask as I grab a shirt and pull it on before coming out of the bathroom.

"Don't be an asshole," Stella says. "Have you heard anything over the Wi-Fi?"

Wi-Fi, you ask? Oh, we have it. No internet, since the apocalypse ruined that, but local Wi-Fi which helps us all stay in touch in the neighborhood.

"I haven't checked my messages," I reply. "Hand me my phone."

Stella crosses her arms and gives me a stern look.

"Please?" I ask. "Sorry for being an asshole."

She hands me my phone and I see a text from Jon Billings, my best friend in the neighborhood and Head of Construction. Jon is one of the few people I truly trust in Whispering Pines. Everyone else we watch with caution and keep at a friendly distance. Makes it easier to shove a crowbar through their heads if you don't get too attached.

"Bums down by the gate," the text reads. "You coming? You know Brenda is going to want you there. I'm sure she'll pick apart any 'weaknesses' she sees in the gate."

"Who's shooting?" I text back.

"The bums," his reply comes quickly. "Where the fuck are you, Hoss? Get your butt down here. Brenda is already trying to redesign the entire gate structure. Jesus…"

Jon is also a minister which cracks me up when he texts. He saves all his cursing for texts to me. No one has a clue, otherwise.

"On my way," I text back.

"Bums," I say to Stella. "I need to bike down ASAP."

"Brenda?"

"Yep. Brenda," I nod as I grab my socks and hurry to the garage. I throw on my sturdy, steel-toed work boots and snag my mountain bike.

I barely wave at the inquiring faces of my neighbors as I speed by, focusing on the twists and turns, dips and rises of the neighborhood. I race down the last hill towards the gate that is set at the entrance to Whispering Pines, blocking all access to the neighborhood from the former State Road Hwy 251. I say "former" because there really isn't a "state" anymore, and I'm pretty sure the DoT has lost its jurisdiction during the apocalypse. Or maybe not. They could be planning to re-paint the yellow lines next week for all we know.

"There you are, Hoss," Jon says as I brake to a stop by him. "Brenda thinks we need more spikes on the outside, because spikes are apparently a deterrent to starving bums."

"Jesus," I mutter.

"Hey, Lord's name and all that?" Jon smiles.

"Smart ass," I smile as I walk past him to the watchtower sitting to the side of the fifty-foot gate.

"I am sorry for your situation, folks," Brenda says, trying to whisper and shout at the same time which comes out as some grotesque croak. "But Whispering Pines is a gated community and we are not taking new residents at this time. You will need to move along please. Again, I am sorr-."

Whomever she's talking to replies with a pistol shot. Splinters of wood explode from the post next to Brenda's face.

"Where is Stuart?" Brenda hisses. "These bums need to be dealt with!"

Bums are what we call the stragglers that come knocking on our quite impressive (if I do say so myself) gate doors. Survivors that have somehow managed to stay alive while avoiding the Zs and the not so friendly groups of people out there. We've been seeing less and less over the months, but they do show up. It isn't hard for them to spot a beacon of living in the darkness of the world around them.

James, "Don't Call Me Jimmy", Stuart, is suddenly at my elbow, looking up at the watchtower with his usual look of pissed off and slightly surprised that everyone else isn't as pissed off as he is. Five feet and eight inches, late fifties, tight crew cut, wiry and strong, Stuart is a retired Marine Gunnery Sergeant. Head of Defenses (not to be confused with Head of Security, God forbid!) he sees anyone without the proper training and understanding of military tactics as a pain in his well-trained and tactical ass. Pretty much that means all of us.

"Gates are holding," Stuart says without looking at me. "What's she bitching about then?"

Stuart likes to end questions in "then" sometimes. It's a strange affectation, but since he can kick the living shit out of me with his perfectly trimmed mustache, I don't question it.

"Bums," I say.

"Bums," Jon echoes.

"Padre," Stuart nods to Jon.

"Yes, my son?" Jon smiles. Stuart doesn't smile back. "Right. Hey."

Stuart sighs with amazing discipline and skill and climbs the ladder into the watchtower. We follow. Once up there, he takes a key ring from his belt and unlocks the steel locker bolted to the watchtower floor.

"How many then?" Stuart asks as his hand hovers over the open locker.

"Eight," a mousy man answers, looking from Brenda to Stuart to me to Jon and back to Stuart. "Three adults and five kids. Look like they've been running nonstop. Didn't think much of them until they started shooting."

"Let us in!" a dry voice cries from below. "Please!"

"Kids?" Stuart asks, his eyes finding Brenda's as he pulls an AR-15 and magazine from the locker. He slaps the magazine home and stares.

Brenda Kelly is our HOA Board Chairperson. Short, fat, ugly as sin, she took control of Whispering Pines in the first few days of the apocalypse, giving some semblance of order in a world that went from normal to "HOLY SHIT I'M GOING TO GET MY FACE EATEN!" in less than twenty-four hours. Despite her lack of everything that makes a human being decent, she does make one damn good administrator. Once you get past that lack of human decency part. That's a tough one to get past, believe me.

"We don't have room or resources," Brenda states, her whisper like the hiss of a hidden viper. "You know that, Stuart. Resolution 856 was very clear on the subject of no new residents allowed. You were there for the vote, Stuart. Do I have to get---"

"Shut up," Stuart says. "I know the resolution. Just wanted to be clear before I do my job."

There are two sentries posted to the watchtower at all times, but they defer to Stuart when it comes to discretionary violence. Stuart is very clear on this point: no one kills the living except him, unless they are defending themselves. I have wondered more than a few times how many people Stuart has killed in his years as a Marine. I've personally witnessed him kill no less than fourteen souls since the apocalypse started. I can't even count how many Zs he's killed.

On that subject, let me explain that the Zs we are talking about are your classic, shuffling, shoot the brain, zombies. The freshly turned ones have some more mobility than the veteran undead, but really can only break out into a half-run at the best. Kind of like a power-walking grandma at the mall. They can be outrun. But, as always, it's about numbers. And the Zs out number our asses by an easy twenty to one. Okay, okay, I'm being delusional. They outnumber us by fifty to one. I just hate admitting that. What? Fine, fine, 100-200 to one. Sheesh.

"Hello, folks," Stuart says as he peers over the watchtower. "I am sorry to be rude, but it has been decided that we cannot take on more residents. I am going to ask you to leave. Please comply. Non-compliance is not an option."

"Fuck you!" a man shouts. "Let us in, old man! We have kids here! We're fucking starving! Stop being assholes!"

Stuart sighs and puts the rifle to his shoulder. "I am not going to warn you again, sir. I am sorry, but you have to leave now. All that noise you are making is bringing the Zs your way. We try to avoid that."

I risk a look and see that Stuart is right, as all of us had expected. From both ways of Hwy 251, the undead are shambling their way towards the small group of bums. If Stuart doesn't take the people out, then the Zs are going to. None look too fresh, which means about a three feet a minute shamble rate. Ten minutes before they're on the bums.

"Is that our old mailman down there with the Zs?" Jon asks, peeking over with me. "Guess I won't have to get him a Christmas present this year."

"For a man of God, you sure are a callous bastard," I whisper to him. He just shrugs.

"Shut. The. Fuck. Up," Stuart grumbles.

"Sorry," I say. Jon just shrugs again.

A gunshot goes off and we all, except for Stuart, hit the floor of the watchtower. I count three shots as Stuart returns fire. Jon and I glance up at him and see he is looking over his shoulder at Brenda. She nods. Five more shots.

"Those were the kids," Jon says as he gets up and walks to the ladder. "Children."

He doesn't make eye contact with anyone as he descends and grabs his own bike, pedaling off up the hill back to his house.

"Brenda," I say, looking directly at her, "really?"

"How will we feed them?" she asks. "This has already been decided."

"Gonna need to clear the road," Stuart says as he hands the rifle to one of the sentries. "Clean that and store it. I'll be back to check to make sure it's cleaned properly. One speck of dirt and you're outside the gate."

The sentry nods, his hands shaking as he takes the rifle.

Stuart looks to me as he takes his phone from his pocket and starts to send the text for his defensive crew. "You in for some Z killing?"

"I guess," I shrug. "I'm already down here."

Back home I have a great baseball bat that I've stuck spikes through and wrapped in duct tape. I call it the Silver Slugger. Stupid name, I know. But I left that in my hurry to the gate, so once down on the ground, I arm myself with a crowbar taken from one of the huge racks of melee weapons that line each side of the gate.

Stuart and I wait only a minute before his defensive crew is there, armed with their own weapons of various sizes and styles. Axes, steel pipes, more crowbars, sharpened to a point baseball bats, even a sharpened cricket bat and a couple of hockey sticks. The crew keeps changing, but their objective never does: keep the road and perimeter clear of Zs so they cannot ever overwhelm Whispering Pines. It's a full time job.

We all silently nod to each other and wait for Stuart's signal. The man stands by the gate and listens, then, almost imperceptibly, nods. The gate is unlatched, unlocked, unbarred, and unbraced, and the right door is shoved open just enough so we can slip through. As soon as we are out, it closes behind us and will not be opened until we are done clearing the road and have checked for bites. A bite is death, for the bitten and possibly for the entire neighborhood. Can't have that.

I count at least thirty Zs coming at us. Most heard the gate open (a part of the engineering I'm still working on; the damn thing is so heavy it's near impossible to keep the hinges quiet) and are shambly shambling their way at us. Stuart points with four fingers at the four members of the crew to his left and they head left, straight at the Zs. He points four fingers at the four members

7

to his right and they move out. Just him and me are going at the Zs directly in front of us.

I get in close to the first one so I can shove my crow bar through its eye and into its brain. I place a foot against the Z's chest and push, freeing the crow bar and sending the now really dead zombie into the group behind it, tangling them up in oozing, undead limbs. Stuart is right with me, using the same move, since he's the one that taught it to me.

Stuart's philosophy on killing Zs is to go through the eye whenever you can. It's an easy and direct route to the brain. If we were using bullets, it would be where we'd aim, so if you have a weapon that can affect the same result, then use it. Plus, cracking skulls not only will tire you out as you raise your arms over your head again and again, but it makes noise. I think we've already covered that noise is bad.

Stab, stab, stab we go, making our way through the throng of Zs. But, as is the zombie way, more keep coming from both directions. Luckily, directly in front of us, about twenty yards away, is the bank of the French Broad River. We don't have to worry about more Zs coming from that way. And Whispering Pines is behind us, so we're good there. That just means we watch our left and right. Stuart splits left, I split right. More stabby stabby.

A half an hour into the slaughter, Stuart raises a fist over his head and whistles quietly. The gate opens again and a new wave of Z killers comes out as our crew retreats up against the gate. We check each other out, making sure we have no bites, and then are let back inside Whispering Pines as the second crew starts its shift of stabbing.

I collapse on a patch of grass by the watchtower, as Stuart takes a seat next to me. He hands me a canteen and I take a couple of long drinks.

"Thanks," I say, handing it back.

Stuart just nods and we sit quietly as a third crew assembles and waits for their turn. The gate opens, they stream out, a few minutes go by and the second crew comes in, dripping with sweat and gore. Stuart does a quick count and nods as he sees the whole crew there.

Then a scream goes up.

"Shit," Stuart says and all eyes fall on him. "Sorry, folks. No more rest. Time to go out in full force."

We all know what that scream is, someone got careless, or were surprised, and ended up taking some Z teeth to their flesh. We all wear long-sleeves and many have leather on, but even still, a hungry Z is a formidable biter. Their jaw strength seems to increase once they rise from the dead, which makes no physiological sense, but is still a reality in this surreal world.

We all pour from the gate and get to work. We have to be fast because a scream and the smell of fresh blood can carry on the wind for a mile. Did I mention that a Z's hearing and sense of smell increases too? Yeah, they do. It's scary as shit. So the key is to wipe out the Zs and get the unfortunate wounded taken care of before we end up with a mob, or a horde, or the dreaded stampeding (a shambling stampede, given) herd of Zs at our gate.

Someone drags the wounded woman inside the gate while crews one, two, and three, move fast through the Zs left. Ten minutes and we're done, leaving the rotten corpses to the ever efficient Edna Strom and her Z cleanup crews.

"Inside and strip down," Stuart orders and we all follow, as we catch our breaths and begin to undress once inside the safety of the gate. "Double and triple checks, people."

We go through the motions of inspecting each other's naked bodies. No modesty is allowed in the apocalypse. You have to be cleared by three people before you get the okay to grab your clothes and make your way home. It's a noble walk of shame, but still pretty shameful, as your nether regions are on full display for the neighborhood to see.

"Looking good, Dad," Charlie says as he comes jogging up to me. "You really should work on your ass tan. No one wants to see those white buns."

"Thanks, bud," I smile. "Way to make your old man feel good about himself."

Charlie leans in. "Mom's pissed. Just a heads up. She didn't think you were going outside the gate."

"The heads up redeems the previous comment," I say. "We are square."

"We can never be square as long as you use the word square," Charlie says, and sprints off towards our house a couple blocks away.

I look and see Greta laughing and pointing at me. Nice kids I have. My wife, however, is not laughing. She is pointing. Pointing daggers at me with her eyes.

I get home, toss the soiled clothes in the "decon" hamper (unless they are really soiled, then it's incinerator time), and grab a shower. Stella is waiting for me when I step from the shower stall.

"Hey, hon," I grin, which instantly slips from my face as I see the look on hers.

"We've talked about this," she says.

"I know, but I had no choice," I reply. "The amount of Zs coming had to be handled. Plus…"

"Plus, what?"

"Plus, I needed to blow off some steam," I say quietly. "Stuart took out eight bums. Five were children."

Stella's hand goes to her mouth and her eyes tear up. "Children?" she chokes. "He did that on his own?"

I shake my head.

"Who gave the order?" she asks when she doesn't need to. Her eyes narrow and her face goes red with fury. "That woman. That crazy bitch. One day, Jace, I'm going to give her what she deserves. I promise you that."

"I know, I know," I say. "She's evil. Kept throwing the last resolution in Stuart's face."

"He didn't have to kill them!" Stella nearly shouts then quiets down, not wanting our kids to hear. "He could have stood up to her."

"He could have, but he didn't. Stuart is a good soldier. He follows the orders of the person in charge. Like it or not, Brenda is in charge. At least until the next election of HOA Board members."

"Which is months away," Stella growls.

"Let it go," I say. "It'll just eat you up. I'm compartmentalizing today in that little black hole in the back of my brain. I'm not going to think about it again until I'm seventy and senile."

Even I know this is bullshit, but it's one of the many lies I tell myself to get through each day.

"How was your day, dear?" I grin as I towel off and get dressed. "Learn them childrens good?"

Stella, having been a schoolteacher for fifteen years pre-Z, has the honor of teaching all eighteen of the school age kids in the neighborhood. She has the dishonor of teaching them in two rooms that we "borrow" from the Church of Jesus of the Light (CJL). Yep, there is a church in our fair neighborhood. But, and this is a huge but, it is not part of Whispering Pines. The first developer for the subdivision actually purchased all the land around this church for a decent price, promising to give right of way to the church in perpetuity. Then the developer went bankrupt. The developer that built all the houses, and truly made Whispering Pines, got the land for a steal, but no matter how hard they tried, they couldn't get rid of the CJL.

That wouldn't have been so bad if the CJL wasn't run by an ancient preacher that honestly believed we were all being punished for our sins by God. And, of course, the Zs were the righteous punishment. He was keen on pointing this out to everyone within earshot at least fifty times a day. Poor Stella had to deal with him all day long. She kept him away from the kids, but it was as much work as teaching was.

"I punched Preacher Carrey," Stella says.

"Shit! You did?"

"No, of course not," she frowns. "But it did come close. I had his ass backed up against a wall and if your son hadn't intervened, I think I would have done worse than punch him."

"And why did you have his ass backed up against a wall?"

"Because he stuck his head in to the younger kids' room and said, and I am quoting verbatim, that each of them 'were going to hell for what their parents were doing at the gate. Good luck burning in the pits, you miserable bastards.' He said that. To kids as young as five, Jace. The man is evil."

"A lot of people are evil in your book," I say. "You may need a new description."

"There's a lot of evil around these days," she glares, "or haven't you noticed?"

"I have," I say.

"Dad!" Charlie calls from downstairs. "Someone's at the door for you!"

"Someone?" I ask. "He knows everyone in the whole neighborhood. He also knows not to yell."

"Be nice," Stella says, "he was my hero today."

"I'll be nice," I reply as I hurry downstairs, "don't worry."

"I am hardly just someone," Mindy Sterling says from my front door.

A woman in her mid-thirties, fat, but not all jiggly fat, strong, but not muscular, Mindy is head of Neighborhood Security. This is like neighborhood watch and the police rolled into one dysfunctional unit. She used to be part of Zenith Property Management, which was the company that oversaw all the enforcement of the HOA covenants for the developer and the HOA. Lucky for us, she was in the neighborhood when Z-Day came a calling. We've been stuck with her ever since. Needless to say, Mindy answers to the HOA Board, which answers to Brenda, which means Mindy is Brenda's bitch. And she actually likes it that way. She doesn't have to think, gets to bully folks around, and pretends she is indispensible. Basically the same job as she had before, but with more death and zombies.

"You left your bike down by the gate," Mindy says, pointing to my bike in the front lawn. "I brought it up for you. You know it's against the covenants of the HOA to leave personal items just lying around. I will give you a warning today, Jace, but next time, I confiscate that bike."

I blink at her a few times and then shake my head. "Uh, thanks?"

"And tell your son to address me as Ms. Sterling when I come to your door," Mindy says as she walks away. "Calling me, 'someone', is disrespectful. I have made note of that."

"Good for you, Mindy," I call after her. "We'd hate for things to get disrespectful in the apocalypse!"

She ignores me, which is really for the best.

My phone buzzes and I see a text from Jon.

"I don't know what Mrs. Hoss did today, but I have Brenda up my ass to come talk to my 'Brother Of God', whatever the fuck that means, and calm him down. He's at her house raving like a mad man and wants your wife brought up on charges."

"Sorry about that," I reply. "Want me to come with her?"

"I want your wife to come with you, so we can sort this out," Jon texts. "And I want everyone to remember that I'm Head of Construction. I gave up my ministering days long before Z-Day. Why doesn't everyone get that?"

"Because of the halo and choir of angels that follow your sorry ass around," I respond. "Tell Brenda you are on your way, but swing by here first. Okay?"

"Sure. Fine. Whatever. Suck my holy dick."

"Your dick only has one hole," I joke.

"At least I have a dick, dick. Now stop texting me. I can't text and walk at the same time. Plus, I'm pretty sure that's illegal and against the HOA covenants. Don't want to get pulled over by Herr Mindy. I can't outrun those Reeboks she got at the last swap meet."

"See ya in a minute."

"I said to stop texting me, so stop! Shit! Are those shoe sirens? Crap, she's coming to get me, Hoss! Police brutality! Police brutality!"

By the time we stopped texting, he was at my front door.

"Hold on," he says, holding up a hand as he types into his phone.

"Eat shit and die," the text says on my phone.

"Okay, all done," he grins. "Where's Stella?"

"Right here, Jon," she says as she comes around the corner. She hugs him and gives a big kiss on his cheek. "Come on in. Jace made sun tea yesterday. Want a glass?"

"I sure would," he smiles. "But let's make it to go. We're going to Brenda's to undo whatever it is you done did."

Stella frowns. Jon frowns. Both look at me.

"You didn't tell her?" Jon asks.

"I thought I'd let you do it," I say, "she likes you better."

"Right now I do," Stella says. "And I'm not going anywhere near that man. Not unless it's to put him down, finally"

"Stella, darling," Jon starts.

"Don't darling me," Stella says. "I don't even let Jace darling me. The answer is no."

"Do I have to say it?" Jon asks. "Do I?" He can see from the look on Stella's face that he does. "The well is on CJL property. If we piss off Carrey, then he cuts off our water. Gone. Dry. No water for houses, no water for crops, no water for anything."

"Then we shut off his power," Stella says, crossing her arms. "Right, Jace? He stops our water, and we cut the power line to the CJL. We own all of the wind turbines and solar arrays."

"People can live without power," Jon says, "they can't live without water."

"The river is just across the road down there," Stella says. "We can get water from there."

"Not clean water, hon," I say, knowing I'm digging my own grave. "The French Broad is contaminated as shit. Literally. The sewage processing plant upstream has been leaking for months since the fail safes started to give out. Pretty soon, it'll just be a river of shit and piss. We need the well."

"Et tu, Jason?" she says.

I give her a weak smile and look at Jon.

"Just three seconds of ass kissing will save us all," Jon says. "You'll be a suck up hero. I'll make sure the whole neighborhood knows it."

Stella grumbles a minute and then calls over her shoulder, "I have to go fight a dragon, kids. Be back with your father soon."

"Okay," they both yell.

Jon and I wince.

"Quiet down," Jon says.

"Mindy was just in the area," I explain. "She's looking for a reason to bust me. Your yelling is a perfect reason."

"Fine, whatever," Stella says as she closes the front door. "Why's your bike in the front yard?"

"It followed me home and then collapsed there," I say.

"Smart ass."

The walk is pleasant, as it has become a nice late summer evening. The sun is still up, but the air has turned and a hint of fall wafts by. We only have to walk a couple blocks before we get to Brenda's house. We can all hear Preacher Carrey bellowing inside.

"Jesus, what did you do?" Jon whispers.

"I let him live," Stella says and barges inside without knocking.

I shrug. Jon shrugs. We follow.

The scene before us is one of wild chaos. It's as if a carnival barker had decided never to wash his clothes, himself, or anything he lived in/on/near. Then, for good measure, decided to take a bath in Old Spice. Preacher Carrey paced in front of us, his hands gesticulating, his wispy white hair standing on end, and his eyes rolling in his head over and over and over and-

"There she is!" Carrey shouts. "The harpy of the dell!"

"Is that an official title?" I ask.

"Don't remember that being in the scripture," Jon says, "and I think I've read it all."

"It's in the unabridged version," I reply.

"Oh, I just have the Cliff's Notes version, skips all the begats and gets right to the sodomy and rape," Jon smiles.

"You...you!" Carrey says, his finger leading the accusatory way across the room at Stella.

I instinctively get in front of her, but Carrey leans around me, reaching with that finger, as if he could burn her at the stake with its touch.

"You are not welcome in my house!" Carrey shouts. We all wince at the noise.

"I thought it was God's house?" Stella asks calmly. Too calm. I know that calm. Not a good calm. I wish I could get away from that calm, but, too late for that.

"You dare blaspheme?" Carrey snarls.

"How exactly am I blaspheming?" Stella smiles. A calm smile. Yikes! "Please, do tell, Preacher. How have I blasphemed?"

"Your unclean presence is blasphemy enough!" he screeches.

"That's not a reason," Stella says, and then looks at Brenda. "Are we done here? He's just going to keep saying that. We've all been here before."

"I call an embargo on your water!" Preacher Carrey yells, his hands above his head, his eyes doing that rolling, rolling, rolling thing.

"Preacher, please," Brenda pleads. "Be reasonable. There are children and elderly to think of."

"Then you should have thought of them before you took up with this lot!" Carrey yells, his arms sweeping towards us.

"Lot?" Jon smirks. "I think you have your parables mixed up, Mr. Carrey."

"You do not lecture me in the ways of God!"

"Wouldn't think of it," Jon replies. "Pretty sure God will sit you down and lecture you on his own, in his time."

"Embargo! EMBARGO!" Carrey leaves.

"Who runs Bartertown?" I whisper. Jon tries not to laugh, but ends up snorting snot out his nose.

"Oh, my God, you two," Stella scolds. "You're worse than the kids."

"People, people!" Brenda cries. "We need to resolve this!"

"Fine," Stella says and clocks Carrey. The man drops to the floor, his mouth bloody and his eyes wide with surprise. She closes on him, shoving me out of the way. "No embargo or I gut you myself, you sanctimonious asshole. I will hunt you down and kill you no matter where you run to. You leave my family alone, you leave the children alone, and I let you live. Cross me again, and I string you up by your balls, and then lower you to the Zs on the other side of the gate."

Carrey stares at her for what feels like several minutes, but is only a few seconds.

"Okay," he says quietly and gets up. "Okay. God will have your reward waiting for you in the afterlife. I have done what I can."

"Uh, so no embargo?" Brenda asks.

"No," Carrey says and leaves.

"Well, that couldn't have gone any better," Jon says. "Can we go now?"

"No," Brenda says, looking at me and then at Jon. "Stella can, now that's taken care of, but not you two."

"Good," Stella says. "I'm going to go take a long bath. In the water I just kicked ass for."

"Mind your rations," Brenda says as my wife leaves and waves. I'm pretty sure there was a middle finger in the wave. "Did she flip me off?"

"No, not at all," I lie. "So what do you need from us?"

"Carl has alerted me to a serious issue," Brenda says, motioning for us to sit down.

We do and wait. She waits. We wait. There is a lot of waiting.

"If this were even remotely suspenseful, I'd be dead," Jon says, "but it's just boring and wasting my time. What do you need, Brenda?"

"Carl has found an issue with the grid," Brenda says.

"I gathered that from your last statement," Jon says. "And the issue is…?"

"We are losing half the grid in the next few weeks," Brenda says. "There were some miscalculations with the battery capacity and, well, to make a long story short, we need to scavenge more batteries if we want to keep the grid at full capacity."

"Maybe cutting back isn't such a bad idea," Jon says, holding out his phone. "I'm not particularly keen on having this thing tethered to me. Do we really need Wi-Fi communications? Or power so kids can play Xbox and adults can watch BluRays? It is the apocalypse you know."

"Keeping the traditions of society is how we keep society alive," Brenda counters.

"A good sharp stick is how we keep society alive these days," I say, but regret it as soon as I see the anger on her face. This is obviously something she wants done. And when Brenda wants something done…

"Let's say we agree," Jon says. "Why us? Why aren't you talking to my wife? She's Head of Scavenging. It's her crew that will go out."

"Because we need her and her crew to go out looking for food," Brenda says. "Stubben has informed me that this year's crops are not up to par. We will need to supplement with canned goods and other found food."

"What has Tran said?" I ask. Tran is my Vietnamese neighbor. His accent is so thick that we mainly communicate with nods and

17

hand signals, because I suck at accents. "He's Head of Food Service."

"He's also a Chatty Kathy," Brenda says. "I tell him and the whole subdivision knows. I can't have that."

A Chatty Kathy? Tran? Now I feel real bad for not being able to decipher what he says. God, I suck as a neighbor.

"I need you two because-" she points at Jon, "-you are head of construction and will know what to look for. And you-" my turn for the pointing, "you are our problem solver. Between the two of you, I know you can get all the batteries we need."

"Last time we saw batteries, they were all the way in town," Jon says. I shiver. "I would rather decline the invitation to go into town."

"Stuart will be with you," Brenda states.

That does make me feel better, but not by much.

"Three of us? That's all?" I say. "I don't think so."

"You will be safe with Stuart," Brenda says, and motions towards the front door as if our time is through. "He'll be in touch in the morning."

"Oh," I say as I realize our time actually is through. "How early?"

"Yeah, how early?" Jon asks. "I like to sleep in on Thursdays."

"Is tomorrow Thursday?"

"Hell if I know," Jon shrugs. "Let's say yes so we can sleep in."

"What's this we? Are you staying over? I'll have to call my mom to see if it's okay. She doesn't like it when-"

"Gentlemen!" Brenda shouts, and then covers her mouth and lowers her voice. "Gentlemen, please. It has been an exhausting day and I still have plenty of work to do before I turn in."

"Our bad," Jon says. "We'll be ready."

We walk a block before we speak.

"You feel good about this?" I ask.

"Fuck no," Jon replies. "It stinks. I don't like it at all."

"Why the secrecy?" I wonder. "Why didn't Carl tell us himself? You'd think he would…"

"We'll talk with Stuart in the morning," Jon says. "Before we leave through the gate. Once on the other side, I'm not making a peep until we are back, safe and sound."

"I hear that," I say as we stand in front of my house. We both know we won't be able to not talk. Talking is our thing. Talking quietly, of course. "Catch ya in the morning."

"It'll be an adventure!" Jon says. "A shitty adventure."

"Night, man."

"Night."

I watch him walk off, and then turn and head inside. I find Stella sitting on the couch.

"I thought you were gonna take a bath?" I ask.

"I just said that to screw with Brenda," Stella replies. "I wouldn't waste water like that." She watches me for a second. "What? What happened after I left?"

"I've been given a mission," I say and sit next to her. "I have to leave in the morning with Jon and Stuart. Apparently we need batteries or the grid goes down."

"So why isn't Melissa going out?" Stella asks.

"Jon asked the same thing," I reply. "Brenda gave us some bullshit answer."

Stella is quiet for a while. She leans against me and sighs. "Who can we trust the most?"

"Why?"

"In case I need allies," Stella says.

"Allies? You've been reading too much John LeCarre from the school library," I laugh. Then I stop. "Tran and his family. Stubben, maybe? Melissa, of course."

"Short list," Stella says.

"Everyone else is in too deep with Brenda. Or Mindy, which is the same as being in with Brenda."

"Tran and maybe Stubben. Great," Stella says. "I may call off school until you get back. Hole up here in the house."

"That could raise red flags," I say.

"I'll just say that Carrey is in one of his manic wild phases," Stella answers. "Which he kinda is."

We sit quietly for a long time before Stella gets up and takes my hand. "Let's tell the kids lights out and go to bed."

"Good idea," I say. I really hope her idea of going to bed is my idea of going to bed. "I'll be right up. Let me double check the doors."

Our little subdivision used to be a never lock your doors kind of place. But this is post-Z Whispering Pines. Even with the gate and all the fortifications, I still make sure all the windows are shuttered and the doors are barred. Once I know the house is secure, then I'll only wake up like twelve times at night, instead of an anxious twenty times.

First, you have kids and never sleep when they are little. By the time they are old enough to take care of themselves in the morning, or even better, sleep later than you do, the damn zombie apocalypse comes and ruins everything. I doubt I'll get a good night's sleep for the rest of my life. And I have a night or two out in the wasteland of Asheville to look forward to. Joy.

CHAPTER TWO

Whispering Pines didn't just happen. It took a lot of sweat and blood to secure the subdivision. Mostly blood. We started with nearly eighty households. We now have less than thirty. The crap Brenda was spouting about us not having enough room, is bullshit. We have plenty of room.

As for resources…

As the gate opens for Stuart, Jon, and myself, I look back up the hill towards Phase One (where Jon lives; Stuart too) and then over to Phase Two (where I live), and think of how long it took us to get things right. Whispering Pines is in the French Broad River basin. This is good. It means it's on a plateau, but not like a flat table top.

The back of Phase One butts up against a fifty-foot limestone cliff. At the top of the cliff is a long, wide meadow. The meadow is filled with row after row of steel fenced razor wire interspersed between long and various ditches. Think World War One battlefields and you get the idea. There is a deck built into the cliff at the top so that sentries can watch twenty-four hours a day for Zs. They do come, and they always get caught in a ditch or the razor wire. None have ever made it to the end of the cliff.

Part of Phase One and all of Phase Two is surrounded on two sides by a 100-yard deep ravine of huge rocks and boulders. Gotta love natural erosion. The ravine sides are covered in steel fencing and razor wire also. If the Zs make it into the ravine, they never make it up the sides.

Hwy 251 and the French Broad River front the gate side. And I've already explained the advantages to that.

Now, the steel fencing and razor wire was my idea. It's the reason I'm head of Engineering, even though I have no training whatsoever. When it comes to structural work, I defer to Jon. But ideas and design? I have a knack for it. Most everything (except for the gate) is steel: the fencing, the razor wire, the steel beams holding both. The reason being? Easy clean up.

Generally, we weave our way through the hidden paths of the razor wire and put down any Zs that are caught. A quick stab through the brain and they are dead. But when a horde tries to get through the wire, then it gets messy. We lost a few people thinking the Zs were caught and they could just go along, one by one, and put them down. Doesn't always work like that.

Edna Strom is Head of Z Cleanup and I worked with her to come up with a simple solution if the Zs are too much to handle. Fire. We burn the fuck out of them until they are either completely dead, or so burned they are incapacitated and easy to pick off. We don't have to worry about the fire spreading, since the ravine is all rock and the meadow above Phase One is pre-scorched so the flames don't spread.

The only problem is the smoke. It's also why I insisted we figure out how to create a sustainable electric grid for Whispering Pines, instead of burning wood or using other means of power. Electricity doesn't send up smoke signals to the world. When we do have to burn through the Zs, we make sure to put that fire out, specifically killing the smoke, ASAP.

There are more than a few factions out in the hollers and coves that would love a chance to come take us out. So far, we've stayed under their radar because we are so close to Asheville and the main population of Zs. The yokels stay clear of the city, as far as we can tell. And I don't blame them. If we didn't have Whispering Pines, I would have packed up the family and booked it way out into the country.

But we do have Whispering Pines and I keep looking over my shoulder as we quietly walk away from the gate and the safety it represents.

"You don't find this fishy?" Jon asks Stuart.

"I find everything fishy," Stuart whispers. "It's why I'm still alive."

"Why us?" Jon asks, more a musing than a question. "I mean, we should be back inside the gate while the scavenger crew handles this. Melissa can be discreet. A select team could keep it all quiet. No need to send us."

"You two have skill sets that will make this more efficient," Stuart answers. "Yours, Padre, is technical. And yours, Jace, is creative. Between the two of you, we'll get what we need and get back home tomorrow. Hopefully without talking too much and getting us killed."

He was right about both parts. Jon will know what batteries we need and what we don't. And, being the problem solver extraordinaire, I will figure out how to get them back to Whispering Pines. Doing both without getting killed, is what Stuart is for.

Not that we aren't capable of defending ourselves. I've been outside the gate more times than I can count, which is the exact same number of times I didn't want to be outside the gate. To keep myself protected, I have the following: Silver Slugger in my right hand. Strapped to my back are a compound bow and a quiver of twenty arrows (Not barbed! These arrows are razor sharp, but can be easily pulled from a Z). I also have a .45 Smith & Wesson with a suppressor (gotta stay quiet in the apocalypse). Slung across my shoulder is my courier bag with canteens of water, some dried food, and a first aid kit.

Jon is similarly outfitted, but he's carrying a steel pipe he's sharpened at one end. He didn't name his pipe. He just calls it a sharpened pipe. Looks kind of like a metal bamboo spear. Four feet long and heavy, he uses it to kill Zs, plus to pretty much crack and break anything he wants. Handy. He also has a pistol, but his is a 9mm Berretta with a suppressor (he made both of ours). No bow or arrows. Jon is a horrible shot with a bow. More likely to kill me than a Z. Not that he's much better with a pistol.

Stuart is, well, loaded. He has at least three pistols on him, several throwing knives, two huge Bowie knives, a machete strapped to his right leg, a compound bow with arrows, a crow bar with the straight end sharpened to a point, two courier bags with supplies, and various other bits and pieces of equipment. It looks beyond heavy, but he hasn't even broken a sweat as we hustle around a curve in Hwy 251.

Which brings us face to face with our first set of Zs. We knew it wouldn't be long. They are everywhere when this close to the urban center.

Six of them, all crouched and feeding on something. We don't know if it's human or animal. In general, about 90% of the time, the Zs won't eat animals; they prefer us delicious *homo sapiens*. But their food source has gotten pretty scarce, so we have seen a few feast on whatever poor, unfortunate varmint they can catch.

As we creep closer -Silver Slugger in my hand, pipe in Jon's, the machete in Stuart's- we see that the meal is human. And still struggling. I take a deep breath and try not to gag, as I watch steaming bits of offal get shoved into the ravenous maws of the Zs. They are so busy feasting, they don't sense us until we are on them.

Six Zs against the three of us isn't much of a match. I bring SS down hard on one Z and immediately yank it back, black blood dripping from its spikes, and nail the next Z. Both drop dead as their brains are pierced by SS's spikes. I flick it to the side like a Samurai sword and the blood splatters across the cracked and weed infested asphalt.

Jon spears one through the skull and pulls back hard, spinning about and cracking another across the jaw. The thing collapses, but the brain hasn't been damaged, so it gets back up and comes for Jon. It's kind of faster than a normal Z and I think about this for exactly 35 seconds before Jon obliterates its head with a mighty swing of the pipe.

We both look at our handy work, and then at Stuart. The guys is nudging the severed heads of his two Zs. The things are still chomping at him even without bodies. You have to kill the brain. He mumbles something and then splits both heads with his machete. The guy still hasn't broken a sweat.

"H-h-h-help m-m-m-me," the half-eaten victim at our feet whispers. "Pl-pl-pl-pleeeeeeese."

Stuart helps him with the tip of the machete through his eye.

"Hopefully, one of the teams will find these guys before they stink up too much," Jon says. "Should we go back and let them know at the gate?" Stuart stares at him like he's lost his mind and his balls. "Just thinking out loud."

"Didn't sound like much thinking going on," Stuart says. "Let's move."

I shrug at Jon and he just rolls his eyes. We move.

The shitty part of going into town is that we have to walk past neighborhood after neighborhood of empty houses. Most we have scavenged clean and marked. Some we haven't. I think about going through the unmarked houses, just to see if we can maybe cut our trip short, but Stuart nixes that idea. He thinks Carl has already had Melissa go through them all. He knows where we are heading.

The dark, blank windows stare at us like the sad portals into the souls that have been lost forever. There is more than just the danger aspect that keeps me from going outside the gate. I hate thinking about the way it was. I hate thinking about all of the people that didn't make it. I mostly hate thinking that I may have met some of the former occupants of these empty dwellings- and stabbed them through their eyeholes.

That part bums me the fuck out.

"You cool?" Jon asks, knowing my tendency towards melancholy. "Not gonna eat the Silver Slugger there, are ya?"

"That would be a shitty way to kill myself," I smile. "And I'm fine."

"Shhh," Stuart scolds.

"Still don't like this," Jon whispers. "My gut is all twisted up and shit. This feels wrong."

"It always feels wrong," I say. "Whenever we leave the gate, I feel like I need to take a long, runny shit."

Jon laughs, but stops as Stuart turns a death glare on him.

The road twists and turns for a good mile before we get to the cross street that will take us up into town. We have a good three miles of road to cover before we get to Merrimon Ave, the main artery for North Asheville. And they are a shitty three miles.

First, we have to get past two churches. The funny thing about Z-Day? It happened on a Sunday. Or at least it became known that it was happening on a Sunday. This meant that many folks were in church when the first real reports came through. And those folks stayed in church to pray and be close to God. Staying put on Z-Day? Not the best idea. One bite became two became four became twelve, and so on and so on.

Instead of clearing out the churches, teams from Whispering Pines had chained the doors and blockaded the windows. After some time, the Zs that were inside stopped trying to get out. They just gave up and went dormant. At least until they caught a whiff of fresh meat walking by.

I look to my right, just before we get to the first church (Baptist, of course) and catch movement. It is brief and quick, but I know I'm not imagining it.

"Hey," I whisper, getting Stuart and Jon's attention.

I point my eyes in the direction I saw the movement. They both look and scan the area, their senses on high alert just like mine. Stuart nods and points. I follow his finger and see the shape semi-hidden behind an oak tree. I take off my bow and nock an arrow, sighting along the shaft at the form.

Then I see movement behind it, deep in the trees. And more movement behind that. Quick, fast. Not Zs. Not Zs!

"Stuart," I whisper.

"I see them," he says. "You catching any signs of metal?"

He's asking if I think they have firearms.

"Too far to tell," I answer.

"Keep moving?" Jon asks.

"They haven't gotten us yet," Stuart says. "We'll stay on mission until they engage. I can't get a clear look at them, so I don't know if they are hostiles or just curious."

I keep my bow aimed at the movement and sidestep along with Jon and Stuart. After a few yards, I don't see any more movement and I lower my bow, but keep my eyes on the spot. Stuart is scanning the road ahead of us and Jon is looking side to side. It ain't always about the Zs in the apocalypse. The people, man. The people...

We pass the church and I can hear the Zs inside, clawing at the doors and windows, their moans echoing through the cracks in the siding. I have to wonder if the people we saw got them worked up. We all keep our eyes on the church, scanning for weak spots that could turn a creepy annoyance into a flood of oncoming death. Best estimate? Close to a hundred parishioners in there.

We get a quarter mile away before I begin to relax. Not that I let my guard down, just ease the tension in my arms and shoulders. I put the arrow back in the quiver and sling my bow over my back. I take SS from the hook on my belt with my left hand and keep my right close to my pistol. Guard still up, tension easing.

However, tension doesn't ease for long as we come to the second church on our Yellow Brick Road from Hell. We all stop in our tracks. I glance over my shoulder, but don't see anyone following. This means I can look at the shit in front of us at my leisure.

"Someone let them out," Jon says finally, voicing what Stuart and I are already thinking. "Who would do that?"

"Wrong question," Stuart says. "I want to know why. You don't go up to a building filled with Zs just for kicks. This was a deliberate action."

"Maybe some nut job just wanted to get into the church," I offer.

"Look," Stuart points. "See the chain on the sidewalk? Bolt cutters did that. You know many nut jobs that just happen to have bolt cutters?"

Stuart crosses the street and approaches the church.

"Fuck," Jon whispers. We both follow.

Stuart kneels down and touches the cut chain, while Jon and I keep our eyes on the church, waiting for the Zs to come shambling out from the shadows.

"This was just cut," Stuart whispers, his head swinging back and forth, eyes scanning our surroundings. "Cut today. Maybe yesterday, but my guess is sometime this morning."

"Then where are the Zs?" I ask.

Stuart shakes his head and stands up. "Don't know. Let's go."

"That rhymes," Jon says.

"It does," Stuart replies.

My gut clenches at Stuart's words. He doesn't glare at Jon for the stupid joke. That means he's worried. I don't like it when Stuart gets worried.

Then he makes my gut feel worse by walking towards the church doors.

"Uh, Stuart?" I ask quietly. Very quietly. "Where are you going?"

"Only more than a couple reasons someone would cut that chain," Stuart answers. "And one of those reasons is to get inside the church."

"Then it stands to reason that they already found what they needed," Jon says. "So let's go find what we need and leave it be."

"After I take a look," Stuart says.

Now, this is the part where someone gets killed. Every movie, book, comic book, TV show, has the macho tough guy walk into the dark, and then the guys that aren't so macho follow and usually one of those not so macho guys gets his head ripped off, or his balls eaten.

"Coming?" Jon whispers, taking me from my thoughts of getting my balls eaten.

"No," I say, "can I wait out here?"

"By yourself?"

"Shut the fuck up," Stuart hisses, "and move ass."

We do and we do, getting right on his heels, weapons ready.

Three seconds. Three long seconds it takes for my eyes to adjust to the gloom inside the church. Unfortunately, my nose doesn't have the luxury of adjusting. A couple years of being a Z pen means a stench that can only be gotten rid of by a cleansing fire. And even then, the stink that soaked into the earth will have a half life of about a million years.

Jon just gags while I think of all the ways to describe the smell.

"It's like someone ate the ape house at the zoo and shit it out," Jon says.

Stuart is ignoring us and leaning, kneeling, sniffing, and, oh, God, tasting, his way through the church. He's halfway up the pews when he freezes. Jon and I instantly go back to back, our eyes searching for the threat.

"Fuck. Me," Stuart says and waves us forward.

We look into the row of pews he's next to and see layers of bones. This isn't anything unusual in the zombie apocalypse.

Bones are lying around all over the place. But both Jon and I see what makes these different: the ends of the bones have been cut. Like by a very sharp meat cleaver.

"Someone was feeding them?" Jon asks. "Why would someone feed them?"

"Another good question," Stuart says. "Only thing I can think of, is…"

He turns and hurries from the church, squatting in the dirt that used to be a nice, well-kept lawn. Just weeds and rocks now.

"Fuck," Stuart says. "Double fuck. I'm an idiot. How did I miss this coming in?"

I want to go to him and say it's all okay and that everyone misses something sometime, but I don't know what he's missing. Jon and I wait until he finally looks at us, his eyes steely and hard. Well, steelier and harder than usual.

"Let's keep going," Stuart announces. "We've lost too much time." He looks at us. "And silence from here on out."

Neither of us argue.

The street is buckled and torn up in many places. Nature has decided to take back what was taken from her. Tree roots, massive weeds, water damage, it all has taken its toll. We navigate through the uneven surface without even a glance. Infrastructure is an anomaly; disrepair is the norm. It's close to half an hour before we get to the next sucky part of our journey: the interstate.

Before us is an overpass that spans four lanes coming and going, or going and coming, depending on your direction of I-26. All lanes are choked with vehicles, most with their doors wide open; ghosts of the occupants that fled on foot. The trouble with the interstate, is that it is a huge part of former society. Which means it is a natural place for Zs to gather.

No one knows why, but the Zs like to be where they think they should be. Absent stimulus or prey, they mainly hang out, or shuffle along slowly, their undead legs taking them through a routine that's lost in the rotten recesses of their memories. Another sad result of post-Z life.

"Where are they?" Jon asks.

I look about and wonder what he's getting at, and then notice that the interstate is sans Zs. Zs don't just follow routine, but also the path of least resistance. The interstate affords them both. On any given day, there should be hundreds below us weaving and lurching between the cars. Today, there are none.

"The cars are empty too," Stuart says.

"Jesus," I say, "someone let the trapped ones out? Zs couldn't do that, right?" I look at them, not even bothering to hide my fear. "Right?"

"Zs can't do that," Stuart says. "They can't cut chains either."

"Oh, fuck," I whisper.

"What the hell?" Jon asks. "Someone's gathering Zs? Is that it? Creating a herd?"

Stuart looks at Jon for a second, a brief hint of suspicion clouding his face. I catch it, but it's gone so fast that I have to wonder if I wasn't just seeing things.

"Could be. Could not. I don't know," Stuart says. "Come on. We have to keep moving."

"You keep saying that, but you keep stopping," Jon shrugs. "Just sayin'."

The silence below us is almost as bad as having a thousand Zs down there. To think that someone took them, moved them, herded them away, makes me shiver. What is the end game there? Is there some mad Z collector taking up residence in the area? Is this some new fad with other survivors? Like silly bands? Or Pokemon? Gotta catch 'em all...?

At least we don't have to hunker down and crawl to stay unseen by the Zs. That's usually how you get across the overpass, on your hands and knees. If you're spotted when there's a few hundred below, they come straight for you. Up the embankments, up the exit ramps, however they can get to you. It gives you only a short amount of time to get from one end to the other before being boxed in. And even if you get across, you still have to deal with the fact that you have a herd of zombies on your ass.

So, despite the uncertainty of the recent discoveries, yeah, I'm stoked, I don't have to crawl or worry about a Z herd.

"Bob and Fam aren't home," Jon says once we are across and back in the neighborhoods again. "That's weird."

Jon raises his hand to shield the sun from his eyes so he can see through the living room window of the house next to us.

Always, whenever anyone comes by here, they see Bob and his family up against the glass. It's a newer house and the double-paned, extra insulated, front window, has refused to break no matter how long Bob, his wife, and two kids smack at it. There has been discussion at HOA meetings about putting them out of their misery, but it never gets enough votes. I always half expect someone just to come do it. The lack of Bob and Fam makes me wonder if someone hasn't finally done it.

"No Bob," I say and shrug, "that is strange."

That look is back on Stuart's face, but now I see worry, not suspicion.

Movement. Again.

"Hey," I whisper.

"Whispers carry farther than just speaking in a low, quiet voice," Stuart informs me.

"I know," I say in a low, quiet voice. "Just thought you should know we have company again."

"Same then?" Stuart asks.

"Don't know," I reply. "I'm guessing yes."

"Does it matter?" Jon says. "A threat is a threat."

We get weapons ready, but keep walking. I can catch flickers of action to my right, back behind some of the houses that line Lakeshore Dr. Just brief flashes of limbs and clothing. I have no idea how many, what size, sex, or age. I just know they are there and they are keeping pace with us.

Stuart's thumb flicks with just the barest of movements and I know he has taken the safety off his pistol. He's ready for a fight. I grip my pistol and SS, very aware of the clammy sweat on my palms. I pray my weapons don't slip from my grasp right when I need them.

Stuart spins quickly and fires one shot. A person cries out in pain and Stuart is off, running towards the sound, his pistol up, his eyes taking in everything, his machete at the ready.

"Fuck," Jon curses, looking at me. "Do we follow?"

"If you were running towards uncertain danger, wouldn't you want your travelling companions coming with you?" I reply.

We follow, basically mimicking Stuart's attack: pistols up, melee weapons at the ready. But before we get more than a couple of feet, they come at us from all sides.

Kids.

"Shit," I shout as four preteens rush at me from my right.

I spin and fire, hitting one in the leg and then I fire again at their feet, hoping it will make them stop and back off. It doesn't. The three left are nearly on me, axes, handmade spears, and twisted clumps of rebar in their hands, ready to split my skull wide open

I fire again and again, emptying my magazine before I realize I took them all down. I stare at the dirty, bloody, malnourished bodies before me. Two are missing half their face, the other is trying to suck air from the hole I put in his chest. The first one I tagged is trying to get up, screaming at me about how he'll rip me open and eat my guts without even cooking them.

Nothing ruins a day like feral, cannibal kids.

Well, not true. Not seeing a fifth kid come at me from my left, kind of ruins the day too.

I feel the pain before I know what's happened. My left leg buckles and I barely get SS up in time to block what would have been the killing blow. I stare up at the teenage girl, maybe sixteen or seventeen, and our eyes fall on our weapons. A smile almost crosses my lips as I see she has a baseball bat with spikes driven through it. But my leg is on fire and I know she can give a shit about the coincidence.

She tries to yank her bat back, but our spikes are crisscrossed and all she does is drag me a foot closer to her. So I kick out as hard as I can, shattering her kneecap. She screams, a real bloodcurdling scream, and goes down hard on the wounded knee. Another scream, almost so loud it hurts my ears, escapes her throat as the shards of patella grind against each other.

I kick again, my foot hitting her in the chest. It knocks her back, but her momentum is enough that she does manage to take SS with her. That pisses me off. Fucking feral cannibal bitch has my baseball bat. I look for my pistol, but it was knocked from my hand and is several feet away. I don't have that kind of time, as I see more kids streaming towards us.

Struggling to my feet, I nock an arrow and fire. It hits her baseball bat. She actually got her bat up in time, and in the right position, to block a mother-fucking arrow. A deadly grin splits her face and I can see the three teeth she has left sitting in brown, rotten gums. I nock another arrow and fire. This one hits the mark. Straight through her throat. She gurgles and coughs while blood pours from the wound. Huge bubbles of blood and snot foam from her mouth.

She's done, so I nock another and spin about. Shit. Too close. Eight kids, various sizes, are almost on me. I let the one arrow go, hitting a kid in the eye, luckily, and then use the bow as a bat. I cringe when it connects with a kid's head, not because I probably split his skull, but because I know it has fucked my bow up. I duck down and swing again, sweeping the legs out from under another kid. Lunging up, my leg screaming in pain, I use the top of my head and connect with the jaw of a boy that is about to stab me with quite the wicked looking hunting knife.

He screeches and I feel something wet fall down my neck and into my shirt. I don't want to think about what it is. Not that I have the luxury of thinking time. I punch the kid in the nuts and shove him back, but his pals are on me and tackle me to the ground. I can see sharpened screwdrivers, steak knives duct taped together, even a fucking gardening trowel, coming at my face.

Then the sound of suppressed gunfire reaches me and I am suddenly pinned under a pile of dead and bloody kids. Trying to free myself from the tangle of limbs, I end up slicing my hand on the fucking gardening trowel (apparently it is very sharp) and shout, "Get these evil munchkins off me!"

"Shut up, dipshit," Jon says as he helps roll the kids off my body. "We've made too much noise as it is."

"They made too much noise," I reply as he gives me a hand up. "All I've done is bleed."

"Let's take a look," Jon says, helping me off the asphalt and onto a patch of moss under a large oak tree. "Any wounds besides the hand and leg?"

"Aren't those enough?"

"Big baby," he smiles as he takes his pack off and pulls out his first aid kit. "Hold still. This will hurt."

It does. I grit my teeth as he cleans and bandages my hand. My leg needs cleaning, stitching, and a bandage, and then I'm good to go.

"Can you walk?" Stuart asks. "Because we need to-"

"Move?" Jon finishes.

"Up there," Stuart says as he points up a winding street that overlooks Beaver Lake.

I glance down Lakeshore and realize I should be able to see the lake, but something is blocking the view.

"We need higher ground to see, don't we?" I say.

And it hits me. Why Brenda asked Jon and me to go with Stuart and not Carl. Why Stuart has been agreeable, but vague. Why we aren't heading towards the college campus and the laptop batteries we need that could be there.

"What are you going to show us?" I ask Stuart.

"Better just to see it," he replies. I catch the hint of a smile. He knows I've figured it out.

Jon looks at me, and then to Stuart. "What am I missing?"

"Help me up and let's get moving," I say.

Jon helps me to my feet and I'm surprised my hand doesn't hurt more than it does. I can't say the same for my leg. It throbs and feels hot. I know Jon cleaned it, but who knows what was on those spikes. I start to walk, but stop immediately. Not from pain, but from revulsion.

"Jon," I say, "pull out the back of my shirt."

Jon looks at me and then at Stuart. Stuart just shrugs.

"Any particular reason, Hoss?" he asks. "I don't think now is the time to get your kink on."

"Please," I say, trying not to shudder, "I think there's something down my back."

I know what it is. Ugh. I know what it is.

Jon pulls my shirt from out of my jeans and I hear the wet flop.

"Oh, damn," Jon says, and then hushes up as he tries not to laugh. "That sucks."

"It's a tongue, isn't it?" I ask. Jon nods. "I feel so dirty."

"Don't be a wimp," Stuart says. "You've had worse splattered on you."

"From Zs," I say, shaking myself a little, trying to get rid of the heebie-jeebies.

"You going to be okay?" Jon asks.

"Yep," I nod.

"Good," Jon says, as we make our way around the dead kids. "What about these bodies? Zs will be on them soon. That's gonna make the area less secure and our way home a little harder."

"I have a feeling there aren't any Zs close by," Stuart says. "At least not free roaming."

"Free roaming?" I ask. "What are they? Chickens?"

Stuart actually smiles at this. It's a little more than off putting.

"You may be more right than you know," Stuart says.

"Don't do that," Jon says. "Seriously."

Stuart's smile goes away quickly and his eyes narrow.

"Come on."

We hike up the long, winding street until we reach a large colonial house. Three stories with wide decks on the back, Stuart leads us through the gate and up the back stairs to the top most deck. As soon as he looks out and below, he hisses and waves us down. My leg hurts like hell.

"You cool?" Jon asks.

"Right as rain," I smile.

"Shit," Stuart says. "Shit shit shit. Get down."

We flatten ourselves on the deck boards and crawl to the edge for a better view. What I see takes my breath away. I can hear Jon's gasp and I look over at Stuart.

"How long have you known about this?"

"Not long," he says. "Melissa and the scavenging crew have avoided North Asheville for months because it's pretty picked over. I came out here a week and a half ago just to be alone."

"You know you can just not answer your door," Jon says. "It's safer to be alone in your own living room."

"Unlike the rest of you," Stuart says. "I have no illusions of safety in Whispering Pines. I come out here to train and stay sharp. I have bags packed and weapons ready at a moment's notice."

"Jeez," Jon says, "that's no way to live."

Stuart grunts in response and then looks down at the lake below. We do also, and I begin to study what I am seeing.

Beaver Lake is a small lake, about the size of an oval football field. It's man made and can be filled and drained in less than 24 hours. Right now, it is drained. Yet it's filled too.

"Are all of those Zs?" Jon asks.

"Yes," Stuart replies, "but they weren't there when I first came here. The wall was, and the guards, but not the Zs."

Surrounding the lake is a massive wall cobbled together from all sorts of materials. Steel, wood, aluminum, car hoods, reinforced chain link, stone, and brick. Guards are posted every twenty feet at least. And these guys look like business. Semi-automatic rifles, body armor, some have helmets and goggles. Even from up here, I can catch the occasional squelch from a walkie-talkie. Which means they have power available to them somewhere.

"You brought us here to analyze and assess what they were building, right?" I ask Stuart. He nods. "But it looks like we now know what they were building."

"The real question is why," Jon states.

"I think I know why," Stuart says. "The real question is when."

"How do you mean?" Jon asks.

While Jon and Stuart talk, I have been busy doing a quick calculation.

"7,000," I say.

"What?" Jon asks.

"God," Stuart responds, "that many then?"

"At least," I say.

Jon looks at me then down at the dry lake. "Are you saying there's 7,000 Zs down there? My Lord." He looks at Stuart. "So you know the why, but want to know the when? I'd like to know the answers to both of those questions."

"They're making a herd," I say. "They are weaponizing the Zs."

"Weaponizing? What for? There's no one to fight. Are they gonna use the Zs against other Zs? Zs don't fight each other. This doesn't make sense."

"Sure it does," I say, tired of looking down into the lake of undead. I roll over onto my back, which makes my leg feel better, and look up at the blue sky above us. "Resources are finite. That includes armaments. If you wanted to lay siege to a place, you'd need a lot of resources to do it. You have to have more resources than the place you are laying siege to. You have to be able to wait them out."

I turn my head and see Jon watching me, waiting for me to go on. I do.

"But in this day, no one can afford to waste all of their resources at one time. The key to survival post-Z, is conservation of resources. So you look for a resource that is not only plentiful, but renewable. And the only resource like that anymore is?"

"Zs," Jon replies. "You don't mean?"

"Yep," I answer.

"They are coming for us," Stuart says. "I didn't know it before, but I know it now. When I saw that lake empty and those guys building the wall around it, I figured at first it was for us."

"That they'd come and take Whispering Pines and throw us in there," I say.

"Yeah," Stuart nods. "But the more I thought about it, the more it didn't make sense. Why keep us alive? They'd have to feed us and give us water. It goes back to a waste of resources."

"You knew we'd find this?" Jon asks. "And you still brought us here?"

"I had hoped we wouldn't find this," Stuart says, shaking his head. "And I didn't want to bring you. But after talking with Brenda-"

"Who else knows?" I ask.

"No one in Whispering Pines," Stuart replies. "Unless Brenda told someone. I told her I'd keep it secret until everyone absolutely needed to know."

"So you talked to Brenda and she changed your mind about coming back alone," I say.

"She said that you two would be the best to bring and help figure this out," Stuart nods. "Padre here can look and see what the structural integrity of the wall is. Maybe find some weak spots. Maybe see if it has a dual purpose."

"Dual purpose?" Jon asks. "Like what?"

"I don't know," Stuart says. "That's one of the reason you're here."

"And I'm here why?" I ask. "You have always known I'm full of shit and just winging it, Stuart. You've never come out and said so, but I've guessed that you don't think very highly of my position in Whispering Pines."

Stuart looks at me for a long time. Long enough for me to grow uncomfortable.

"I've stopped trying to figure you out, Jace," he finally says. "You don't fit any mold I know of. I'm a military man and I like everything to fit perfectly. Everything in its place and all that. But you are all over the place."

"Thanks?" I smile.

"You can seem like the laziest asshole in Whispering Pines, but then you show these bursts of creativity and industry, and all of a sudden, we have a new innovation in the neighborhood. Wi-Fi communication. You spearheaded that. The gate structure. That was you. And the razor wire and fencing is quite possibly the simplest, most genius use of natural topography I have seen."

"I didn't come up with any of that," I say. "Those ideas have already been invented. I just put them into use."

"No, what you did was search through that wild, information hoarding brain of yours and found solutions, and then," Stuart said. "And post-Z, solutions are as valuable as bullets."

"More so," Jon says. "You can run out of bullets. There's always a solution."

"Not always," Stuart says. He points towards the lake of the undead. "But I'm really hoping there's a solution to that. I'm counting on it."

We watch the lake for a long while, each lost in our thoughts. Unfortunately, this internal focus screws us. I know Stuart's senses are tuned to pick up anything coming for us. He has a sixth sense about danger. But no matter how well trained he is, he never sees this coming.

"There is a gate," Jon says and we look over at him.

I don't see the problem at first, but Stuart does. He grabs the binoculars away from Jon's face and shoves back from the edge.

"Move! Move!" he hisses.

"What? What is your problem?" Jon asks.

"The reflection, you moron!" Stuart says, standing up and hurrying down the stairs. "They saw the damn reflection off your binoculars!"

"How do you know they saw it?" I ask as Jon and I follow him down to the street.

The sound of motorcycle engines revving up answers my question.

"Fuck," I say as we follow Stuart across the street and up a muddy incline. "Fuck fuck fuck."

CHAPTER THREE

I lied to Jon, obviously. My leg isn't right as rain. It hurts like a motherfucker, and I know I only have so much in it before I fall behind. There's a stabbing pain where the spikes pierced my flesh and I have to wonder if there wasn't something on the metal more than just dirt. Did that crazy little bitch poison me?

Doesn't matter. I have to shove the burning agony from my mind. I have to focus on Stuart and Jon scrambling hand over hand in the mud above. I have to pay attention to where I grab and where I set my feet. I can't fall.

But…

Of course, I do fall. I feel my leg giving out just as I reach for a rhododendron root only inches from my hand. My leg slips and I swear I can feel the flesh around the wound tearing. Years of living in the zombie apocalypse keeps me from crying out, but also keeps me from alerting Jon and Stuart to my situation. I've slid halfway down the hill before Jon glances over his shoulder.

"Stuart!" he hisses. "Jace is going down!"

"Fuck," I hear Stuart grumble just as he gets to the top of the hill. He looks down at me as I slide the last few feet back to the road. He raises his eyebrows; I shake my head. He nods.

"Where are you going?" Jon screeches, looking up at Stuart and then down at me. "Stuart? We have to wait for Jace!"

"Go," I say, "go!"

Jon begins to protest, but the sounds of motorcycle engines make his eyes go wide. I can see the conflict in those eyes.

"GO!" I shout, waving him on. "I'll be okay! Fucking go!"

Stuart doesn't even wait; he's already gone.

"You want to die too?" I say to Jon. The motorcycles are so close I don't know if Jon can hear me over the engines. "Save yourself, dammit! FUCKING MOVE!"

Jon hesitates, and then closes his eyes. I see his lips moving and I know he's said a prayer for me. Then he's scrambling the last few feet and up over the hill.

So…on my own with some crazies heading in my direction. What to do?

I take off my shirt and tear one of the sleeves off, pulling and tying it tight around my wound. The pain is excruciating. But it also does what I need it to do: clear my head and pump me full of adrenaline.

I'd be lying if I said I was lucky enough to live the post-apocalyptic, suburban life without getting my hands bloody. Before we secured Whispering Pines, I had to make some hard choices and do some morally questionable things to keep my family and myself safe and alive. Most of us did. I think back on those first few weeks of Hell as I prepare for the motorcycles.

SS in one hand, my pistol in the other, I pound my fist against my wound, over and over and over, letting the white hot pain drive me, change me, get me ready for-

"THERE!" a man yells over the sound of his motorcycle, as he sees me standing in the middle of the road. Half his face is covered by goggles so I can't see his eyes (why do these guys always wear goggles? Is it the cool thing to do?), but his mouth is twisted in a grin of blistered lips and snaggleteeth.

I plan on helping him with his dental issues.

He revs the engine and guns his bike for me. He pulls a machine pistol from his waist, but never has time to use it. The dipshit is going too fast and gets to me before he can pull the trigger, but not before I slam SS into his face. He flies off the motorcycle and the bike drives up the muddy hill and flips over, the engine cutting off instantly. I make note of where the bike is, but don't waste time in finishing the guy off. Two hard whacks from SS and his face has less solidity than the mud behind me.

Two more motorcycles crest the hill and fly at me. I lift my pistol and fire before they can do the same. I tag one rider in the chest, his shirt blooming with blood, and he tumbles from his bike.

41

The second rider, a mad-eyed (no goggles!) woman, with a mass of tangled, matted hair, ducks to her right and avoids my shot. Not a problem. I duck under her arm as she swings a huge knife at my head and SS shreds her left leg as she tries to speed past me.

Three down. Three motorcycles to choose from.

Okay, quick admission: I've only ridden three-wheelers, four-wheelers and scooters. Never a motorcycle or dirt bike like the one the woman fell from. But no time like the present to learn, right?

I grab her bike and swing my leg over. Of course, the ignition button doesn't work. Looks like I'll have to kick start the thing. With my bad leg. I wail on that foot lever and gas it until the engine catches and the motorcycle roars back to life. I briefly think about heading down the hill and towards home, but the sound of more engines means I have to go deeper into Asheville. Sucks to have your options taken from you.

I spin the bike around and twist the gas. It takes all of my strength and balance not to topple right over. I get it under control and realize the engine is whining in a way it shouldn't. Fuck, this thing isn't an automatic. I haven't had to hand clutch and foot shift since my three-wheeler days when I was twelve. But when your life is at stake, it's funny what memories and skills come back to you. Like riding a bike.

I shift into second and fly up over the hill, nearly missing the turn in the road. I lean into the turn and avoid plummeting down to Lakeshore below and the fence. With the guards. And the lake of the undead. Part of my plan is to stay as far away from all of that as possible. Not in the mood to put a pretty bow on my head and present myself as a gift to the crazies.

I assume they're crazies. They look like crazies (did I mention the stupid goggles?) and from their screams of rage and anger behind me, I'm guessing they really are crazy. At least these ones are. I have a sinking feeling that whoever is behind the organization and planning of the lake of the undead, isn't so crazy. Well, maybe insane, since there's, well, a *lake of undead*! But not the unstable crazy of the perpetually goggled motorcycle gang on my ass.

I race down the long, twisting road until I'm suddenly spit out onto Merrimon Ave. The street is still clogged with cars from Z-

Day. The bodies the Zs haven't eaten lay half out of their vehicles, mummified and still. I crush the skull of what had been a toddler, as I kick my rear wheel out and fit my bike between a row of cars. I'm racing along, watching in front of me while also trying to keep track of my pursuers. I don't know how many are after me, but one is too many in my book.

I see ahead that a car is cutting me off and I hit the brakes. I slowly wiggle the bike between the car's front bumper and SUV to my left. I just get it clear when I hear the shot and then the ricochet, as a bullet takes off the side mirror of the SUV. Then I hear more shots. I gun the engine and hunker down over the handlebars, as I turn left down Evelyn St.

The street takes me deeper into the more affluent neighborhoods of North Asheville. On both sides, houses start changing from one and two story brick ranch style to two and three story brick and stone mansions. The yards get bigger and the abandoned cars get more expensive. I race past a Land Rover and really wish I had time to switch vehicles. My leg is not happy with my pitiful Easy Rider impression, and I'd much rather be escaping in a heated leather seat than on a Yamaha, whose shocks have seen better days.

More shots and I see the bullets hit the asphalt in front of me. I would do that dodge and weave thing I used to see in action movie chases, but my leg won't take it and I don't have the control to pull it off. I'd just crash and break my neck. Which might be better and quicker than taking a crazy bullet in the back. But sometimes, you don't get to choose.

The street has become more and more choked with weeds and plants. It looks like someone's "decorative" ivy has decided to move across the street, and I see a blanket of green ahead of me. I'm not too worried since I'm riding a dirt bike, which is supposed to be able to handle all types of terrain. Why worry about some ivy?

Then I see it's not really ivy so much as kudzu gone rogue. Covering the trees and stone mansions just isn't enough for this overachiever of the plant world. Nope, Mr. Kudzu has to take the street too. But, no worries, right? I have a dirt bike!

But a dirt bike, just like all motorcycles, has open wheels. No hubcaps on a dirt bike. Nothing to keep the kudzu from kicking up and wrapping itself like a tight, green ball inside the wheels as I speed over the greenery. I feel the pull and can tell I'm in trouble just before the bike is yanked from underneath me, and I go flying over the handle bars.

I'm able to tuck my shoulder and roll, but that doesn't help much. Even though I land in the kudzu, it does nothing against the hard asphalt beneath. I scream as I feel my right shoulder separate. The pain is white hot. Just like the pain from my leg as it slams into the ground. I watch the sky above me tumble past as I roll and roll, and then come to a spine-crunching stop against the (kudzu covered!) curb.

Shit, I'm fucked.

Four motorcycles are coming at me. They've seen what the kudzu can do to their bikes, so they stop just before it, grab their various weapons of chains and sledgehammers, machetes and sharpened rebar, and take a casual stroll towards me.

"Oh, you gonna pay," the lead biker snarls. His skin is so bad that he looks like a serious case of acne is trying to take human form. "You think you can spy and kill ours and not get fed?"

Get fed? Does he mean they're going to feed me? I am a little hungry. We never stopped to eat. But I don't think he means that. I'm pretty sure he meant to say that I was going to be fed to the lake of the undead. You know what? Just because the world comes to an end, doesn't mean we have to let our communication skills go. How did this dipshit speak before Z-day? I mean he couldn't have been this stu-

The kick to my ribs brings me out of my thought loop right quick. I guess my mind tried to take a vacation from the pain and forgot to tell me. Suddenly, they are all standing over me, their weapons raised and their lips back, showing their less than stellar dental hygiene. Take care of your teeth, people! The world is over, but that doesn't mean you shouldn't floss!

Another kick brings me around again. Damn, mind! Stop trying to check out!

"You hear me, meat?" the biker asks. "We are going to fuck you up and hurt you. But we ain't gonna kill you. We'll leave that to the flock."

"Flock?" I ask. "Of seagulls?"

This makes me laugh. Nothing like some good old-fashioned sarcasm when facing death.

They don't get the joke and tell me so by lifting me up, punching me in the face, lifting me again, punching me in the gut, lifting me and kicking me in the nuts, lifting me- Well, you get the picture.

This lift and beat routine goes on for a while. These guys are good. They keep me in agony, but don't let me pass out. Stuart would probably applaud their professionalism. Then he'd rip their throats out. Man, I wish Stuart was here right now. He'd be a sight for sore eyes.

"What you looking at, scrounge?" the main biker asks.

This question confuses me. I'm not looking at anything, because both of my eyes are swollen shut. You know, the beatings and all.

"Move along," the biker orders, "this ain't your concern. Be glad about that. We're letting you live. Unless you want this to be your concern? Then we co-"

I don't hear the rest of his words. I do hear gagging and choking. Very wet. Then the hands on my right side let go. I'm able to get my eyes open a slit and see the bikers spinning about, pulling out pistols and unslinging rifles. Then one by one, they drop. Blood pours from their throats. The shafts of crossbow bolts bounce and wiggle as the bikers take their last struggling breaths.

So, if they are dead on the ground, then who is holding me up?

I turn my head and see a beautiful, yet extremely dirty, young woman next to me. Her hand is on my upper arm and is surprisingly strong.

"How are you doing that?" I ask. The look on her face tells me that my words actually sound like, "Hew uh ya duh det?"

She cocks her head a little and smiles, as she looks me up and down. I try to smile back at her. Then I realize she isn't holding me up. It's the hand on my other arm that's really holding my weight. I turn my head and see the opposite of the young woman.

Sure, this person is just as dirty, but not a beautiful young woman. More of a grizzled, old man. With one eye, no hair, and half of the right side of his face flayed open and healed in a horrifying tangle of skin and tendons.

"I can see your tongue," I say. He just nods. I don't think he understands me, but oh well.

Then he smiles and I really wish he hadn't. Smiling with only one intact cheek and half your face gone, is not flattering. Not in the least. I get over my shock at the grin and then wonder what he's smiling at. I'm not really given the opportunity to find out, as the next thing I see, is his fist up close and personal.

Then it's goodnight, Jace, sleep tight.

I dream of tacos.

I can smell the crispy corn tortillas. I hear the sizzle of the taco meat in the pain.

"Better stir that or it will scorch," I say to the nothing of my dreamscape. The taco meat is stirred.

Onions, cilantro, garlic, and then tomatoes. All it needs is some salt and it'll be an amazing salsa. Fresh and refreshing. Yum!

Oh, but there's guacamole too! Creamy avocados with just a hint of cumin. I am so ready to make some tacos. I want to fill those shells until they are ready to crack. Fill them with all the stuff that makes for great tacos. I don't care if they do split and crumble all over my plate. That's what forks and tortilla chips are for! To catch the droppings!

God, I miss tacos.

I don't miss pain, though. And that's what waits for me as my taco dreams turn to wakefulness. Slowly, excruciatingly, I am brought back to consciousness. And know what? I still smell tacos. Not beef though. No. More like pork. Mmmm, carne asada.

"He's coming around, Pa," a woman says. "Should I knock him back out?"

"Nah," a man replies. "He's roped tight. May be good to talk to him for a spell and see what he knows."

"Hey," the young woman says. Then she slaps me. "Hey, you awake? Pa wants to do some talking with ya."

"I'm…awake," I croak. "Can…I…have some…water?"

"Can he have some water, Pa?"

"No, don't waste it on him."

"No, you can't have no water," the young woman says.

I get my eyes open and see her sitting in front of me. Damn, she is beautiful. You know, once you get past the layers of dirt and post-apocalyptic disarray. And the smell. She isn't pleasant smelling. I can smell shit and piss plus something tangier that I'd rather not identify. Her mouth is a bellows of yuck and just her short breaths are almost enough to send me back into unconsciousness.

I try to move and realize I'm down on my knees and bound to a metal post, my arms tied behind my back and around the post. My shoulder hurts, but isn't dislocated anymore. There's a plus. I look about and can see we're in a wide basement. There are no windows, or if there are, they're blacked out, and only a small fire in the corner lights the room. I can see a camp rig set up over the fire and the man is standing there, slowly turning a spit.

The other thing I notice is the thick and cloying smell of copper. Like pennies in the rain. Which doesn't make sense. When have I ever smelled pennies in the rain? I mean what is that all ab-

"Hey!" the young woman says, slapping me again. "Stop drifting. Stay awake while Pa talks."

"Where you from?" the man asks as he motions for the woman to go to him. She takes over the rotating of the spit and he walks over to me. He looks me up and down with his one eye. "You're looking pretty healthy. Where you holed up? You got food? Where's your water coming from? There others with ya? How many? Kids? *Ladies*?"

Yeah, not liking how he says *ladies*.

The questions all muddle together in my muddled brain and I stumble for muddled answers.

"I have a penthouse," I say. "Right downtown. In those new condos off Biltmore. Great views. I can see the apocalypse for miles from my bedroom."

The man stares at me for a second and then grins that half-face grin. I have to wonder how he lost half his face on one side, but then the eye is clouded on the other side. The bizarre questions of the apocalypse...

"You're playing with me," he states and chuckles. Bits of spit fly from his open cheek as he laughs. "You're a funny guy, are ya?"

Uh-oh. Never good when the guy with half a face calls you the "funny guy." I learned that from bullies in middle school. Once they call you "funny guy", then there's usually some type of violence and the inevitable question, "You find this funny, funny guy?" I never did.

He squats down in front of me, a very sharp boning knife in his right hand. He slowly moves the blade closer and closer until the tip is right by my left eye.

"Let's see how funny you are with only one eye," he says and laughs. More cheek spit. "Get it? *See* how funny?"

"That's a good one," I smile. "We're two funny guys. Just a couple of jokesters hanging out and telling jokes."

"You know any?"

"What?" I ask, the need to shit myself with fear probably keeps me from understanding the question. "Know any what?"

"Jokes, stupid," the woman says from the fire. "Pa likes jokes. We always like to get new jokes when we meet new folk."

"We do, Elsbeth," Pa says as he stands, slipping the boning knife into a sheath on his belt. "What was that one we heard last week? You know? Those two kids kept telling it over and over while I cut their mama up."

Oh, sweet, God...

"Oh, oh, I remember," Elsbeth says. "It was...it was... Oh, wait... I forget."

She starts to smack the side of her head over and over and over before Pa can stop her. He grabs her wrist and yanks it away hard enough for her to cry out.

"Too pretty to be hitting yourself, Elsbeth," Pa says as he pushes a stray strand of hair away from her forehead. "Don't hurt that beautiful face."

"I'm very pretty," Elsbeth says.

"Where was I?" Pa asks himself as he turns to me. "Oh, right, jokes. You heard this one?" He clears his throat. "Knock, knock."

I wait and then realize that he wants me to answer. I was thinking he was talking to pretty and stinky Elsbeth.

"Who's there?" I ask.

"Interrupting zombie."

"Uh, interrupting zombie-"

"Rarrrr!" Elsbeth shouts, interrupting me.

"Good one," I smile.

Pa whirls around and punches Elsbeth in the chest, knocking the breath from her. She falls to her knees, but gets up quickly and keeps turning the spit.

"Sorry, Pa," she gasps. "It was your joke. I ruined it. Ruined the joke."

She starts smacking herself again.

Pa stops her and pulls her to him, stroking her hair. She doesn't stop turning the spit. Pa's hair stroking gets faster and faster until I notice he's kind of grinding against her. Ah, fuck, seriously?

"My kids told me that joke," I say quickly. "But it's with an interrupting cow instead of a zombie. I like yours better."

"Ain't mine," Pa says, his hips stopping their obscenity. "I told you it was from two kids. Are you stupid, mister? Do you have to be told things twice?"

"Stupid," Elsbeth says, looking around Pa at me. "You're stupid."

"Pot meet kettle," I mumble.

"What's that?" Pa asks, and he moves at me faster than I think he can. His hand grabs my chin and pulls hard. "You say something to my girl?"

"I think dinner's ready, Pa," Elsbeth says, taking some rags and lifting the spit off the fire.

She walks it over to a dirty work bench and sets it down. Grease and juices start to drip over the edge and the smell makes my mouth water. Pa watches me and then nods.

"I'm guessing you're hungry," he says. "Elsbeth, cut our guest a hunk. After today, we got plenty to feed a third mouth."

Elsbeth rips a chunk of meat from the roast and walks it over to me. The meat has to be burning her hand, but she doesn't show any sign. Her eyes are bright and glassy and she just looks at me, a simple smile on her face.

"You gonna like this, mister," she says. "Long pork is good. The best."

The smell is incredible. I haven't smelled fresh roasted meat in forever. We don't keep livestock in Whispering Pines other than chickens. They take up too many resources. Easier to just grow beans for protein. And chicken does not smell like this. My mouth is drooling, but...then...I realize...

"Long pork?" I ask.

"Yep," Pa smiles, "best kinda pork."

He laughs and Elsbeth laughs with him.

"I, uh, think I'll pass," I say, "long pork gives me the runs."

He backhands me and my head snaps to the side.

"Don't be crude," Pa snarls, "no potty talk like that in front of my girl."

"You should eat what's offered," Elsbeth says, the meat right under my nose. "Never know when you're gonna eat again. That's what Pa always says. Eat when you can, it may be the last you see for a while."

The boning knife comes out and my eyes are drawn to its wickedly sharp looking blade. I follow the blade up to the hand, up the arm, and to the shoulder, and then to the half-cheeked face. Pa looks at me with his one eye and I know he knows I know what the meat is. There is a lot of knowing going on. I really, really, wish I had none of it. The knowing, that is.

"I'd rather not," I say again. "I am sorry, but my stomach...it gets touchy with too much grease."

Elsbeth wipes the hunk of meat against her pants leg, leaving a shiny streak of fat. "There," she says, offering me the meat again. "I wiped the grease off. It's a shame since that's where the flavor is."

She shoves the meat against my lips. I try to keep them closed, but she just keeps pushing. Then she takes her other hand and grips the back of my head.

"Eat it!" she shouts. "Eat the fucking meat! It's good! GOOD! LONG PORK IS GOOD!"

She keeps screaming at me until I can't hold back anymore. My lips are forced apart and the hunk of meat is shoved inside my mouth. I'm about to spit it out when Elsbeth brings out her own knife and pushes it up one nostril until I can smell and feel the trickle of blood.

"Eat," she says, "ain't telling you again, mister. Eat what's good for ya."

Oh fucking Jesus on the cross with a head like a hole black as my soul oh fuck shit fuck.

I chew.

I swallow.

I struggle.

I lose.

I puke.

Elsbeth barely gets out of the way. She stands and looks at her pa. He shakes his head.

"Too bad, mister," Pa says. "I thought we'd keep you around for a while. I kinda like you." He looks at Elsbeth. "And she's more than I can handle sometimes. Would be nice to have another man help take care of her."

He pulls his boning knife and looks at the reflection of the fire in the blade.

"But I ain't gonna keep ya around if you're going to starve yourself," he says quietly. "You'll just waste away to nothing and then what would you be good for?"

"Gonna kill him now while he's plump?" Elsbeth asks.

"Seems like the smart thing to do," Pa replies. "Help me get him up and trussed. And go get the buckets. We lost half the blood from the biker woman. Can't waste blood like that."

"No, sorry, Pa," Elsbeth says as she helps pull me to my feet. My body and arms slide up the pole and I'm looking her right in the eyes.

"You don't have to do this," I say. "You don't have to live like this. There's better places to live than this basement."

"Is there now?" Pa says as he pushes Elsbeth away. "The buckets, girl!"

"Right, Pa!" She hurries through a side door I hadn't noticed. The smell of pennies gets stronger as the door swings open. I glance over. Wish I hadn't. Bodies. Hanging. Dripping...

"You were saying there's better places to live than here?" Pa asks. "Where would those places be? Up in that penthouse of yours?" The knife nicks my cheek. It is wicked sharp. "I don't appreciate you filling my girl with lies and dreams. Cotton candy and pinwheels, that's all you are. A fading game on a summer night."

Okay, he's lost me.

Elsbeth comes back in with two large, five-gallon buckets.

"Ain't gonna lose the blood now, Pa," she says.

"Take your knife and cut his clothes off," he orders. "Get him naked and we'll wipe him down. Don't want to taint the meat."

I'm pretty sure the workbench that hunk of whomever is resting on isn't very sanitary, but decide now is not the time to quibble about what taints what.

It takes her less than two minutes to get my clothes cut off. I stand there, arms bound behind me, cock and balls free for all to see, and shake my head.

"What?" Pa asks.

"Just wasn't how I thought I'd die," I say.

"Really?" Pa laughs. "You had other plans? What? You planning on dying in your sleep in a feather bed up in that penthouse?"

"That would be preferable," I say. "Or you could let me go and I can just die out there somewhere. We can just skip the slicing and the dicing."

"It even cuts cans!" Elsbeth says out of the blue. "That's Shakespeare."

Pa rolls his eye. "Sometimes it's all I can do from killing that one." He shrugs. "But you can't always pick your family."

"I have a family too," I say. "I'd really like to see them one last time before I die. You already said you have plenty of food. You don't need to carve me up."

"Waste not, want not," Elsbeth sing songs.

"She has a point," Pa says. "I smoke you up and wrap you in oil cloth and you'll last us through the winter. How can I pass that up?"

"I get it, I do," I say, panic setting in. "We all have to do crazy shit to live. But you can't keep eating people. You'll get sick. People aren't supposed to eat people. There are these things called prions-"

"Called what?" Elsbeth asks.

"Prions," I repeat.

"That's a funny word," she says and starts saying it over and over.

"Shut up, will ya!" Pa barks, whirling on her, the knife slashing out and just missing her by a hair. She stumbles back and cowers against the wall. "It ain't a funny word, it's a science word." He looks back at me. "You a teacher, mister? You trying to teach me and my girl?"

"Uh, I could be a teacher," I say. "I do know a lot of stuff-" The knife cuts across my cheek. Deep. I scream and wish I could clamp my hand to the flap of flesh I can feel flapping away. "Fuck! FUCK!" I scream some more, you know, just in case they didn't get the point.

"I don't need no one filling my girl's head with science," Pa smiles. "It's all lies. Science couldn't stop the Zs from coming, but the Bible predicted it would happen. What's the point of science if religion is always right?"

"Gotta get you some religion," Elsbeth whispers and nods. "Gotta get ya some."

"Listen," I plead. "Man to man, father to father, you can't do this! Please! I just want to see my wife and kids again! Please!"

"How about you tell me where they are and I'll go get them for ya?" Pa says. "I'll keep you alive long enough so you can see them one last time. Then you and your family can die together. How's that sound, Mr. Science?"

"I think I'll leave them out of this," I say.

"Fine," he nods then looks me up and down. "Where should I start? I hate to kill and butcher you now. Your fear is gonna make the meat all gamey. I like the quick kills. Or a kill in a fight. The adrenaline tenderizes the meat for me. Less pounding of the tough cuts."

"Maybe we can put this on hold? I can get some sleep. Letting me rest will do wonders to the flavor."

"Don't think so," Pa says. "I have a lot of work to do before I sleep, and I'd like to get started."

"No...please..."

I may have just peed a little.

"That's disgusting," Pa says.

Yeah, I peed.

"Just kill him, Pa," Elsbeth mutters from the wall. "I don't like him talking no more. Makes my head all flunky spin like."

"You heard the girl," Pa says, placing the knife against my groin. "Better get to it."

"No! NO! WAIT! NO PLEASE NO DON'T-!"

I go deaf and blind suddenly as bright flashes fill my eyes and gunshots fill my ears. I'm pretty sure I'm still screaming for mercy when Jon slaps me.

"Will everyone please stop slapping me?" I yell in his face.

"You were hysterical, Hoss," he says as he cuts my hands loose. "Something had to be done."

"You hurt?" Stuart asks. I just stare at him. "Besides the leg and the hand and that flap of loose skin on your face, I mean."

"Nah, I think that covers it," I say. "But I am going to need some clothes."

"I'll see what I can find," Stuart says as he leaves the basement.

I catch Jon eyeing the meat and shake my head. "Don't."

"Looks and smells good," he says. "Goat? Wild boar?"

"Biker," I say.

He takes a couple steps back.

I look down at Pa's body and give it a kick. It hurts my bare toes, more than it does me any emotional good, but it had to be done. I look around, but there is no sign of Elsbeth.

"You looking for the girl?" Jon asks. "Tucked out the window as soon as we hit the stairs. Fast thing, pretty too. Was she his captive? She left this behind. Looks just like yours, but better."

I see a spiked bat on the ground that he's pointing at. I guess it's all the trend for North Asheville cannibal girls to have spiked bats. One gets one, and then the girl down the street has to have one, and pretty soon, they're more popular than skinny jeans and Uggs. Wonder what that says about me? How soon will I want to wear skinny jeans and Uggs? All the cool girls are!

"Hey!" Jon snaps, his fingers right in my face. "Earth to Jace!"

I blink then glance around again.

"Ugly thing is more like it," I reply. "And she wasn't a captive. She was his daughter. They were going to eat me."

"Well, good thing your girly screams carry," Jon says. "Stuart heard you and booked it straight for this house. I'm guessing you had seconds before this guy slit your femoral artery. See the nick?"

I look down at my leg and see the tiny trickle of blood on the inside of my thigh.

"Stop looking at my junk," I say to Jon, and then take a deep breath and struggle not to collapse.

"You okay?" he asks. "Need to sit?"

"No, no, I'm good."

"I found some clothes that should fit," Stuart says when he returns. "But you won't like them."

"I don't care what they look like," I say. "I just want to get dressed."

"Okay," Stuart nods as he tosses me a bundle.

I look at the shirt and pants and frown. Looking from the clothes to Stuart to the clothes to Jon to the clothes, I shake my head.

"No way," I say.

"That's all I could find that will fit you," Stuart says. "Must have been a single mom and her kids that owned this place. No men's clothes."

I hold in my hands a pair of bright pink yoga pants and a purple t-shirt with a glittery butterfly. I sigh and start to put them on.

"Well, at least we'll be able to find you in the dark there, My Little Pony," Jon laughs.

"I've had a hard day and could do without the sarcasm," I say, "it hurts my feelings."

"Time to go," Stuart says. "We can't stay here. Too much noise. The bikers are looking for us. Only a matter of time before they find this place."

"Where to?" I ask. "We can't make it back to Whispering Pines before dark."

"It's already dark," Jon says.

"Jesus, how long have I been missing?"

"Hours," Stuart says, "hours we couldn't afford to lose."

"Oh, I'm sorry," I snap. "Did I make you miss your flight or something? Did you have someplace better to be?"

Stuart closes on me and I remember just how dangerous he is.

"I think we all have someplace better to be, Jace," he says, "but we aren't going to get there by being a little bitch, now are we then?"

I sigh and shake my head. "No, Stuart, we aren't. My bad. Thanks for saving my ass."

"Your life," Stuart says, "I want nothing to do with your ass."

"A joke!" Jon laughs. "Miracle of miracles!"

"Come on-"

"We need to move," Jon and I say at the same time.

"I don't know why I bother," Stuart says. He looks around the basement. "Anything worth salvaging then?"

"No clue," I say. "I was busy being prepped for dinner."

"Fine, let's go," Stuart says as he puts a full magazine into his pistol. "You stay close to me, stay down, and don't make a sound. Got it?"

We both nod at him.

"Good," Stuart says as he heads for the basement door.

He opens it and then closes it quickly, but quietly, his finger to his lips.

Shit. Guess we didn't move fast enough.

We all look up at the basement ceiling and that's when I hear the footsteps. They are careful, moving methodically through the house. There's a creak over by the far corner telling us there's two people in the house. Then another creak in the opposite corner. That makes three.

"What now?" I mouth at Stuart.

He cocks his pistol, aims it at the door, and waits. I give him a thumbs up.

"Shit," Jon hisses, "your leg."

I look at my leg and see the bandage is soaked with blood. There isn't a speck of white.

"His face isn't looking so good either," Stuart whispers.

I reach up and feel my cheek and my hand comes away drenched in red.

I'm a fucking mess.

"He needs help," Jon says, his voice barely louder than the crackle of the fire. "We have to get him home."

"We have to get us all home," Stuart says. "But we can't now. Get him settled and redress that leg. See if you can clean his cheek and dress that too."

"What are you going to do?" Jon asks.

"I'm going to watch that door," Stuart says.

"We'll do it in shifts."

"No, you watch him. If he goes into shock, he could die. You have to make sure he stays breathing and doesn't bleed out. Watch the wounds, change the dressings, and keep him alive."

"How will you stay awake?" Jon asks.

Stuart opens his bag and pulls out a blister pack of pink pills. He cracks open two pockets and takes out the pills. He dry swallows them, and then hands Jon the pack.

"You'll need some too," he says.

"I can't swallow these without water," Jon says, "I'm a pussy that way. Bad gag reflex."

"There's water over there," I say and point at the workbench. My stomach clenches at the sight of the meat. "Can you cover that or something?"

Jon goes to the table and swallows the pills, taking a drink of water from a large gallon jug. He brings it over and hands it to me.

"I'll do better than cover it up," Jon says as he goes back to the meat, grabs it, and tosses it on top of Pa's body. He covers him with a moldy tarp from one of the basement shelves. He stands there and whispers a few words and then nods, looks up at the ceiling, nods again. "Amen."

"Amen," Stuart repeats.

"Amen," I say more out of superstition than any spiritual need. Plus, I have no desire to really send his soul along in peace. Jon and Stuart weren't here. They didn't see them, hear what they said, know what they'd done. What they were going to do. He can rot in fucking hell, thank you very much.

"I don't hear them anymore," Jon says.

"That means they are good at what they do, not gone from the house," Stuart says. "They're either figuring out how to take us or have decided this house is a good place to hole up in until morning." Stuart looks around the basement then at me. "It is a good house to hunker down in. It's how we found you. It looked like the right house."

"That and the screams," Jon says.

"Those helped," Stuart says. "Get some rest, Jace. We'll need you at your best in the morning. We may be doing a lot of running."

"I'll try," I say.

"To rest or run?"

"Both," I nod.

I lean back and close my eyes, but all I can see is Elsbeth's laughing face. My eyes shoot open and I see Jon watching me. He cocks his head and I shake mine.

I don't expect to sleep much at all. Who would?

That's the last thing I remember until Jon is shaking me awake. I look about and see the basement door open and Stuart gone. I start to speak, but Jon puts a finger to my lips. Then I hear them.

Engines. Big engines.

"Okay, kiddies," a voice booms from above. Someone has their very own PA system. "You are in there and I would like you not to be. I'll count to ten, because I'm generous and nothing gets done in five, and then you have to come outside. Arms up. Weapons down. This is something you have to do. Have to."

"Guys," Stuart says from the door and waves us over.

Jon still has to help me, but the rest must have done me some good, because I feel stronger than before. We follow Stuart upstairs. The sun is just starting to make an appearance and the front room of the huge house is bathed in pink dawn light. There's no sign anyone stayed in the house. They must have gone for reinforcements because outside the front window, I can see two huge dump trucks, backed up to the front yard, their tailgates pointing at us.

"I'm at three now," the voice booms. "Oh, did you think I was going to countdown for you? Why would I do that?" The voice laughs. "That would ruin all the fun."

The dump truck beds start to lift and the tailgates open. And out come the Zs. Lots of Zs. Like a whole lot of Zs. I would be safe in saying a shit ton of Zs.

Jon and I stare at the Zs, and then cringe as red liquid is sprayed up on the porch, the front windows, the whole house.

"They're baiting us," Stuart says. "That's blood. The Zs will go insane and be in here in minutes."

"Upstairs?" Jon asks.

Stuart turns and looks at him, puzzled. "Why? You think Zs can't climb stairs? It'll just prolong the inevitable."

Stuart walks past us and we follow him into the kitchen. He looks out through the window over the sink into the sprawling backyard. He sighs. We look too and see men and women wrangling Zs into the backyard, baiting them with hunks of meat. I don't even want to know where they got the meat. Sucks to be bait.

"Now what?" Jon asks.

Stuart goes to the range and turns one of the knobs. It's not much of a surprise that the burner flicks to life and blue yellow flames dance before our eyes. As we all know from Whispering Pines, apparently the gas stays on in the zombie apocalypse. Stuart blows out the flames, but keeps the gas flowing. He does the same to all of the burners then opens the oven and gets that gas going.

"Let's hope the basement will hold," Stuart says. "This is a pretty old house, which means it wasn't built by the lowest bidder. Should be strong."

He starts to tear up a kitchen towel and soak it in olive oil. He ties strip after strip together and pushes us towards the basement door.

"Get down there and get secure," he says as he closes the door. He pulls a lighter from his pocket and stuffs the oil soaked rags under the door. "To put it in terms you understand, this is going to suck."

"I'd also understand it if you made booming noises and flashed your hands in the air," Jon says.

"That would work for me too," I say. "How much suck, exactly?"

"Big suck," Stuart says and flashes his hands in the air while making a booming noise. Another joke? Will wonders never cease?

He sets the lighter next to the cloth. We don't wait to watch him light it and hustle down the stairs and into the farthest corner.

"Should we cover ourselves with something?" I ask.

"Yes, let's pre-pile the debris," Jon replies. "Good idea."

"Asshole."

"Dickhead."

"Get down!" Stuart cries as he runs down the stairs.

He's halfway across the room when all hell breaks loose above us.

CHAPTER FOUR

"Get up," I say as I shove debris from Jon. "Come on. Gotta go, gotta go."

"Ugh," Jon grunts as he shoves me away and struggles to his feet on his own. "Are we alive?"

"We are," Stuart coughs from behind me. "And we have limited time to use our distraction." He points at a shattered basement window by the top of the wall just above us. "Out. That way. Now."

He staggers a little, then shakes his head and pushes past us.

"You okay, Stuart?" I ask.

"No one is okay in this Hell," he snarls as he grabs the sill and heaves himself up and through.

I can see a large wet mark on his lower back, but he is out the window and turned around, his hand extending to us, before I can see how bad he's wounded.

"Hold on," I say and look about. The bat. I don't want to leave it behind and have the neighborhood girls laugh at me because I'm not cool like them.

"Hoss!" Jon calls taking Stuart's hand and is helped up and through. "What the hell?"

I take a second to look at Elsbeth's bat. And as much as I hate to admit it, hers is better. Bigger, sharper spikes set more solidly than mine were in SS.

"I dub thee, The Bitch," I say as I run/limp to the window.

They both reach for me and I'm out of the basement of death and breathing semi-fresh air for the first time in a long time. Stuart motions for us to crouch and follow him around to the front.

"Seriously?" Jon asks, looking at the bat.

"Don't mock The Bitch," I smile.

"You are one fucked up dude," he grins.

"Shut it," Stuart hisses.

We get to the corner of the house and peer around. Stuart's plan took out half of the fucking mansion! Zs and bikers lie everywhere in various states of death and woundedness. Men and women are running about, their eyes wide with shock. The bullhorn guy is shouting orders, his bullhorn forgotten and dangling from his hand, pointing at the mansion and waving his hand left and right, trying to organize his people in the face of fiery chaos.

"Good job," I say as I clap Stuart on the back.

"Job's not done yet," Stuart says and stands up and walks right into the chaos.

Jon starts to call to him, but I grab his shoulder and shake my head. Barely anyone notices Stuart as he walks to the closest dump truck. The few people that do look at him, he just snarls and barks orders at; they turn and run, not willing to get in trouble. Stuart is up and in the dump truck, its bed open and holding pieces of flaming debris.

Bullhorn looks over at the truck as the engine roars to life. He watches it back up and turn, coming straight for us. His eyes go wide and he lifts the bullhorn to his mouth, but all that comes out is ear-splitting feedback. He throws it aside and begins to shout and scream, pointing at the dump truck that is almost to us.

Bullhorn is not what I thought he'd look like. Dressed in an immaculate (or was before things went boom) double-breasted suit, his hair is pitch black and slicked back on his head. A long, sharp nose, and piercingly blue eyes, he looks more like an older male model than the guy in charge of these crazies. As Stuart comes to a halt and the passenger door opens, Bullhorn's eyes meet mine. I want to puke, shiver, and cry at the same time.

"Holy fuck," I say as Jon and I climb up and jump into the dump truck's cab.

"What?" Jon asks as Stuart puts the truck into gear and guns the gas.

"I just saw evil," I answer, "like with a big E."

The dump truck clips the corner of the mansion and we hear boards and brick cracking. Then we hear the gunfire. Bullets ping off the metal beast and we duck our heads. Or Jon and I duck our heads, Stuart is cool as cucumber. Doesn't even flinch as the sounds of ricochets get more and more frequent.

He glances into his side mirror and turns the truck to the left, taking something out. We hear a scream and a small explosion. I'm guessing one less motorcycle, and rider, to deal with.

Then Jon and I grab the dashboard, bracing ourselves as Stuart heads straight for a line of cedars.

"Uh, Stuart?" I say. "The trees? The trees! THE TREES!"

"Fuck the trees," Stuart says as we plow through them and into the next yard. He slams his foot down on the accelerator all the way, heading for the wrought iron fence across the huge lawn.

"Okay," Jon says. "Fuck the trees. Fuck that fence. Fuck the roads." The ping of bullets echoes in the cab. "And fuck those bullets! Fuck it all!"

"Language, Padre," Stuart says as we hit the wrought iron fence and rip it from the ground.

A huge chunk is twisted up over the grill and hood of the truck, but it doesn't slow us. Stuart keeps going, demolishing a white picket fence then a hedge of fire bushes. More cedars, some junipers, and we are out on a side street. Stuart whips the wheel to the left and slams against a Honda sitting halfway across the road. The little Civic never stood a chance.

Stuart casually pulls one of his pistols (the motherfucker is still fully armed where I only have The Bitch and Jon doesn't look like he has anything, not even his pack) and starts firing through his side window. Two motorcycles drop as their riders take slugs to their chests. He steers us around a rolled over pickup, and then hops the curb into the front yards of the row of houses, avoiding the other vehicles blocking the road.

I look about and realize we are on Kimberley Ave. On our right, set behind the yards we are driving through, is mansion after mansion, huge fucking houses that lookout across the street at the Grove Park Inn and its long dead golf course. I look out Stuart's window and am amazed to see people lining the balconies of the Grove Park.

"Look," I say and point. Jon follows my gaze and even Stuart risks a glance.

"The Grove Park has a new owner," Jon says. "You think it's Wall Street back there?"

"You mean Bullhorn?" I ask.

"I prefer Wall Street," Jon says. "Anyone can have a bullhorn. Then it gets confusing."

"Why do you get to name him?" I ask.

"Shut the fuck up," Stuart says. "Padre is right. Wall Street is best."

We demolish a stone fountain and bits of rock and sludge water splash up against the windshield. Stuart casually turns on the wipers, smiling slightly when washer fluid comes squirting out.

"It's the little things," he says quietly. We nod in agreement.

We get to Farrwood Dr. and Stuart hooks a right. The street is pretty clear, so he keeps to the asphalt. We can still hear motorcycles, but they are a ways back.

"Where are we heading?" Jon asks.

"Campus," Stuart says.

"The fuck we are," I protest, "that's Z central, man!"

"We'd have had to go there if this mission really was about batteries," Stuart says.

"Which would have been a quiet mission," I say. "Three guys creeping along, taking care not to wake the undead co-eds."

"You know of a better route?" Stuart asks as we cross Merrimon Ave and up Edgewood. Stuart downshifts to get us up the hill. We crest it and he hits the gas as we speed downhill. "If you do, then I'm all ears, Jace."

"Jesus," I say, knowing he's right. "We can hit the field behind the athletic training center. Then cut down to 251."

"Why not head to the meadow?" Jon asks. "Ditch the truck up there and use the path to get through the razor wire and ditches."

"Because we want this thing," I say. "Right, Stuart?"

"Right," Stuart says.

"Something I need to know?" Jon asks. More ricochets and part of the side mirror by Jon is torn off. "Fuck these guys! Give me your pistol!"

Stuart hands it over without taking his eyes off the road. Jon leans out the passenger window and starts firing. Stuart glances in his side mirror and frowns.

"You're missing," he says. "Stop that."

"Shut up," Jon replies as he takes aim and squeezes the trigger. I hear a crash then a whump as the motorcycle goes up in flames. "How's that?"

"Still two more," Stuart says, taking a hard curve to the left before having to take an immediate right. Jon and I slam into each other, our heads knocking together. "Quit fucking around and fire."

"You suck," I say as I rub my head.

Jon leans back out and hits another biker as the guy comes around the corner. We wait, but the third motorcycle is nowhere.

"Lost the last one," Jon says, "must not have been good enough to take those turns."

"You were saying?" Stuart says as we watch a motorcycle fly off the hill to our right, directly in front of us.

It is a spectacular stunt, and everything kind of goes in slow motion as the guy, still in the air, aims his pistol right at us. Jon and I open our mouths to scream, but bring our arms up to cover our face instead, as the world goes back to regular speed and the truck nails the motorcycle in midair.

The rider tumbles across the hood, his clothes on fire from the burning gas of the motorcycle. He looks at us, shocked and confused. Then looks around at his situation.

"Hey." Jon waves as he leans out the window and puts two bullets in the guy's face.

Stuart is happy he gets to use the windshield wipers again.

We take another hard right and the truck struggles up the next hill as the engine starts to make a loud banging noise. Ahead is the University of North Carolina-Asheville sports arena (Go Bulldogs!). To our right is the road to the athletic training center. To our left is a horde of Zs, probably a hundred strong.

"Oh, crap," I say, looking past Stuart. "Homecoming committee is here."

"Go team?" Jon says. "Can we go faster now?"

"The truck didn't like eating that motorcycle," Stuart answers.

"I don't like getting eaten," Jon replies. "We could get out and run faster than this thing!"

"Speak for yourself," I say, my wounds reminding me that running isn't at the top of my options.

"We'll make it," Stuart says, "I want this truck."

"Why?" Jon says. "Not like we can go joyriding in it! And it makes a shit ton of noise! Every time we start it up it'll bring the Zs, so why keep it? We might as well park it in front of the gate and leave it there!"

Stuart glances over at Jon.

"What?"

"We won't park it in front of the gate," I say. "We'll park it on one side, blocking Hwy 251. Then when they come for us, we'll only have to worry about the other side of the road."

"Oh, good idea," Jon nods. "Wait…when they come for us?"

"Wall Street," Stuart says. "This shit ain't done yet. Trust me."

The horde of Zs is almost too us. I can actually make out the logos on some of the kids' clothes. Popular brands pre-Z. But this ain't no Benetton ad. This is real life and the kids are really just one color of dead grey.

"Move, move, move," Stuart says as his hand rhythmically slams against the steering wheel. The Zs get closer and we can hear their moans over the engine. "Come on!"

"MOVE!" we all shout.

The truck crests the hill and Stuart aims for the sports center. He tries to steer around the building, but we're blocked by a long steel bar across the access road. The brakes squeal and we stop.

"Rock, paper, scissors?" I ask.

"I'm on it," Jon says as he opens the door and jumps from the truck. He sprints to the bar and pulls on it, trying to swing it out of the way, but it won't budge. "Rusted!"

"Can't we ram it?" I ask.

"9-11," Stuart says.

"Not following."

"It looks harmless, but after 9-11, shit like that was reinforced." He looks at his side mirror. "We hit that and the already groaning engine will be toast."

"Shit," I say as I hop down from the truck too.

I limp over to Jon and we both start shoving against the bar. We can feel it start to give, but it's not fast enough. Behind the truck, the horde gets closer and closer. We shove more, putting our whole bodies into it. No dice. Just a creak and a cloud of red dust from the hinge.

"We'll have to figure something else out," Jon says. "We're out of time!"

Stuart shakes his head and we hear the truck's gears grind. Then the thing starts moving in reverse with Stuart looking at his side mirror. The dump truck plows into the Z horde and squashes about twenty of them before Stuart pulls forward again.

It gives us a minute longer and we use that to our full advantage. Jon and I get our hands against the bar and dig with our legs. It creaks, it groans, metal on metal shrieks, and then finally, it starts to move out towards the truck. Just as we get it clear, Stuart hits the gas and starts rolling quickly. Jon jumps into the cab and reaches for me.

I catch his hand and am almost up when I slip, my legs dragging on the ground.

"Stop!" Jon shouts.

"No," Stuart says, "we can't. I don't think this thing will get going again."

"Then fuck the truck! We're gonna lose Jace!"

"No, we aren't," Stuart says, "pull."

"I like the pulling!" I shout as my feet scrape the pavement. I look over and the horde is at the truck's rear. "Please, for the pulling now!"

Black, congealed blood drips from several undead mouths as they raise their arms towards me. I can see the hunger in their dead eyes. It's always surprising how much "life" they have when they're all riled and close to feeding. You can see them just perk right up, all set to get their chomping on.

Then Jon yanks me into the cab and I slam the door closed.

"Thanks," I say, catching my breath.

"Any time," he smiles, then points. "Behind that shed. The access road leads across the soccer field and down to Riverside."

Stuart takes his eyes off the road long enough to give Jon a look of disdain.

"What? I didn't know if you knew which way to go."

"I know which way to go," Stuart says. "This was my idea."

"Well, maybe you had a different route in mind," Jon says. "How am I supposed to know?"

"What route would that be, Padre?" Stuart asks. "How many routes are there then? You have a list on you?"

"Okay, okay, don't get all touchy," Jon says, lifting his hands in surrender. "Same team, Stuart."

Stuart just frowns and grumbles a bit.

"I think he needs a nap," I whisper.

"Screw you, Jace," Stuart says. "I'll sleep when I'm dead."

"Not necessarily," Jon says, hooking a thumb over his shoulder. "I'm sure that's what half those dorm rats thought pre-Z and now look at them. Never gonna rest again."

"Speaking of," I say as we hit the soccer field and rip through the long grass. "How many do you think are back there?"

"I know, I know," Stuart says.

Jon rubs at his face. "Can't lead them all back to Whispering Pines."

"So...?" I ask. "We make a stand?"

"Yes, but not here," Stuart says. "Wait until we get down to 251. Then we pick one of the spots that's closest to the river with a cliff on the other side."

"Box them in?"

"Narrow their charge and take them out," Stuart says.

"With what?" Jon asks. "Jace's bat?"

"The Bitch," I say. "She is called The Bitch."

"I don't care what she's called," Jon says. "We don't have enough weapons."

"Then we look for some," Stuart says. "This isn't our first rodeo."

"True, but I'd rather be the bull in this than the clown," Jon says.

"Me too," Stuart nods, "but clowns serve a purpose too."

"I hate clowns," I say. "Why'd you have to bring up clowns? Zs aren't enough? Gotta talk about the smiley creepy guys too?"

"I like clowns," Stuart says. "My wife used to collect them."

Jon and I look at each other. It's the first time we've ever heard Stuart talk about pre-Z other than his Marines days. As far as we've known he was immaculately conceived and just showed up fully grown in the middle of Camp Lejeune one day, rip roaring ready to kill, kill, kill!

"What?" Stuart asks. "You know those little ceramic clowns? Not the big ones with the sad faces, but the small ones that are busy doing tumbles and cartwheels? She liked those. I always brought her as many as I could carry when I was deployed."

"I thought you trained Marines?" I ask.

"That too," he says. "She loved those clowns. Hold on!"

We are so busy listening to him that we don't see that he is heading straight for the edge of the field and a drop off.

"Fuck!" I shout as I hold my hand to the ceiling of the cab, bracing myself for the drop.

"Dammit!" Jon yells next to me.

The front of the truck seems to hover in mid air then fall forward, slamming and bouncing against the side of the hill. It's almost a straight drop and I am seriously worried that the truck is just going to start tumbling end over end. That stops being my worry when I realize that the bottom of the hill isn't a nice, gradual grade, but a straight shot at the asphalt.

"Shit," Stuart growls as he turns the wheel slightly.

We feel the truck start to turn, but we also feel the wheels start to leave the hill.

"Ah, shit," Jon says.

I agree with him 100%.

Stuart is able to angle the truck just right so that the front wheel, and not the grill, hits the pavement first. The back bounces up in the air and we wait for it to flip us over as it lifts, but all of our cursing/praying works, because then it slams back down in a teeth jarring crunch.

The engine stalls and Stuart turns the key over and over.

"Shit," he says.

"Dead? Or flooded?" Jon asks.

"Not a clue," Stuart says and jumps from the truck. He unlatches the hood and flips it up, bracing it with its bars. "Come give me a hand!"

We follow and climb up the wheel wells until all three of us are looking into the engine.

"Do you guys know what we're looking for?" Jon asks.

Moans and the sound of breaking underbrush tell us that the Zs are coming. They'll be down the hill pretty quick, since most of them will probably just trip and fall their way down. We have a very limited time to trouble shoot a dump truck engine none of us knows how to work on.

"I don't smell gas," I say, trying to work it out, "and I don't see smoke."

"It could just be dead," Stuart says. "It sounded like it was going to throw a rod soon anyway."

"We would have heard that happen, right?" I ask.

Stuart just shrugs.

"Okay, so what happened?" I stare into the engine, my brain working on overdrive. I'm the problem solver. That's why they keep me around. I figure shit out with the barest of information. I can do this. "We took a hard bounce, right?"

"You need me to confirm that?" Jon says. "You were in the same truck we were."

The Zs are even closer.

"Dammit," Stuart says as he hops down, machete in hand. "I'll buy us time. Figure it out, Jace."

"Right," I nod, "figuring it out."

"You were asking about the bounce," Jon says.

"Thanks. Yes, the bounce," I say. "It could have loosened something. What looks loose?"

"It's a piece of shit engine," Jon replies. "It all looks loose."

We hear a thwack and then a body drop. I don't have time to look behind me. I just have to trust Stuart to do his job.

"Something specific," I say. "Look for loose wires. Loose cables. Loose belts. Anything that is hanging down or disconnected that shouldn't be."

"Again, I don't know what should or shouldn't be hanging down," Jon snaps.

Thwack, drop. Thwack, drop. Thwack…thwack, drop.

"You aren't helping," I say to Jon.

"I don't know how!" Jon says. "I know nothing about engines!"

"Fine, fine, fine," I mutter as I scan and rescan the engine, going over everything with my eyes.

Thwack, thwack, thwack. Drop, drop, thwack, drop.

"Gonna need to get moving," Stuart says, slightly out of breath. "No pressure. Just letting you know we have about fifty seconds."

Nope, no pressure there.

"Get in the cab," I order Jon. "Turn the key when I say so."

"Okay," he says.

I study the engine one more time, and then reach as far down as I can and grab a handful of thick wires. One is connected, a second is connected, a third and a fourth. The fifth isn't connected, neither is the sixth. I follow the wires back and realize what I'm looking at. Distributor cables.

"Well, shit," I say as I plug cables five and six in. The rest are good to go. "Crank it!"

Jon turns the key and the engine sputters, sputters, sputters, kicks over, sputters, dies.

"FUCK!" I yell. "Do it again!"

Thwack, thwack.

"Son of a bitch!" Stuart shouts. "Fucking die!"

Thwack, drop.

Jon turns and the engine sputters, sputters, catches, revs, revs, stays running!

"Let's go!" I yell at Stuart, but he's already on the other side of the hood and helping me slam it down and latch it.

"Move," he says to Jon as he hops into the cab.

I look back as I climb up and see several Zs with their heads split open sprawled on the ground, goo pooling about them. I also see quite a horde coming at us and coming down the hill. The first horde has grown; they must have texted that there was a meat party, because it looks like half the campus is on our asses.

"Can we get this thing up to speed?" I ask, slamming the door. "Because the game just got out and the frat boys are coming our way."

Stuart looks over at me and frowns as he prepares to shift into second gear. "Make sense, Jace."

"Big horde O' Zs crawling up our tailpipe," I say.

"Yeah, I saw them," Stuart says.

"Then why'd you tell me to make sense?"

"Because I wasn't sure if that's what you meant."

"Really, guys?" Jon says. "Is this the time?"

Stuart shoves the gear shift into second and a huge grinding sound echoes from under the truck. The stick pops back on him and he snatches his hand away.

"Ow! Dammit!" he shouts.

He tries again, but the truck won't shift into second.

"That's not good, right?" Jon asks.

"No," Stuart says. "It means we can't get above about five miles an hour without burning out the transmission or the engine."

"Still faster than the Zs, though," I say and lean out the window for a look. "Or not."

"What?" Jon asks as he leans past me and has a look. "Crap."

"Zs can't go faster than five miles an hour," Stuart says. "We'll stay ahead of them."

"But we won't have a lead," I say. "We need to get rid of this horde before we get to Whispering Pines."

We all three sit there while the truck rumbles along at its snail's pace.

"There is one way," Jon says.

"No," Stuart and I say at the same time.

"I'm pretty fast," Jon says. "I just draw them away in the other direction. We're close enough to home that I can double back without them getting me. Not the first time I've been solo out here."

"No," Stuart says.

"No way," I agree. "We aren't splitting up."

Jon starts to rummage around in the cab and comes up with a nasty looking tire iron. Long, thick, strong. Way bigger than the one that comes with the free jack in your average sedan. This guy is easily three feet long with an already wicked point on the straight end. The wrench end is as big as a fist, ready to work the huge lug nuts off the truck tires.

"Look at this," Jon says. "Come on, guys. I can do this. It's our only option."

"No, the other option is we get to the gate and let the sentries pick off the Zs," Stuart says.

We can tell he doesn't believe his own bullshit. The amount of ammo that would be wasted? It would be devastating. This horde has become a fucking herd. While I'm pretty sure the gate would hold, it would be put to the test.

And we still have Wall Street and his Day Raiders to deal with.

"Ha," I chuckle.

"What?" Jon asks.

"Wall Street and the Day Raiders," I say.

"Is that some rock band?"

"Nah, it's the name I came up with for Wall Street and those bikers."

"Good one," Stuart says. "Clever."

"Thanks," I smile.

"So…about the bait thing?" Jon asks.

"No," Stuart and I repeat.

"Not even with this?" he says, holding up the tire iron, waving his hand over it like a sales model.

"No, Vanna, not even with that," I say.

"You guys are no fun," Jon says, "which means, sometimes you have to make your own fun!"

He grabs the handle and shoves me back against the seat, pinning me so I can't stop him. Out he jumps, tucking and rolling into the small ditch by the side of the road. Even over the truck engine, I can hear the moans of the herd grow louder as they catch sight of him.

"You fucker!" I shout and start to go after him, but Stuart's hand clamps down on my shoulder and pulls me back.

"No, you don't," he says. "He may have a chance, but you won't limp fast enough. You'll be eaten before you get twenty yards."

"FUCK!" I yell as I slam my fists against the dash. "Ow…"

We can hear Jon hooting and hollering. I look back at him and he's waving his hands over his head, getting the Zs attention. He looks at me and winks, then goes back to taunting the Zs. Most of them shuffle towards him, but some stay after us. I guess that's better than all of them.

"Come on, come on, go," I say quietly. "Fucking run. Dumbass, run."

"Timing is everything," Stuart says.

Finally, FINALLY, Jon turns and books ass up a small side street. I can see him huffing and puffing as he fights the weed-choked road as well as gravity. Maybe three quarters of the Zs go for the bait. That leaves a quarter for us. That's still a lot of Zs.

We come around a bend and Stuart points.

"That downhill grade could give us enough speed to get ahead of the ones that didn't follow Jon," he says. "How many do you guess?"

"Seventy, probably," I reply, staring straight out the windshield.

He looks over at me. "Really? That many?"

I shrug. "That's my guess. How many can you take?"

"Jesus," he sighs, "maybe twenty before my arms give out."

"I can probably do that many," I say and he chuckles. "What? You think you're better at killing Zs?"

"I am better at killing Zs," Stuart replies. "I'm better at killing in general."

"Good point," I say. "So I guess I can take ten."

"If I knew the transmission wouldn't give out, I'd just back over them again," Stuart says. "But I don't dare stop this thing and shift into reverse."

"How far are we?" I ask.

"A mile, maybe," he says.

"That's not far. If we are going to stop them, we have to do it now or we'll be too close to Whispering Pines."

Then it hits me.

"You could run up ahead," I say. "I'll keep driving and you run to the gate. Get your crew and head back this way. That'll give us the numbers to take them and we can still keep the truck."

"So we split up even more?" Stuart says. "Bad tactics."

"Any other plan you can think of?"

He sighs and shakes his head. "No."

"So we do it," I say. "Let's switch."

He shifts into neutral and scoots towards me. I crawl over him and get into the driver's seat. I depress the clutch and shift back into first. The truck lurches and comes close to stalling, but I give it enough gas and it keeps moving.

"Don't even try to shift into second," Stuart says. "I know you, Jace. You like to test things for yourself. Don't."

He opens the passenger door and climbs out onto the steps. He swings the door shut easily, avoiding getting hit. I have a feeling he's done that move before. He gives me a quick salute, and then jumps down. He may be older, but the man can book it. He pumps his arms and sprints well ahead of me, and then is gone around a curve. But, not before I notice the dark stain on the back of his shirt has grown.

I reach behind me and can feel the sticky wetness of his blood on the seat.

"You fucker," I say. "You knew you were hurt, but went anyway."

I keep glancing over at the passenger side mirror and all of the Zs behind me. Is it me or are they getting closer? Can't be. Zs can't move fast enough. It's probably that thing with mirrors where objects are closer than they appear.

Wait...

That would be the opposite. God...are they getting closer?

I try to shove the thought from my mind and focus on the road ahead, but I can't help and sneak glances. They are gaining. The fucking Zs are gaining on me.

"At least I'm still moving," I say aloud. "That's something."

You know what? For a smart guy, I'm pretty fucking stupid. I'm not a big believer in the afterlife or heaven or God or anything like that. But one thing I do believe in is karma. I've just experienced it too much to ignore it. My whole life has been one long chain of spiritual cause and effect events. I should know better than to jinx myself by saying, "At least I'm still moving."

The truck sputters, sputters, lurches, and dies. I try to turn the ignition as the truck slowly comes to a stop, but it does nothing. I crank and crank and crank, hearing the battery get weaker and weaker.

"What the fuck?" I say. "What's wrong now, you piece of shit? Huh? You need a binky? Baby need its fucking binky?"

I look at the dashboard and slap my forehead.

No, baby needs to be fed.

"Out. Of. Fucking. Gas," I say, "or diesel. Whatever."

I can see the mini-herd (mega-horde?) behind me, maybe ten yards back and getting closer. I take inventory of my weapons: The Bitch. I count again and come up with the same number. One. Nothing I can do about that.

"Better roll 'em up, kids," I snicker with nervous laughter as I roll the windows up tight. I lock the doors for good measure. Not that a Z could open the doors, they can't work latches, but it makes me feel better.

Dead hands begin to slap against the sides of the truck, and pretty soon I feel the weight of them pressing in. Their bodies, their constant shambling movement, slowly rock the dump truck from side to side. Not a lot. Not like kids jumping on the bumper of a car, but enough that I know there's trouble in River City. That starts with T and rhymes with Z, and stands for, uh, well, Zs.

The slapping gets louder. Then the moans, the groans. And that wet sound that happens when their flesh gets stuck on something and rips right off the bone. I hate that sound. That sound is the worst.

I can see them in the mirror, getting closer to the cab, their mouths hanging open, congealed bloody drool dripping from their lips and chins. Those that have lips and chins, at least. Some don't even have lower jaws and the viscous fluids just drop from their palates. Flaps of flesh hang in random strips from faces, necks, shoulders, arms, breasts, and bellies.

Hey, a cheerleader! I can't wait to tell Stella I saw an undead cheerleader. She's always hated cheerleaders. Like I hate clowns. Well, maybe not exactly like I hate clowns.

The slapping! Ugh, I want it just to stop. I try to keep the Stella train of thought going, try to think of the kids, home, the neighborhood. I even try to envision what the next HOA meeting will be like. "Hey, guys! Guess what? We have more neighbors! And they aren't really into the HOA covenants. In fact, they aren't into letting us live! Whatcha think of that, huh? Huh? Guys?"

The face that appears at my window is scorched from the scalp down to the eye sockets. It looks like someone set its hair on fire, but the thing got lucky and dunked itself in a toilet or something. Really weird. Then I have to wonder, looking at the burn pattern, if that isn't what happened. And the way the skin looks, I then have to wonder if the poor soul was alive when the burning and the dunking happened.

"Go away please," I mouth. I don't say it out loud. Voices, living real voices, tend to get them wound up, stir that hunger and shit.

The face is pushed aside as more and more Zs get to the window. Scorch Scalp decides to move to the front of the truck and climb on. Hmmm, it's actually climbing onto the hood. That shows some athleticism. Maybe he died when a hazing went wrong? "Welcome to the lacrosse team! Now we burn your hair off! Oh, shit, and you're coming back from the dead? Eeeeeeek!"

Ah, man, Scorch Scalp isn't wearing pants. Or underwear. Don't puke, don't puke.

It sees me and pushes right up against the windshield. Scorch Scalp hisses, showing his teeth...and the meat stuck in them. He's fed recently. Like really recently. Jesus. Do you think that makes them stronger? More agile? Like a flesh battery recharge? Fuck, I hope not.

Slap! Slap! SLAPSLAPSLAPSLAP!

"Stop it!" I cry, then clamp my hand over my mouth. What the fuck was I thinking? Why? Why did I do that?

The Zs like it, though. It seems to energize them, give them new hope that they can crack this cab like a walnut and pick the tasty nut meat (me) out and have a tasty treat. The slapping is now banging. The windows don't look as strong as they did just seconds ago. And look! Scorch Scalp has a buddy! Oh, two buddies? Sure there's room, why not. Three? Four? Five, six, seven? Fuck...

Slapping to banging to...cracking?

Shit, the passenger window is breaking. I stare at the spider cracks that are slowly spreading as hand after undead hand slams against the safety glass. Safety glass? Not feeling so safe, thank you! The cracks spread more, not so slow. Not slow at all. Pretty fast, actually. Huh. I think this shit is going to-

"FUCK!" I scream as the glass crumbles inward. I kick and kick and kick at the hands that reach for me. I jam The Bitch at the hands, stabbing, gouging, and trying to shred them. "Stay back! Fuck off! Fuck you! FUCK YOU!"

The hands keep reaching, but there are so many of them attached to so many bodies that they clog the window. They can't get bodies in. And bodies are where the teeth are. Okay, okay, this could be fine.

CRACK!

I slowly turn my head and see the split in the windshield. The Putrescent Seven will not have a problem getting through that window when the glass goes. Not going to get clogged there.

A hand grabs my foot and I scream. I don't yell like a man or below in a deep voice. I scream in a high-pitched way only dogs can hear. I'd say I scream like a little girl, but that would be an insult to the marvelous screaming ability that little girls have. My scream can only be described as a supersonic attempt at shattering every piece of glass in the world.

Speaking of shattering glass... There goes the driver's side window and here come the Z hands. Not to be confused with jazz hands. Those are kinda fun. Who doesn't love a little song and dance in the apocalypse?

Aaaaaaaaaah! The hands that grab my head are wet! Slimy wet! Like a dog bone left out in the rain after a day of gnawing. Not jazz hands! NOT JAZZ HANDS! Skin sloughs off in my hair as I jerk away. Oh, but I can't jerk too far since there are those supersonic scream inducing hands on the other side of the cab. So I settle in the middle, turning from side to side, smashing what I can with The Bitch. Soon the cab is covered with the oozing drippings of a thousand spike wounds. I keep bashing and smashing with The Bitch, but I'm not really helping my cause. I'm just creating more of a mess. The Zs don't give a shit if I prick their fingers with my mighty spikes.

Back and forth, back and forth; smash and bash; spike and drip.

CRACK!

The windshield. The fucking windshield! Aren't dump trucks supposed to have windshields made of like super glass? Indestructible glass that can stop a boulder at sixty miles an hour? I mean, dump trucks are around nothing but construction work. Can't they stop falling girders and shit?

CRACK!

Apparently not.

CRACK!

Oh shit, oh fuck, oh shit, oh fuck...oh shit.

The windshield is buckling under the weight of the Zs on the hood and I can see more climbing up and joining them. Great.

All I can do is close my eyes and pray I hear gunshots. Come on, Stuart. You were running pretty fast. You have to have gotten to the gate by now. But then, there was that dark stain on his back. Oh, shit, did he fucking keel over and die before getting to the gate? Did a Z catch him in his weakened state? Oh, shit. Please let there be gunshots. Please, I have never wanted to hear the sound of gunpowder igniting so much in my life.

But as I hear the windshield start to give, the sucking sound of the seal giving way around the frame, the crackcrackcrack of the glass crumpling under the weight of the Zs, all I can think about, besides the fact I'll never see my family again (which I really try not to think about), is that I'm going to fucking die wearing bright pink yoga pants and a purple shirt with a mother fucking glittery butterfly.

Fuck!

CHAPTER FIVE

Okay, so I have to open my eyes. I can't just die like a fucking pussy, all curled into a ball and whimpering on the bench seat of a dump truck. I have to open my eyes and face death like a man. Yep, just need to open my eyes. Come on now, Jace, open those eyes.

But I really don't want to. God, how I don't want to see what I hear. So I do the next best thing and roll off the bench seat and continue my cowardly curling on the floor, jammed up underneath the dashboard. At least a dump truck has a lot of legroom. I get fully wedged into the passenger's side and cover my head with my arms, as chunks of windshield fall over me. The hungry groans and moans of the Zs get louder and louder as they crawl through the windshield and the windows.

Half-rotted, and even fully rotted, fingers grab for me, their blackened nails digging into my forearms. Can I get turned from a scratch? Is that true? I know bites are death, and everyone has been told that being scratched can mean infection from germs and shit, but I don't think I've ever known anyone to turn from a scratch. And I've known a lot that have turned since Z-Day.

What the fuck am I talking about? I'm not going to live long enough to get give a shit! I am only a couple minutes from being buried under a mound of undead bodies all trying to get a piece of my sweet, sweet meat. They are going to fill this cab and eat me bit by bit, as I lie on the floor and scream like a prom queen in a slasher movie. Oh, am I screaming again? Yeah, I may be. Don't think it's the Zs hitting those decibels, not with their putrid vocal chords.

So, here I am, my forearms bleeding from the Z fingers that can reach me, trying not to think of the family that is at home worried about me and may never know my fate, dressed in the most ridiculous outfit a man can die in, screaming like a madman, and what do I hear?

A war cry.

That's the only way I can describe it. This undulating wail of violence and anger. There is no fear in this scream; unlike mine which is pretty much 90% fear and maybe 10% stress relief. This scream/wail/yell/call to kill echoes over the dump truck and I decide now is a good time to open my eyes. The Zs have started to retreat. Well, they try to, but they have jammed themselves in the windows pretty damn good. Too stupid to back out one at a time, the Zs thrash and flail, conflicted between their need to eat me and their need to eat whatever is outside the truck. For being undead, they have a lot of needs and conflicts. Fucking Zs...

I feel the truck rocking as Zs start moving towards the war cry. There are too many for me to have any hope that the cab will clear out. I can see rotted bodies climbing over the crushed windshield, trying to get to the floor and my flesh. I try, god how I try, to shove myself up inside the dashboard, but it doesn't make any difference as cold, cloudy eyes turn on me and rotted mouths open in a single hiss of hunger.

"Fuck off!" I shout at them. "You want a piece of my pink ass? Come and get it, fuckers!"

And boy do they. Or try. Engineering not being their forte, the Zs have actually blocked access to me by pushing what's left of the windshield down against the seat. It won't hold long, I can see, that but it gives me a few more seconds of screaming time.

Then I notice that I'm the only one screaming. The war cry is silent. Poor bastard, whoever he was.

Then a Z is gone. Like gone. Yanked out of the truck. Then a second. And a third. A fourth. The windshield brigade of death is out of sight, pulled away, they are no more. All that's left are the Zs wedged into the side window frames. And in seconds they start to shudder. First the driver's side window: gone, gone, gone. No more Zs. Then the passenger window, right above me. Once again, no more Zs.

"You gots to stop screaming," a voice says from outside the truck. "I didn't kill these Zs so you can bring more."

I see a couple of hands grab the window frame then a face is there. Hey...I know that face.

"I know you," I say. "You're Elsbeth."

"Hey, Long Pork." She grins and I don't quite feel safer. But I'm not screaming anymore. "You're truck is broke. Why'd your friends leave you? They hates you or something?"

"They didn't leave me," I say. "One ran off as a diversion and the other went to get help."

She looks over her shoulder. "Help? But there's only like fifty of the Zs out here. Grown men can't kill fifty Zs?" Then her eyes light up and the hugest grin comes across her face. "My stick! You got my stick!" She reaches in and snags The Bitch from the seat. "Thanks, Long Pork!"

She jumps away and I listen closely, not sure I can uncurl from my heroic fetal position. I hear a few whacks and...laughter? Yeah, she's out there laughing and I'm in here whimpering in pink yoga pants. Not wet with pee. Not at all.

I finally shove the broken windshield out of the way; it just folds in on itself, and I climb out of the truck. I stand there on the asphalt, in my not wet with pee yoga pants and purple butterfly shirt, and gape at the carnage. There are dozens and dozens of Zs strewn everywhere, their heads crushed or ripped off. Many are missing limbs and I can see said missing limbs buried in the skulls of other Zs.

One girl did all of this?

"What are you doing?" I ask Elsbeth, as I watch her going through the still Zs' pockets. Those that have pockets. "Are you robbing the undead?"

Elsbeth looks up at me, squinting against the sunlight, and cocks her head. "Robbing? What you mean by that?"

"You're going through their pockets. Why?"

Elsbeth shrugs then holds up her hand. A few coins, a paper clip, and a Swiss Army knife.

"Never know what you might find," she says as she stands up and lets the coins fall from her hand. She puts the paper clips in her pockets and opens the large blade on the knife. "Still sharp."

She hands it to me and hoists The Bitch over her shoulder. I look at the knife and the size of the blade compared to the bat. "I'd rather have The Bitch."

She looks at me and I can see her trying to figure out what I mean. I nod at the bat on her shoulder. "The Bitch. That's what I call your bat. It's like mine."

"This is better," she says and takes it from her shoulder, looking at it. "The Bitch. Good name. I never named it. Thanks."

"Uh, sure," I nod then look around. I can hear moaning coming from around the bend and know more Zs are on the way. "Uh, Whispering Pines is just up the road." I point ahead. "Not far. We should get going."

Elsbeth looks at me then at the road. She does this a few times and nods. Then starts walking away. I follow her, but can't even come close to keeping pace as my leg feels like it's on fire. And, well, Elsbeth is a really fast walker. She looks over her shoulder at me and smiles.

"You're a gimp, Long Pork," she says as she comes back and takes one of my arms and drapes it over her shoulders. "I wouldn't have saved your gimp ass if I'd known you'd be so slow, but Pa's gone and I just got you. Still, slow don't deserve to live."

"Well, I'm an exception because I'm so awesome," I say.

"That right?" she laughs. "Don't you mean because you're so pretty? What with those pants on and all. Damn, Long Pork, I lived in that house for a long time and I wouldn't be caught dead in those things. They were left upstairs for a reason. Even if Pa wanted me to wear them."

"Not really my choice," I say. She's pretty talkative, a different person. I have to wonder how much of the stupid was just an act for her pa. "And don't call me Long Pork. My name is Jace. You can just call me Jace."

"Nope," Elsbeth says as she helps me hobble along. "I save your pinky ass and I get to name you. Long Pork is your name now."

"I don't think my wife will like that," I say. "The kids will think it's funny, but my wife won't be too pleased that you named me after your cannibal cuisine."

"Cooz-een?" she asks. "What's that mean?"

"Cuisine? Like the way you prepare food. A style of food. You know, like Mexican cuisine, Italian cuisine, stuff like that."

"Only one way you prepare foods," she replies. "Over a fire. That's my cooz-een."

"Yeah, I was made quite aware of that," I say.

We walk for a few minutes before I notice the landmarks that tell us we're close to Whispering Pines. "Just around the corner," I say.

She stops and lets my arm fall away. "Good luck, Long Pork," she says and starts to take off up the hill and into the brush.

"Hey!" I shout. "Wait!"

"Holy cripes, Long Pork," she hisses. "You's got to shut the hell up."

"Where are you going?" I ask. "Whispering Pines is this way."

She shakes her head. "They won't let me in. We tried once. Killed Uncle Jeb with one shot and then said they'd kill us if we didn't move on."

"Ah, shit," I whisper. *Jesus...* I shake my head back and forth. "They won't shoot you now. You're with me. They'll let you in. They have to."

She laughs loud and then closes her mouth, her eyes wide and senses alert. When she's satisfied she hasn't brought Zs down on us she gives me a hard look. "Nobody has to do nothing no more, Long Pork. Ain't you got no sense in your head? Nobody has to do nothing."

She has a point.

"Jace? Jace!" Stuart says as he and part of his defensive crew come jogging up to me. "Damn, man! How'd you get away?"

"And what the hell are you wearing?" one of the crew asks, a guy named Harlan Tobias, as the others just stare at me.

"It was hot yoga night," I say. "I didn't have time to change before being surrounded by Zs." I hold up the knife. "But they were handing out knives to the first lucky dozen. So that's a plus."

"I think Jace has gone over the edge, man," Harlan whispers to the man next to him.

"You," Elsbeth snarls and the men all see her a few feet away for the first time. She had just stopped being there for a minute, almost invisible, until she wanted to be noticed. "You killed Pa."

Stuart turns and gives her the full weight of his stare. For the record, Stuart's stare, when it is on full blast and without any mercy or compassion, is terrifying. Other than a mob of Zs, it's the only other thing that would make me piss my pants. Not that I pissed my pants. I'm not admitting that at all. But Elsbeth doesn't wither under his eyes. Instead, she seems to puff up, her body filling with confidence as she slowly walks over and gets face to face with Stuart.

"Uh, boss?" Harlan asks. "Should we shoot her?"

Before anyone can do anything, Elsbeth sweeps Stuart's legs out from under him. The others move on her and in a blink, they're down on the ground, clutching body parts, mainly their crotches, and all writhing in pain. Elsbeth raises The Bitch over Stuart.

"Say you're sorry," she orders.

"For what then?" Stuart asks.

"For killing Pa," Elsbeth says.

"No," Stuart says.

"Uh, dude," I say, "just say you're sorry."

"I'm not, though," Stuart says as he lies on the asphalt. "I'd do it again in a heartbeat to save your pink ass, Jace."

"Okay, I need to get home and change," I say. "I'm really sick of everyone commenting on my pink ass."

"You ain't gonna say you're sorry?" Elsbeth asks.

"No, young lady, I'm not," Stuart says. "Are you gonna kill me with that thing?"

"Maybe," she says.

"But maybe not then?"

"Maybe not."

"I think you're leaning towards the maybe not part," Stuart says. "Because since I did kill your Pa, you don't have anyone else. You kill me and Jace can't take you back to Whispering Pines."

"I'd be fine on my own," she replies. "I can handle the Zs."

"I can attest to that," I say.

"For a time, I'm sure you would be," Stuart nods. "But not against the people. There's a lot of them and they aren't looking to make friends."

"I don't make friends with food no how anyway," Elsbeth shrugs.

Stuart suddenly kicks out at her, but she jumps his legs and comes down with one knee on his chest, the spikes of The Bitch pressed against his throat. They stare at each other and I'm pretty sure I witness the first ever successful example of nuclear fusion outside the Sun itself. What I mean to say, is that staring shit is intense.

Stuart gives her a slight nod. Elsbeth watches him for a split second and then nods back. She gets off his chest and he pushes up onto his elbows. He looks over at me and frowns. "Gonna need some help, Jace."

I see the bloodstain on the asphalt and remember that he's wounded. The motherfucker runs to get help and then hikes it back while bleeding from god knows where. Adding that to the long list of why I don't piss off James "Don't Call Me Jimmy" Stuart.

I get him up and Elsbeth steps past us and starts to help the others. They warily take her hand, one at a time, but don't argue with the olive branch. I highly doubt any of them will ever argue with Elsbeth.

"Let's get you home and fixed up," I say to Stuart, "you look worse than I do."

"Not possible, ma'am," Stuart smiles.

"No, seriously, Jace," Harlan says, "what the fuck is up with the outfit?"

"You are welcome to shut your pie hole," I say. "No, seriously."

"You can't be dressed like that and not expect questions," Stuart says.

"I didn't dress like this!" I protest.

"Quiet down, Long Pork," Elsbeth warns. "Still gotta watch for Zs."

Stuart's crew eyes Elsbeth then me, when she says Long Pork.

I let the name slide by and glance at Stuart. "Jon?"

"I don't know," he says. "We're gonna get back home and then work out how to go look for him."

"You aren't going anywhere," I say.

"Neither are you, limpy," he replies.

"I don't think Stella's letting me out of her sight any time soon."

"Who's Stella?" Elsbeth asks. "That your wife that won't like me calling you Long Pork? She a nice lady or a ball buster?"

The guys all laugh. A little too hard for my taste.

"I wouldn't call her a ball buster," I say. Harlan snorts.

"Hey, now," Stuart snaps. "Show some respect for the lady. She takes care of the children and keeps their brains from turning to mush. When one of those kids is grown and fighting next to you, you'll be thanking her up and down for making sure that kid has a brain in his or her head."

"Didn't mean nothing by it," Harlan grumbles.

"So, does she bust your balls?" Elsbeth asks again.

"Why do you keep asking that?" I say. "What's up with the ball busting?"

"Pa said women are ball busters and can't be trusted with nothing 'cept cleaning, cooking, and fucking."

"Jesus," I say. Everyone is silent for a minute before I respond. "No, she's not a ball buster. She's the best thing that ever happened to me and I'd die for her in an instant."

"Huh," Elsbeth replies. "Die for her? Guess she's good at fucking, because no one is gonna die for cooking or cleaning."

There is dead silence for a brief moment before everyone bursts out laughing.

"Oh, shit, man," Harlan says. "That's the funniest thing I've heard in a long time!"

"What?" Elsbeth asks, honestly perplexed. "What's so funny?"

This gets everyone laughing even harder and I give her a big smile so she knows she's not the butt of the joke. I really don't want her pissed off when we are so close to home.

Speaking of, we come around the last bend in the road and it starts to dip down to the entrance to Whispering Pines. I have never been so glad to see that gate.

"Open up," Stuart orders.

"Gotta check for bites," a sentry replies.

"Yes, you do," Stuart says. "So open up and let us in so we can get checked then."

"Outside the gate," the sentry says.

"Inside ain't the procedure anymore," the other sentry replies, obviously uncomfortable with how the conversation is turning.

"Like hell it's not," Stuart barks. "I made the damn procedure! Open the gate!"

"Gotta get checked first, James," Brenda says, appearing at the watchtower. "New rules."

"That makes no damn sense, Brenda!" Stuart shouts and Brenda looks like she's been physically slapped by his voice.

"You hush now!" she warns. "Or none of you are coming inside. Just get checked and you can be done with it. All checks happen outside the gate now. New rule in the covenants. The Board just approved it."

"Whoa," I say, "you can't just call a Board vote without giving the full HOA notice."

"Emergency measures," Brenda says. "You'll be informed once you are inside. After you get checked."

"Jesus," I grumble as I start to strip off my clothes.

"And what are you wearing, Jace?" Brenda asks from above. "That outfit is ridiculous."

"Yeah, yeah, I know," I say.

We all stand there naked, checking each other over. Except for Elsbeth. She refuses to undress.

"They won't let you in otherwise," I say. "It's to make sure there are no bites."

Elsbeth eyes me for a minute (luckily her eyes stay up) and then looks at the gate. She squints up at Brenda and frowns.

"If she doesn't undress right now," Brenda says, "then she isn't coming in ever. I'm not keen on someone new being allowed into Whispering Pines."

"She saved my life," I say, "and she's going to undress." I look at her. "Don't be shy. It's all good. No one is going to act like a pervert."

"I don't know what a prevert is," Elsbeth says. "But y'all have to promise not to stare at me. Sometimes Pa would stare at me when he was done with a new…"

"What?" I ask, not sure I want to. "Done with a new what?"

She doesn't answer, just starts removing the many layers of filthy clothing from her body. When she is naked, we all try not to stare like she'd asked, but it is very hard.

"Pa called them my beauty marks," Elsbeth says. "But I know they ain't beautiful. Even I know that."

I have said before that Elsbeth is a gorgeous young woman, but it isn't her muscular body that we all try not to stare at. It's what covers that body.

"Oh, my…" Brenda whispers from above.

Without us saying anything, the gate opens and we all wait for Elsbeth to go first. She looks at me and I nod. She avoids everyone else's stares and slips inside the gate. I'm right behind her, followed closely by the rest, their eyes glued to what covers her skin.

Burns. Layers of burn marks. Circles, squares, triangles, s-shapes, spirals. All deliberate and covering nearly every inch of her skin, from wrist to shoulder, calf to thigh, across her back, her belly, and her breasts.

"Holy Mary, Mother of Joseph," Mindy says as she surrounds Elsbeth with a group of her security officers. "That ain't right."

"Don't stare," Elsbeth says, and I can hear many emotions in her voice, not the least of which is anger.

I have a pretty good idea what the woman is capable of and I step in between Mindy and Elsbeth. "She's going home with me," I say, surprised at the words even as they come out of my mouth. "She's going to get cleaned up and then fed. You can do your interview at my place later."

"Dude."

"Whoa."

"Stella is gonna kill him."

I hear all of these comments behind me and ignore them. I especially ignore the last comment. Stella *is* going to kill me.

"Can't let you do that, Jace," Mindy says. "Express orders from Brenda. She is to come with me and be debriefed."

Stuart laughs and inserts himself between Mindy and me. "Debriefed? Exactly what does that mean? Please, I'd love to hear this."

Stuart may be a guy that follows orders, but he has never been one to condone incompetence or insincerity, both traits that Mindy seems to possess in full.

"Well, she has to tell us what she knows," Mindy says.

"And?" Stuart prompts. "Go on."

"Well, she could have vital information about the people coming after us," Mindy says. "Those people you ran into."

Stuart looks over his shoulder and up at the watchtower. Brenda is against the rail, staring directly at him.

"Those people…" His voice trails off.

He gently takes Elsbeth by the elbow and directs her over to me. She tries to press against me, her anger having turned to confusion and fear. I keep my forearm between us, making sure certain parts don't, well, touch.

"I think the young woman will be going home with Jace, so Stella can get her cleaned up," Stuart states, his eyes still locked with Brenda's. "Then Dr. McCormick will examine her. Once she gives the okay, I think a debriefing is a good idea."

"Stuart," I start to say, but he holds up his hand.

"With Jace and me present," Stuart says, his face turning back to Mindy. She quickly sees he's very serious. "That work for you?"

Mindy looks up at Brenda, as we all do. She nods slightly and Mindy steps aside.

"I'll be by later," Mindy says, "I want to get it done before dinner time."

"We'll see," Stuart says. "I'm going to speak with Melissa. Jon's still out there."

"I'll accompany you," Brenda says. "I'd like to hear what you have to say. Then you and I can sit down with our Head of Security here and have an even bigger conversation."

"That works," Stuart says.

"Does it now, Mr. Stuart?" Brenda asks as she descends from the watchtower. "How kind of you to acknowledge that."

"Um, I'm going to have to veto that," I say, pointing to the ragged wound on Stuart's back. "Dr. McCormick will need to look at that first. That looks deep."

"I'm fine," Stuart says, "I've had worse."

"Bullshit," I say. "Well, sure, you may have had worse, but you aren't fine. I know how much blood-"

"Thank you, Jason," Stuart says. "The doctor lives by you so I'll let you walk me there. Then I go straight to the Billings' house."

"After fetching us," Brenda says, "right, Mr. Stuart?"

"Yes, ma'am," Stuart nods and walks off. "Coming, Jace?"

I steer Elsbeth away from the crowd, dropping our clothes in the fire bin by the watchtower, no need to decon those. I wait until we have crested the small hill and are turning towards Phase Two before I speak up.

"How did they know about the people?" I ask. "Did you fill them in when you got here?"

"No," Stuart says, "glad you caught that. Wasn't sure if maybe I misheard."

"When have you ever misheard something?" I laugh.

He gives me a very weak smile and I realize just how badly he's hurt. He's completely naked and there's quite a breeze blowing across the plateau, but his forehead is covered in sweat.

"Stuart? You need some help?"

He starts to wave me off, but I can see his legs shaking.

"Maybe."

I get on one side and tell Elsbeth to get on the other. We are pretty much carrying him by the time we get to my house. Well, Elsbeth is carrying him. I'm more like hobbling next to him adding to the weight of the effort.

"Hey, babe," I say as Stella opens the door.

Her eyes and attention don't know where to go: me naked and wounded, Stuart nearly unconscious, wounded and naked, or Elsbeth and her scars, naked. But there's a reason I married her long ago in a different world.

"Charlie!" she yells. My son comes running to the door. His eyes, of course, go straight to the naked woman. Stella snaps in front of his face. "Go get Dr. McCormick. Now."

"Hey, Dad," Charlie smiles and claps me on the shoulder as he runs past.

"Get him in on the couch," Stella says. "Greta! I need a sheet!"

Greta peers over the second floor landing. "Mom, I'm drawing right now and the light is- Holy fuck knuckles!" Her head disappears and seconds later, she's barreling down the stairs with a sheet. She hands it to Stella who covers the couch with it so Elsbeth and I can set Stuart down. "Hey, Dad."

"Hey, sweetie," I say.

"New girlfriend?" she grins.

"Greta," Stella warns. "Towels. Now. And put water on to boil."

"Right," Greta nods, not willing to argue with her mother.

"Thanks," Stuart croaks. "Just a scratch. May need a stitch or two." He drifts off.

Stella turns to me, starts to reach for my face then pulls back, shakes her head, turns to Elsbeth and holds out her hand. "I'm Stella Stanford, Jace's wife."

"You're Long Pork's woman?" Elsbeth asks. She looks my wife up and down. "You look like you're the boss." She looks at me. "Is she the boss?"

"She's the boss," I smile. I look at Stella and the smile falls from my face. "Maybe Greta can show her to the bathroom so she can get cleaned up?"

"That's a good idea," Stella says. "Greta?"

"Fine," Greta says as she hands Stella a stack of dishtowels. She sighs and looks at Elsbeth, her eyes studying the scars. "Come on, Queen Tut. I'll show you where you can shower and pee."

"Queen Tut?" Elsbeth asks, very confused.

"You know," Greta says as she waves her hand at Elsbeth's body. "All the hieroglyphs and shit."

"Greta, be a good host," Stella says, "and be nice."

"I'm always nice," Greta says, leading Elsbeth upstairs, "unless someone interrupts me when I'm drawing and the light is going away."

"Thanks, G," I smile. "Maybe grab some of Mom's old clothes from the closet? They should fit Elsbeth."

We wait until they are upstairs before speaking.

"You have got to be fucking kidding me," Stella says. "Really, Jace? Really?"

"Long story," I say, exhausted. "I need to get clean too and then we can talk."

Stella gently puts a hand on my arm, but I can still see anger in her eyes.

"Get showered then get your ass down here," she looks at my wounds. "You need to see Dr. McCormick too."

"Yeah, I know," I say as I start for the stairs. "I love you."

"I love you too," she says, "but you aren't even close to being off the hook."

"Baby, I've been on the hook since I met you," I smile.

She frowns, but some of the anger leaves her eyes. She turns and starts to put some towels under Stuart to catch the blood.

The shower is heaven. A painful, excruciating heaven, but still heaven. It takes me a while to get all of the grime off of me and before I know it, I'm soaping up in cold water. Which is weird since our water heater never runs out of hot water. Even in the zombie apocalypse, we have the best water heater in the world.

Luckily for Whispering Pines, all water heaters and stoves/ovens are natural gas. Whatever the infrastructure is for that, it never shut off even well after the power went out. Stuart has mentioned it a million times that we need to send out an expedition to the natural gas distribution center. But life and undeath keeps getting in the way.

Shivering, I rinse off, towel off, and get dressed. I limp downstairs in time to see Stuart looking up at me from the couch, his face a rictus of anger and pain, as Dr. McCormick probes the wound in his back.

"Jesus H. Christ, James," Dr. McCormick says. She's a young doctor, in her thirties, pretty, but plain in a clinical way. No makeup ever, her hair pulled up in a tight bun at all times. She lives alone in her 3,600 square foot house, so it doubles as the infirmary. She never talks about what happened to her partner and their three little girls. Never.

"How bad is it?" I ask.

"I need to get him to my exam room," she says, without looking at me. "But not before he gets some blood. His kidney is nicked for sure."

"Shit, Stuart," I say. "What the hell, man? You ran here and back with your kidney all ripped up?"

"Thank you, Stuart," Stella says. "That's what Jace meant to say. We owe you big time."

I grab a chair and limp over to the couch, rolling up my sleeve as I sit down. "O negative to the rescue," I smile, "this will make us even."

"No, it won't," Stella and Dr. McCormick say together.

"I was kidding," I say as the doctor preps my arm. The needle is huge and I give her a questioning look. "You plan on bleeding me dry?"

"Only gauge needle I have left," she says. "Sorry. I put in a request with Melissa, but none of her scavenging crews have come across med supplies in weeks."

"Somebody is hoarding," Stella says. "And I have a good idea who."

"Maybe, maybe not," I say. "There are new players in town." Stella raises an eyebrow and I shake my head. "Later."

"If we don't get more med supplies, then I'm going to be back to the horse and buggy days when it comes to medical care. I do not need to tell you all that medicine in the horse and buggy days was less than reliable."

I sigh and lean back into the chair as I pump my fist a couple of times, while Dr. McCormick gets the blood collection bag situated on the chair.

"I'm going to stitch what I can here," she says. "Can you text Mindy so some of her folks can help carry him down the street to my place?"

"No, don't," I say to Stella. "Just go ask Tran. He can get Stubben and some of the Ag folks to help carry Stuart. I don't want Mindy to know how bad Stuart is."

"I'm fine," he mumbles.

"Yeah, you are, tough guy," I say. "Just the picture of health."

"Can still kick your ass," he whispers. "Try me."

"I'll pass on that," I say. "You probably can."

"While you fill that bag, how about I look at you?" Dr. McCormick asks. I roll up the leg of my sweats and Dr. McCormick frowns at me. "I can't get to it that way. Drop 'em."

I pull my sweats down, wishing I'd worn better boxers, and the doctor looks at the spike wounds on my leg. "I can clean those, no problem." She looks closely at the wound on my cheek. "This is going to take a lot of stitches. And I'll have to irrigate it and change the dressing a few times before it can really heal." She leans in. "God, what did you get in there? You're lucky your face hasn't fallen off with the amount of dirt in that wound."

"I just kept pressing it until the skin stopped falling over," I say.

That's the last Stella can handle. She walks away, her hand to her mouth, trying not to gag. "I'm going to check on Greta and our, uh, guest."

"Elsbeth," I say.

Stella tries to kill me with her eyes. "I remember her name."

"Guest?" Dr. McCormick asks.

"Stella didn't mention her?" I ask, wincing and trying so hard not to cry as the doctor swabs out my cheek. "Ow, shit, Doc. Yeah, a guest. Found her in town. Or she found me." I give the doctor a hard look. "Cannibal."

She pulls back and looks over her shoulder up at the second floor landing. "How old?"

"I don't know. Maybe twenties? Not sure."

"She sane?"

"Debatable."

"Yes, but is she coherent? Or is her speech pattern off? Maybe has a hard time tracking with her eyes? Not so perfect motor control?"

"No, no, she's coherent and has no problem with motor control," I answer.

"Good," she nods, "then she hasn't damaged her brain eating human meat. She's too young, really. But you never know nowadays."

"No shit," I laugh and then want to cry as it stretches the skin on my face.

"Okay, shut up while I stitch," she says.

I want to scream as the hooked needle slips into the tender flesh on my cheek. Tender, tender, OH FUCK, THAT HURTS, flesh. She stops and I sigh.

"Don't get comfy," she says. "Just changing the blood bag. One more pint and that should do it."

"Shit."

Then she starts in again OH FUCK MY FACE OW!

"Quit squirming," she says. "There. Done. Keep it dry and clean for the next couple of days. Hear me, Jason? Dry and clean."

"Yes, doctor," I say. "Oh, wow."

Dr. McCormick turns and sees what I'm looking at. A freshly washed, and cleanly dressed, Elsbeth, standing at the bottom of the stairs with Greta and Stella. Despite herself, Stella is smiling.

"Elsbeth, this is Dr. McCormick," Stella says. "She's gonna look you over and make sure you're healthy."

Elsbeth lifts her arms, stretching the t-shirt she's wearing, and flexes her biceps. "I'm plenty healthy. Pa always said I'm healthier and stronger than most men folk. It's because I eat so many of them. I get their strength."

Yeah, that brings the room down quickly.

"Okay then," Stella says. "Doctor? You can use the office here."

"Pinch this clamp when the bag is full," Dr. McCormick tells me, pointing to the second blood bag still filling from my vein. She checks the first bag, which she hooked up to Stuart's arm, and nods. "I'll be right back."

Stella walks the doctor and Elsbeth into the office, and then shuts the door behind them. She turns and looks at me, and then at Stuart.

"How's he doing?"

"Fine," Stuart says quietly. "I can leave if you need to talk."

"Funny," Stella says. "Greta? Go find what's taking your brother so long. Tran should have only been down the block picking beans. That's what he said he was doing this morning."

Once Greta is gone, Stella focuses on me, her face a mixture of emotions.

"I didn't think you were coming back," she says finally. "When I heard Stuart was at the gate alone and why I just...you know..."

"Sorry," I say. "It got weird out there."

"Very," Stuart says.

"Something isn't right," I say. "Stuart knows it too."

"Yep."

"Like how?" Stella asks.

"Like Brenda knows more than she's saying," I say. "Like she sent us out there and knew maybe we wouldn't come back. Did you know the Board held a special vote?"

Stella frowns. "No, when?"

"Last night," I say. "I don't know what all they voted on, but they changed it so everyone has to strip outside the gate before they can come in. That's just reckless."

"Easier to pick people off that way," Stuart adds, his voice muffled by the couch. "Good strategy if you want to put someone down without there being many witnesses."

"What the fuck are you saying, Stuart?" Stella asks. "You think Brenda wants to kill someone?"

"I think Brenda has a plan," Stuart says. "I think she's putting that plan into place. It's been a long time coming."

"I know she's a little heavy handed," I say, "but what plan could she possibly have?"

"I don't know," Stuart says, "but I want to talk to Melissa before I talk to Brenda and Mindy."

"Mindy?" Stella asks. "Is that cow part of it?"

"I doubt she knows details," I say. "Whatever those details may be. But she's Brenda's bitch, that's for sure."

The front door opens and Tran and half a dozen men come tromping in. They get close to the couch and Tran nods at me.

"Hey, Tran," I say, "Dr. McCormick will be right out and then you can haul this sorry sack down to her house."

He nods knowing I'm crap when it comes to accents. I feel like such a dick.

"Stella, can I speak with you?" Dr. McCormick asks as she peeks her head out of the office.

"Sure," Stella says, following her inside.

Tran and his crew just look about the house.

"I'd offer you guys something to drink, but I'm kinda hooked to this," I say, pointing at the blood bag which I have just pinched off. "Go ahead and grab some water if you need."

"We're good," one of the guys says.

"I got a board," Charlie says as he comes inside carrying one end of a long piece of plywood. "To carry Stuart on."

"It was my idea," Greta says as she comes in carrying the other end.

"It was not," Charlie snaps. "That's why I was gone so long! Because I was looking for this!"

"You were looking for boards," Greta says. "This is plywood, not a board. It's bigger. This was my idea."

"This specific board was, but the general idea was mine," Charlie says.

"It's not a 'board'," Greta counters.

"Yes, it is!"

"No, it's-"

"Enough," I bark, too tired to deal with the bickering. "Thank you to both of you. Set it down right there and head up to your rooms."

"To our rooms?" Charlie asks. "Why?"

The look on my face gives him all the answer he needs and the kids book it upstairs.

"Okay, let's get this done," Dr. McCormick says as she walks over and gets the second bag and line from my arm. She ties the line around it, puts it in her bag, and then grabs the bag hooked to Stuart. "I'll hold this while you scoot him onto that board. That was a good idea. Who's was it?"

She looks to the Ag group for an answer, but Greta answers from above.

"Mine!"

"It was mine!" Charlie shouts.

"In your rooms!" I bellow.

"Kids, man," one of the crew smiles.

Dr. McCormick gives my face one last look, and then gets the ball rolling with Stuart. He looks at me while he's lifted onto the board. I give him a wink so he knows we are on the same page.

Stella helps Elsbeth upstairs to the guest room. By the time she comes down, the house is empty of non-family (except Elsbeth). She sits down on the couch and leans forward looking at me. I haven't bothered to get up from the chair. Just too tired.

"You should go up to bed," Stella finally says.

"Can't," I say. "My brain is in overdrive."

"She's a sweet girl," she says, "but completely fucked up."

"Yeah, cannibals aren't known for their stability or sane life choices."

"She said her dad did that to her skin. And he let others do it too. Before they killed and ate them."

"Fucking A."

"Yeah."

"She doesn't have to stay here," I say. "I just had to keep her away from Mindy and Brenda."

"Why? You think they'll hurt her?"

"I don't know what to think right now. There's something rotten in Whispering Pines."

"There's something rotten everywhere."

We sit there for a minute before I summon the strength to get up and plop next to her on the couch. She reaches for my cheek and touches the bandage.

"How close was it?" she asks.

"Which time?" I say.

"Fuck, Jace," she sighs. "I don't want you leaving the gate again."

"I can't make that promise. You know that."

"Leave the outside to Melissa and the scavengers," she insists, "and to Stuart and his defensive team. Once he's healed. You're a brain. And brains need to be kept safe and protected by a hard shell like Whispering Pines."

I debate telling her. I don't want to scare her, but the reality of what's out there can't be kept secret.

"We made some friends while we were gone," I say and look at her.

"Oh? Invite to dinner friends?"

"No. More like shoot on sight friends. Killed a few of them before we got away. They've got this leader, or I assume he's the leader, that Stuart calls Wall Street. I like Bullhorn because he kept shouting into a bullhorn, but Stuart likes Wall Street because he looks like that guy from the movie, but younger."

"Shia LeBouf?" she asks.

"What? No, Michael Douglas."

"Old school Wall Street."

"Yeah."

"Does he actually look like him?"

"He dresses like him."

"Then he's Wall Street. Bullhorn can be any asshole."

"Thanks for backing me up."

"Stop stalling. Tell me what's going on."

I do. I fill her in on the entire ordeal. Even the pink yoga pants and purple butterfly t-shirt. I could have just left that part out, but there can't be secrets in a marriage. Especially not in the zombie apocalypse.

Stella is still and quiet for a long time before she stirs and grips my hand.

"You think Brenda knows Wall Street?" she asks.

"I think she knows of him," I answer. "But whether they've communicated? I don't know. How would they? Brenda never leaves Whispering Pines. Only Stuart and his team and Melissa and her crew do, really. And neither of those two have any true love for Brenda."

"But you said Brenda gave Stuart the real mission, right? Maybe she gave him something to leave somewhere and he didn't even know what it was?"

"I think that's stretching it," I say.

Stella's phone chimes with a text. She reads it and laughs. "Charlie wants to know if he can come out of his room."

I smile. "Yes, he can come out of his…"

"What?" she asks.

"The Wi-Fi," I say. "It's strong enough to reach outside Whispering Pines. Landon has it jacked up so no matter where we are in the neighborhood, we always have full signal."

Landon Chase, a scrawny little fuck of a man. Even after the apocalypse, he thinks that tech is the answer to everything. He wired the neighborhood and made sure the Wi-Fi was working. He troubleshoots everything tech. Sure, Carl handles the grid and electrical, along with Jon, but Landon makes sure the phones go beep when they are supposed to.

I'm about to elaborate when there's a loud knock at the door. Stella starts to get up and answer it, but doesn't have to as the door opens and we hear someone come stomping in.

"Jace!" Melissa Billings shout/whispers. She's spent enough time outside the gate that she can make her voice carry like a shout, but only have it loud as a whisper. "Jace!"

"Hey, Mrs. Billings," Charlie says from the stairs.

"In your room, Charlie," Stella says.

"Ah, for fuck's sake, I just came out!"

"Go," I say.

"Fine. Whatever."

We all wait until we hear the door close.

"Where is he?" Melissa asks. "Where's Jon? I can't believe you left him out there!"

Before Stella can get pissed and try to defend me I dive into the whole story.

"So he's still out there?" Melissa asks. "Alone? With the Zs? And those others?"

"Yeah," I say. "But you know Jon, he's scrappy and resourceful."

"And a shit shot," she says. "Man never could hit a damn thing."

Melissa Billings is a handsome woman. Grey/white hair that she keeps tied back in a pony tail. She's lean and muscular, looking exactly like what she is- an ex-farm girl. She is Western North Carolina through and through and grew up not far from Asheville. Knowing the area, having the strength and guts, and always keeping a cool head, Melissa Billings is the perfect choice to lead the scavenger group.

She paces back and forth in front of us and then sighs heavily, her hands planted on her hips.

"So when do we go find him?" she asks.

"Uh…"

"Jace isn't going anywhere," Stella says. "He just got back and look at him. His leg is in bad shape and he has to keep his cheek clean or it will get infected."

"Oh, I'm sorry," Melissa laughs. "Is that scratch an inconvenience for you, Jace? What a man you must feel like. Your wife telling you what you can and can't do. She probably makes you piss sitting down, huh?"

"Too far," I say. "Never insult a man's pissing style." Melissa doesn't laugh. Stella just groans.

"Melissa, I know you are scared and hurt right now," Stella says. "I understand that. Until Jace showed up at the gate, I didn't know if he'd ever come back. So I know how you are feeling."

"You don't know shit, Stella," Melissa snaps. "You have your man back. Mine's still out there."

"And he'll make it back," Stella says. "I'm sure of it."

Melissa cocks her head and studies Stella. I have a sinking feeling she's gonna haul off and punch my wife, so I get right in front of her, ready to take the hit myself.

"He took off to save me," I say. I swallow hard, knowing what I'm about to say is gonna bring a shit storm down on me like never before. "You get a team together and I'll go out with you."

"Like fuck you will!" Stella shouts, grabbing my arm and turning me about. "Are you fucking crazy, Jace? You just got back. Barely." She points up to the landing. "And you want to leave? When you brought that crazy cannibal twat into my house? You fucking piece of shit."

I look up at the landing and freeze. Shit. Stella sees the look on my face and turns her head to look also. Elsbeth.

"I ain't crazy," Elsbeth says, looking down on us from the landing. "I ain't. Pa always said I just have different wiring in my head." She taps her temple over and over. "Different. But not crazy." The tapping starts to get rougher and rougher until she is smacking the side of her head. "Different! Different! Different!"

"Jesus," Greta says and smacks Elsbeth in the back of the head, "knock it off."

We three adults just stand and stare at this thirteen year old girl taking on this obviously disturbed young woman.

"What?" Greta asks. "She was losing it. You want her to crack her skull?"

Elsbeth looks at Greta and smiles. "Pa used to have to smack me. Thank you, little girl."

"Greta," my daughter answers. "I already told you that. Don't be stupid. Or crazy. Different is fine. Just no more crazy, got it?"

"Yes, Greta," Elsbeth nods. "Got it." She gives a thumbs up and Greta just rolls her eyes before she turns and goes into her bedroom, slamming the door behind her.

"Can I come out?" Charlie calls.

"No," Stella and I say.

"I'll go," Elsbeth says. "I can track your man, lady."

Melissa looks at us and then back up at Elsbeth. A million emotions and responses filter across her face until she says, "Can you shoot a bow?"

"Don't need to," Elsbeth smiles and lifts The Bitch up for Melissa to see. I don't even remember her bringing that into the house. How did I not notice that?

"Where the hell did she get that?" Stella asks. "It looks like yours, Jace."

"It's better," Elsbeth grins. "I can use this and these." She taps her eyes, ears, then nose and her grin widens. "Ain't no one got away from me. Not ever. Pa says that's part of what makes me different. I don't lose prey."

Holy shit, I think I brought home some cannibal savant or something. Rain Man with a taste for people. Great?

"Is she for real?" Melissa asks.

"She killed about fifty Zs by herself getting me from that truck," I say. "That's pretty fucking real in my book."

"Then we leave in the morning," Melissa says. "I'll pick the ones from my team I can trust 100%. We do this and Brenda is going to have a shit fit. She may not let us back in."

"Are you kidding?" Stella says. "You have got to be kidding! Jace? Don't even think about it!"

"If Jace was lost out there and you were standing in my living room with me and Jon looking at you, what would you want, Stella? Be honest. What would you want? For us just to sit on our asses and hope?"

Stella starts to answer then closes her mouth. "I don't like this."

"No one does," Melissa nods. "But I have to go get Jon. There is no point in any of this for me without that man." She glances up at Elsbeth and then at me. "Are you in?"

"I am," I say, looking at Stella. "I have to."

"Your leg is shit," Stella says. "How are you going to run? If the Zs swarm they'll take you down."

"I'll watch him, lady," Elsbeth says. "He won't fall behind. And if we get trapped and I can't kill our way gone, then I'll put a blade through the back of his neck and then through my heart so we don't get ate and turned." Elsbeth is smiling as she says this last part like it's a wonderful plan.

"Oh, sweet Jesus," Stella says. "This is all shit."

Our phones chime as a text comes in. We all pull them out and frown, then Stella and I look at Melissa. Her face is white, but her eyes blaze.

The text is from Mindy and says, "We need all security and defensive personnel to the gate now! We have a situation! And someone go get Jason Stanford! This is his fault! Oh, and no one tell Melissa Billings. She doesn't want to see this."

"Fucking dumb bitch sent it to the whole neighborhood," Stella says. "That stupid cow."

"It's Jon," Melissa says. "He's back."

The way she says it chills my bones. She is assuming the worst. And I can't blame her.

"We better get down there," I say. "Are you staying here?"

Stella shakes her head. "I'm coming with you. The kids will stay."

"What about…?" I nod up at Elsbeth.

"She comes. I'm not leaving her with the kids alone."

"I won't eat 'em," Elsbeth says. "I don't eat friends." She turns to the stairs and her words become muffled. "Never had friends. Good rule. Don't eat friends. Rules is good."

"Jesus," Stella says, shaking her head. "Weapons?"

"Bows," I say. "I'll have to take Charlie's until I get a new one."

"He's dead," Melissa says quietly as we walk to the garage for the bows.

"Maybe not," Stella replies as I push up the garage door. "It may not be that bad."

"It may be worse," Elsbeth says. "He could be turned."

"Fucking A!" Stella snarls. "Just stay quiet, okay? No more talking unless I say so."

Elsbeth nods, her eyes wide with fear. Yep, my wife can scare the shit out of a cannibal savant.

It takes us longer than it should because of my leg and we have to push our way through the crowd at the gate to get to the watchtower. The whole neighborhood has turned out thanks to Mindy's incompetence. I look around, but don't see Brenda anywhere.

"This is quite ridiculous," a voice blares from the other side of the gate. My belly clenches at the sound. "All I need to do is speak to your leader. A Brenda Kelly, I believe. A simple request that should not be taking so long!"

I know who is at the other end of that voice before I get up into the watchtower. Stella, Elsbeth, and Melissa are right behind me.

"Who told her?" Mindy snaps as she sees Melissa. "I said not to tell her."

"You sent a blast text to the whole neighborhood," Stella says. "You moron."

"I did?" Mindy asks, pulling out her phone and looking at the text. "It wasn't supposed to be." She taps at the screen a couple times. In a second, every phone in the crowd chimes. So does one outside the gate. "Oh, poop."

I push Mindy out of the way and look down into the road. Bullhorn. Or Wall Street.

"See," I say to Stella, "he has a bullhorn. That's why I think Bullhorn is a better name."

"Shut up," Stella says.

The man is looking at his phone and shaking his head, laughing. Surrounding him are at least twenty heavily armed men and women. And kneeling in front, his hands and feet bound, and quite a few wraps of duct tape around his mouth, is Jon.

"JON!" Melissa shouts.

"Oh, you must be Missus Smart Ass," Bullhorn says. "Your husband has quite a mouth. I had to close it for him."

The bullhorn comes down and slams into the back of Jon's head. He crumples to the asphalt, but a woman reaches down and yanks him back up onto his knees.

"Now, where is Ms. Brenda Kelly?"

"Here, here," Brenda says as she steps from the ladder and onto the watchtower platform. "I'm here!"

"The deadline has passed, Ms. Kelly," Bullhorn says. "You were warned. Now things have to go my way." He waves a hand at the road. "And you folks get to go the highway."

"I haven't…," Brenda has to struggle to catch her breath. "We haven't had time to speak to the HOA. The Board just met last night. These things take time to discuss. I told you that."

She doesn't look at any of us as our eyes bore into her. I told you that? What the fuck does that mean?

"Brenda. Brenda, Brenda, Brenda. I was very clear on the time frame of my plans," Bullhorn shouts. "But for the sake of everyone else up there, and behind that gate, I'm sure, I will explain myself further."

"My name is Edward Vance," he says. "Since Z-Day, I have been a very busy man. I have done everything in my power to make a safe place for myself." He spreads his arms wide, indicating the men and women around him. "And, as long as my safety comes first, I make sure things are safe for those that believe in me."

"Believe in me?" I whisper. "That doesn't sound good."

"I know him," Melissa says. "I know that man."

I look from her to Jon. Something passes between them and he nods.

"Oh, shit," Melissa says. "Shit shit shit."

"What?" I ask.

"Am I boring you?" Bullhorn shouts. "I hope not. May I continue? Thank you. You see, I have many, many followers. Many of my flock needs more space and resources than the world can provide."

106

He grins and lowers his bullhorn. When his voice booms at us, I realize he doesn't even need the thing. Shit. Maybe I should call him Wall Street? "Whispering Pines is what community is all about. And I want that for my people. I want that to be our home. So…you have to leave. You leave and I won't have to make you leave."

He waves his hand and points at Jon.

"If you don't leave?" he says as the crowd parts and a man comes forward with a Z secured by a catch pole around the neck. Bullhorn/Wall Street nods and the man shoves the Z at Jon.

"NO!" Melissa screams as the thing's teeth clamp down on his shoulder, ripping a chunk from him.

Even with the layers of duct tape, we can all hear him screaming. The man yanks the Z away and a woman steps up and puts a bullet through its brain. It crumples to the ground, black blood oozing from its shattered skull. Jon has stopped screaming and is just staring down at the pavement. Stella and I grab Melissa before she can jump off the watchtower. She is ready to leap to her death to get to Jon.

"That was just to punctuate my point," Bullhorn/Wall Street says. "And my point is that we have thousands of Zs ready and waiting to come into your community and do that to all of you. Husbands, wives, children, grandparents. And you, Ms. Kelly. Especially you. I'd rather not, since it is a pain to have to corral and clean up after the buggers, but I will do what I need to do to secure the future of my flock. It's God's will and the American way."

He circles his hand in the air and his people start to head out. He lingers for a moment and watches us watching him. "Please know how serious I am. I don't want to kill all of you, but I will. You have 48 hours to voluntarily leave before I send in the Zs."

"You'll never break our defenses!" Mindy shouts down at him.

"Shut up!" most of us shouts at her.

"Wise advice," Bullhorn/Wall Street says. "48 hours, Ms. Kelly. That is all. Not a second longer. And those defenses? While they are impressive, one of the many reasons I'd like to acquire Whispering Pines, they can't stand up to wave after wave after wave of the undead. Nothing can. Until then, I bid you farewell. You have a lot of work to do before moving day."

He casually saunters off. I look about and wonder why the hell no one put a bolt or arrow between his eyes. Jesus, are we sheep?

"Jace," Stella says quietly as she looks down at Jon. He's just laying there in a pool of his blood. "Is he…?"

"I don't know," I say. "But I've got this."

I open one of the cabinets in the watchtower and pull out a rifle. I load two rounds into the breach and head to the ladder.

"Where do you think you are going with that?" Brenda asks.

"You weren't authorized to take that weapon," Mindy adds. Just before Melissa's fist hits her square between the eyes. Mindy kinda stands there for a second, and then drops to her knees before falling on her face.

"I can't do it," Melissa says.

"I know," I nod. "It's because of me. It's my duty."

The crowd parts as I step from the ladder and walk to the gate.

"Open it," I say. The two men manning the gate look up at Brenda. "You want that bitch to be the last thing you see?"

They both look back at me quickly and open the gate. I walk through and kneel next to Jon. I manage to get the duct tape away from his mouth, but he isn't saying anything. Not anymore. I look over my shoulder and see Stella and Melissa watching me. I shake my head. Melissa wails then buries her head in Stella's shoulder.

"You need help?" Elsbeth asks, suddenly at my side. I startle at how quiet she is. I didn't even know she had followed me.

"No, no, I got this," I say as I stand up. "Farewell my friend." I place the barrel of the rifle to his head and pull the trigger. No hesitation, no remorse other than the fact that I feel to blame. I won't regret the shooting, but I will regret everything that led to it.

"Help me carry him," I say and sling the rifle over my shoulder. Elsbeth looks at me and I nod towards his body. "He was my friend. I won't leave him out here. Please."

She shrugs and grabs his legs while I grab his shoulders. We carry him to the gate and everyone moves quickly out of the way. There are murmurs in the crowd, but they are drowned out by Brenda's hisses.

"You can't bring an infected body into Whispering Pines!" she snaps at me. "It is strictly against everything in the covenants! No infected past the gate for any reason!"

"He's dead," I say. "Dead dead. We're going to have a service and then burn his body. No burying, no body left to rot. He'll be burned and that will be that."

"I can't allow it," Brenda says. "Mindy? Mindy!"

The moron comes waddling up, her hand to her face. She can barely focus on Brenda and me as she tries to play catch up.

"Mindy, please have your team arrest Mr. Stanford," Brenda says. "If he doesn't turn around and put that body back outside, arrest him. This is blatant sedition and cannot be tolerated!"

"You want me to what?" Mindy asks. I honestly think she doesn't know what is going on. "I can't do that? Can I?"

"You can and will," Brenda says and turns to the crowd, pointing at Jon's body. "This is unfortunate, but the rules are here to protect us! To save us! How many of you had relatives turned outside that we had to put down and leave? Why should this man be held higher than them all? Why risk our lives?"

I look about and see a lot of confusion as people try to decide what to do. But most of all I see fear. And that fear is directed at the corpse in my hands.

"You all knew Jon," I say. "He helped build this place into what it is today. He deserves some respect."

I start to move away from Brenda, but several members of Mindy's security team block my path.

"Come on, guys," I say. "You don't have to do this."

"Arrest him," Brenda hisses. "If you disobey the Board and the covenants, then you are guilty too and will be cast out."

I can see muscles tense and know what is close. I look over my shoulder and see Stella and Melissa coming towards me. I look across Jon's body and see Elsbeth staring right at me. She is smiling.

"No," I say to her. "Don't." She frowns, but nods. "Set him down."

Elsbeth sets Jon's legs down, but I keep a hold of his shoulders. Stella is at my side.

"What is your plan?" she asks.

"Same as before," I say. "I just need you to make sure Elsbeth doesn't hurt anyone."

Stella stares at me for a moment and then nods, kissing my unwounded cheek. She walks over to Elsbeth and takes her elbow, leading her away from the crowd. I start dragging Jon's body.

"Mindy," Brenda snaps, "do your job."

"Jason Stanford," Mindy says, trying to sound authoritative, but just sounding loud, "if you do not stop this moment, you will be under arrest."

I don't stop.

Hands grab me and I try to fight, but they overpower me quickly. I'm on the ground, my hands being tied behind my back when I look up and see Brenda smiling.

"You're wrong about this," I say, "all of it."

"Not for you to say," she says.

They haul me up and drag me away. Brenda barks orders and a couple sentries gingerly pick up Jon's body and carry it to the gate and they are lost from sight.

CHAPTER SIX

The "jail" is just an empty house that sits next to Brenda's house. The room I'm in is what would be called the "media room" on the developer's floor plans. Ground floor room with double windows looking out onto the back yard and double doors leading to the living room. Same exact floor plan as my house. Other than the guard sitting outside the double doors, it's not really very secure. I could probably crawl out the windows if I want.

I'm actually thinking about doing this when I see the first rays of dawn start to pierce the early morning fog. Sleep didn't come at all in the night, but my situation has my adrenaline up and I just lie on the carpeted floor in the bare room, watching the sky go from deep purple to slightly pink to bright orange. My eyes actually begin to close when there's a knock on the door.

I twist around and see Stella and Melissa standing over me, the guard in the background.

"We're leaving," Stella says. "The Board met last night, called an emergency HOA meeting and it was overwhelmingly in favor of abandoning Whispering Pines."

"What?" I say, getting to my feet. "Why the fuck would everyone go along? We can fight this out!"

"We can," Melissa says. "Most of my team and a few others, sure. We have guts. But the rest? They've only survived because of the strong in the community. They'd be slaughtered sheep if left on their own. And sheep only know how to follow."

"Brenda was very convincing," Stella says.

"So that's it? We abandon Whispering Pines? And go where?"

"I said we're leaving," Stella frowns. "Not abandoning Whispering Pines. We'll be back."

I look from Stella to Melissa.

"I'm not following," I say. "What's going on?"

"While everyone is packing up and figuring out the next move," Melissa says. "I am taking your family, my team, that cannibal girl, and a few others on a trip. We're going to get reinforcements."

"The Farm," Stella says.

"Seriously?" I laugh. They don't. "Oh. What makes you think they'll take us in? Or help us in anyway? Brenda has rejected them time and time again when they've come to trade. She pissed them off last time pretty bad. They haven't been back for a year or so. Why would they give a shit?"

"Tell him," Stella says to Melissa, "you've kept it secret long enough."

"The Farm is my home," she says, "it's where I grew up. My daddy and brothers run the place with those they took in."

"Your home?" I ask. "What the fuck? Why are you here?"

"Because of Jon," she says. "He wanted to live close in to town. That's why we bought a house in Whispering Pines. We always knew the Farm was a back up if things went to hell here."

"They've now gone to hell," Stella says. "We're leaving and coming back with our own army."

"It's thirty miles away," I say. "It'll take longer than 48 hours to get there and back."

"We know," Melissa says. "Those fucks will have moved in and taken over by the time we show up. And be busy figuring it all out. They won't see us coming."

I shake my head, rubbing my tired face. "This isn't going to work. First, do you honestly think you can convince your family to help us?"

"We have tech they need," Melissa says. "Landon is coming. So is Carl. They'll share what they know with Daddy and he'll see what we have to offer. We should have done this a long time ago, but that Brenda cunt was always in the way."

I look past the women at the guard standing there, his eyes wide and mouth open. "Are you going to be a problem?"

The women turn around. He looks from them to me and back. "We're really being forced to leave?" he asks.

"Yes," Melissa says.

"Can I go with?"

"Yes," Melisa nods. "Kirby, right?"

"Yes, ma'am," he nods, leaning his rifle against the doorjamb. He takes a bandana from his back pocket and wipes the fear sweat from his face. "When do we leave?"

"Good question," I say.

"We leave now," Stella says. "We have provisions packed. Everyone is meeting at the gate."

"Brenda isn't going to like this," I say. "She hates it when people disagree." I wave my hands at the room. "Case in point."

"We'll be taking problems off her hands," Melissa says. "The less people to deal with, the less variables she'll have to calculate. And Brenda may be devious, but she isn't smart enough to calculate variables."

"That's why she's always needed you," Stella says to me. "So let's get you out of here and get gone."

"Here," Melissa says as she hands me a handled, carbon steel pole. "I keep these on hand when we are out scavenging. Good weapon plus helps you move when you got a bum leg. These things have saved more than a few of my team out there. They'll keep your gimp ass moving."

"You sound like Jon," I say.

"Thank you," she smiles.

We step out of the house and Charlie and Greta rush towards me. Hugs all around and we are off.

I'm surprised, since we were right next door, that Brenda didn't see us and try to figure out what we were up to. When we get to the gate, I see why.

"I will not allow this," Brenda says, standing in front of Mindy and a dozen of the security team. "You are valuable members of this community and wherever we end up, you will be needed."

"You can't stop us," Carl says, at the front of the group that is facing off against Brenda and her lackeys. "You voted that we are leaving. This shit is over, Brenda. You aren't the Board Chair of us any longer."

"I am as long as you're inside these gates," Brenda says. "And even when we leave these gates. That was the resolution passed last night. We maintain our HOA structure and covenants even when we leave. It is for the good of the group as a whole."

"We're leaving," I say as we get closer. "Just move out of the way, Brenda. Like Carl said, you can't stop us."

"I can and will," Brenda says, puzzled. "And you are supposed to be locked up. Whoever let you go will be tried for sedition."

"Oh, for fuck's sake, it's over, you overbearing twat," Stella snaps. "Just move your fat ass out of the way."

Brenda raises her hand. Mindy raises hers and the security officers raise rifles to their shoulders. Then Elsbeth is in the mix. She has The Bitch shoved up against Brenda's windpipe. Brenda is trying to protest, but all that's coming out of her mouth is a strangled wheeze. Drops of blood start to trickle down her throat.

"These people want to go," Elsbeth says. "I want to go. We're gonna go now."

"Goddamn she's fast," someone says.

Elsbeth looks over her shoulder and finds me. She cocks her head and I shake mine.

"Take the rifles," I say to the others. They look at me and back at the security team. "Go ahead. They won't shoot. Right, Brenda? Right, Mindy?"

Mindy looks to her boss. "Should we shoot?"

Brenda starts to answer and Elsbeth presses harder. Brenda shakes her head, careful of the spikes puncturing her skin.

"Take 'em, team," Melissa says as her scavengers rush forward and snatch the rifles. The security team is shoved out of the way and Melissa gets the gate open. "Ready?"

"Elsbeth," Stella says, "let the ugly troll go."

Elsbeth jumps back, startled. "She's a troll? Like in the story books?" She rubs her hands on her pants. "Yuck."

And this is the girl that can kill a horde of Zs without batting an eyelash. It's a fucked up world.

Clutching her bloody throat, Brenda rasps, "You'll be dead out there. You'll never make it with such a small group. How will you survive? Where will you go?"

"Home," Melissa says.

"The Farm," Stella adds.

Brenda's eyes go wide and I can see she didn't even think of this possibility.

"Wait!" a voice yells. "Wait!" Tran and his wife and three kids are hurrying towards us. "You take us with!" Stubben is right behind them.

"Not a problem," Melissa says, smiling at Tran and Stubben then over at Brenda. "You'll fit right in on the Farm."

We all slip through the gate and turn to the left. A few miles up the road is a bridge that will take us over the French Broad and towards Leicester, where the Farm is. Just as we are about to go around the bend and up the short hill, I look back and see Brenda and Mindy looking at us from the watchtower. I can see on her face that Brenda knows she fucked up. She never even thought of the Farm as a refuge. Her suburban, bigoted mind just couldn't even go there.

Tough shit for her.

"Keep it tight and quiet, people," Melissa whispers once we are well away from Whispering Pines. "Team? You know what to do. Eyes up, ears open, nothing for granted."

There is a murmur of agreement and then all are quiet.

I look around and take stock of who is with us:

Stella, the kids, and Elsbeth. Melissa, of course.

Carl Leitch and his partner Brian. Brian is a quiet fellow. I haven't spoken with him much over the years, but when I have, he's always been warm and funny.

Tran and his family.

Landon Chase, the punk ass.

Stubben with a large walking stick and a pack the size of Greta. The guy is used to manual labor, so I guess he knows what he can carry and what he can't.

That Kirby guard. I don't even remember seeing him around before. It's strange who you mix with and who you don't.

The rest of our crew is made up of Melissa's scavengers: Alison Woods, Tony White, Lanny Smithfield, Tara Johnson, Steven Grimes, West Bullock, and her right hand, Andrew Crespo. None of them have families, which is why Melissa picked them for the scavenger crew. She was the only one with a spouse, but no longer.

I don't see any of Stuart's defensive team with us, which sucks, but I guess they stayed back with their boss. I am glad for that since I know Stuart is in no shape to travel. Forcing him to move in 48 hours is going to be rough enough.

We're a motley crew, but nothing unusual in this day and age. The zombie apocalypse makes for strange bedfellows.

A true fact of human nature: you can only keep a group quiet for so long. Doesn't matter if their lives are on the line or not, get more than four or five people together and someone is going to feel the strange pull to start chattering. Of course, Landon is the one that starts it off.

"What if they reject us?" he asks. "They just turn us out. Leave us to the Zs."

"They won't," Melissa says. "Now hush." She points to the dump truck I abandoned. "There are going to be extra Zs around here. Shut it."

"I was just asking," Landon says. "I have a right to speak."

"No, you don't," someone says.

"Shut the fuck up, Landon," another whispers.

"We aren't in Whispering Pines anymore," Landon says. "I don't have to answer to you."

"Should I kill him?" Elsbeth asks. A few heads turn to look at her. Some seem to be eager to see what I have to say while others look appalled at the question. "Should I? He's stupid."

"That may be true," I say.

"Hey," Landon protests.

"But the first rule of survivor club is you only kill Zs," I say. "Unless you have to kill humans. Then you kill humans. But stick with Zs."

"That really cleared things up," Stella says. She looks at Elsbeth. "Do not kill anyone living unless I say so, got it?"

Elsbeth nods, but her eyes bore holes in Landon's head. Stella smiles at Landon and he cringes and shuts up. Good man. Not the day to piss off my wife.

We're maybe ten yards past the dump truck when the first few Zs come at us. There're ten of them, all fairly new looking, with all limbs attached. They come from the riverside of the road, stumbling and crawling up from the old railroad tracks. Melissa holds up her hand and we stop. The scavengers circle around us.

"Lanny. Tara. West. Keep everyone moving," Melissa says. "We can't lose daylight. The rest of you with me. We'll take these down and catch up."

But it isn't needed. Elsbeth walks right up to the Zs, The Bitch gripped firmly in her hand. The closest one hisses and reaches for her and get's a spike through the brain for his effort. The next two lose their heads as Elsbeth goes all batter up on them. By now, the other seven have gotten up to the road and are converging on her fast. She doesn't even seem to care.

She takes out the legs of one, slams another back a few feet with a hard kick, decapitates two more with well placed swings, shatters the face of one, spins about and jams the butt of the handle through the gut of the sixth, snapping its spine in half, then reaches out and literally rips the head off the seventh.

We all just stare.

The couple she hasn't killed die quickly under some well placed and efficient bashes. She stands over the last one, the one with shattered legs, and looks down on it. Honest to God pity is on her face. We all watch her mutter something then she lifts her foot. The thing gnashes its teeth and groans at her just before she squishes the undead life from its skull.

"Sorry," she says as he walks back to us, interpreting our stunned faces as disappointment. "I'll be faster next time. I'm tired."

"Yeah, not a problem," Melissa says. "You can have point if you want."

Elsbeth just stares at her.

"It means you can go first," Stella explains.

"Oh, no," Elsbeth says, shaking her head. "I have to stay close to them."

Everyone looks at us: The Stanfords.

"Lucky you guys," Carl says and Brian nods.

"Let's keep moving," Melissa says. "More will be on the way."

We do keep moving, making a steady pace (lucky for my leg Tran's little ones can only walk so fast), everyone's eyes peeled. You can smell the fear off the folks that haven't been outside the gate. Carl and Brian are sweating profusely, as is Landon. Tran and his wife seem to be right at ease, but Stubben is looking back and forth like a beaten dog waiting for the next kick to deliver the familiar pain. The scavengers are keeping a good perimeter around us, rifles in the crooks of their elbows, ready.

Elsbeth is kinda smiling to herself, like she's have some internal dialogue, and she giggles quietly every few minutes. At first Stella looks at me like there's a crazy person next to her, but soon her and the kids are smiling and trying not laugh when the giggles come. I gotta say that despite our rather rough introduction, the cannibal savant is growing on me.

It's nearly noon by the time we reach the bridge.

"We'll lunch in the middle," Melissa says. "Easier to defend. Anyone that wants to catch a few minutes of shuteye, now is the time. Forty-five minutes, people, then we're back on the road."

"Where are we going?" Elsbeth asks as she sits down next to Charlie and Greta, looking at her sandwich like it's the one that's going to do the biting. She sniffs it and looks around. "The food farted."

"It's egg salad," Greta says. "Eggs have sulfur in them which is why it smells like a fart."

Elsbeth just shakes her head and takes a bite. Her eyes go wide and then she crams the whole sandwich into her mouth. She chomps, chomps, chomps, and then swallows.

"Farts taste good," she says. She looks around. "Is there more?"

"That's all the egg salad ones," Stella says. "But I have a blackberry jam sandwich, if you want it."

Elsbeth nods her head and takes the sandwich Stella holds out. She crams that one in her mouth and her whole face lights up. I'm guessing sweets like jam and stuff weren't on the menu in her basement.

"That beats long pork any day," she says when her mouth is clear and she can finally speak.

"Lots of things beat long pork," I say.

"Pretty much every other food on the planet," Charlie says.

"Except for zucchini," Greta says. "Fuck that shit."

"Yeah," Elsbeth nods. "Fuck that shit. Fuck it. Just fuck it in the shit. Shitty fuck it."

"Great," Stella says. "She's learning from our kids. She's doomed."

"Ah, come on," I smile. "We've taught them well. By the time we get to the Farm, she'll know way more words than just shit and fuck. Right, kids?"

"Vocabulary is important," Greta says.

"Fucking A right it is," Charlie nods.

"The Farm?" Elsbeth asks. "Are we gonna fuck that shit?"

"I sure hope not," Melissa says as she sits down next to us. "Daddy isn't fond of cursing. He's a righteous man and follows the Lord's path."

"We're screwed then," Charlie says.

"We are not," Stella says. "I've taught you to respect God and all beliefs. You will be respectful when we get there and mind your mouths and your manners."

"Manners," Elsbeth says, her brow furrowed. "Wait your turn to chew on the bone. Don't pee in the corner, go outside. Those are manners."

"Jesus," Stella says as the kids giggle.

"The Farm is wonderful," Melissa says. "My kin has every acre locked down. Daddy keeps an organized house. Waste is not allowed."

"Are there chickens like back home?" Greta asks.

"Oh, there's chickens, and pigs, and cows. Probably ducks and rabbits too," Melissa says. "Not to mention dogs and cats."

"Dogs?" Greta beams. "I miss our dogs."

"We all do," Stella says. Charlie nods.

We try not to think of the early days of the apocalypse. The hard days. The scary days. The days before the gate and the fences. We lost two great dogs in those days; they fought to death keeping us safe. I'm not a praying man, but every once in a while I say a couple words of thanks to them, hoping they found peace.

A low whistle gets all of our attention. Zs.

"Riverside," Tony White says. He carries a six foot pike with a nasty barbed blade on the end. He swings it off to the Hwy 251 side of the bridge. "About twenty coming from UNCA."

"Those would be part of the herd that Elsbeth saved me from," I say. "I'm sure there are more than just those on their way."

The scavengers are already up and watching as the Zs approach the end of the bridge. Melissa quietly goes from group to group, getting everyone moving. It doesn't take much since the first of the Zs have already turned onto the bridge, their shuffling feet scraping against the weathered concrete. Stella and I have the kids between us with Elsbeth in front, as we make our way to the far side of the bridge.

"We keep moving we can lose them up the hill," Melissa says, pointing to the winding twists and turns that make up Pearson Bridge Road. "They'll slow down quick."

"But the little ones," Stella says, looking at Tran and his family.

"We'll have to carry them," Melissa replies. "Switching off so no one gets bogged down."

The scavengers take the rear, their eyes watching the Zs as we get across the bridge and start up the road. In seconds, Elsbeth stops and holds out her hands.

"No," she whispers, "not up the road."

"What did she say?" Melissa asks, her voice quiet also. She knows nothing about Elsbeth really, but she can sense the survivor in her. Plus, the little show earlier certainly added some respect. "What's up?"

"The Zs," Elsbeth says, turning to look at the hillside and the thick underbrush. She points over her shoulder at the bridge. "That is the small problem." She points ahead of us. "Big problem coming fast."

Then we hear them. A lot of them. Even with their shuffling gait they make quite a noise as their feet hit asphalt. Gravity is on their side as they come around the corner downhill. Some look like they are ready just to topple forward as they struggle to keep up with their feet and the decline.

"Shit," Melissa says. "How many is that?"

"Gotta be a hundred," Stubben says. "We are fucked."

"This way," Elsbeth says and dives into the bushes that cover the hillside in front of us. "No more road."

Stella and I help the kids find handholds and Elsbeth shows them where to grab vines and roots to scramble up and away from the road. She points them to the right and they obey instantly, following a natural path made by water erosion and small animals. Stella goes with them then looks back at me. I wave her on, giving her a big smile. Tran and his family are next followed by the rest. The scavengers are pulling up the rear and Melissa grabs onto my arm as her people close in behind us.

"You think your leg can make it up this?" she asks me.

"Do I have a choice?"

"No," Tara Johnson says, her eyes watching the two groups of Zs. I know she is timing when they'll come together. The others are busy sizing up the weaker and the stronger of them.

Melissa goes first and reaches down. I grab her hand and she helps pull me up the hillside. I grab onto anything that will hold me and struggle against the weakness in my leg, but I don't crumple. I don't let it take me down. I'm sweating and could really go for a shot of whiskey and some aspirin, but I make it to the small path. The carbon pole helps too as I jam it into the soft earth here and there for purchase.

"They see us," Andrew says. "Gotta hustle."

I dig deep and pull out some hustle so we can get some distance between the Zs and us. By the time the two groups come together, we are a good forty yards above them, moving parallel with the road above us. The path seems to be a natural switchback, keeping us from the Zs and the Zs from us. They'd have to be great climbers, which they aren't, to get up the hillside.

Unless they just fall from above.

"MOM!" Greta screams up ahead.

My instinct is to run towards her, but Melissa keeps me back. One of the first rules of surviving the zombie apocalypse, is that you don't rush in to anything until you know your situation. Otherwise, you're dead too. I can hear Charlie yelling and someone telling him to shut up. I try to push past Melissa, but she holds me firm. A couple nods and half the scavengers scoot past us and sprint up ahead.

"Melissa," I growl.

"No," is all she says.

Branches are breaking and there is crying and screaming and yelling. For those Zs that don't know where we are, they have just been told. Today's lunch is a panicked party of twenty-plus suburbanites. Enjoy.

I can hear the grunts of the scavengers as they engage the Zs. The undead groans get louder and louder as I move forward. Only about ten yards up, the path twists and I see what happened. The road turns at a sharp angle about twenty feet above us. The Zs are just tumbling over the edge. Like undead lemmings, they keep coming, falling, and then getting up immediately, many of them snapping their legs in the process. It cuts down on their mobility, but there are just so many of them that they create piles of gnashing teeth and reaching hands blocking our way.

I can see Elsbeth killing and shoving, trying to clear a way, but even her skills can't keep up. Charlie is fighting alongside Stella with Greta between them. Carl and Brian are hacking away at anything that moves, while Stubben is busy swinging like a madman, doing absolutely nothing productive.

Then that Kirby guy goes down, his throat ripped out by a reaching Z. I've seen a lot, but never a man's windpipe yanked right from his body mid-scream. One second it's being pumped full of air and wailing, then it's cut off like hitting the power on a stereo.

"Fuck," I say.

I shake it off and move forward. I see Tran and his wife. But I don't see their kids. His wife (God, I'm such a shitty neighbor that I can't even remember her name) is screaming at the top of her lungs, her hands on her head, pulling at her hair. Tran is yelling and lunging forward, but he is stopped by a pile of undead mouths and hands, teeth and nails.

Then she dives in.

One second Tran's wife is there, hysterical, and the next she is in the pile, her arms thrashing and fighting, trying to get at something. I'm not close enough to see the something, but there are very few things in the zombie apocalypse that would make a screaming woman willingly dive into a pile of death.

Her screams become wails of pain, the shrieks of agony and anger. Z parts start flying everywhere and Elsbeth shoves Stella and Charlie back out of the way. Black blood splats against tree trunks and rhododendron leaves as Tran's wife goes full on Tasmanian Devil. I can see her arms and hands grabbing and tearing, ripping and rending. There goes a hand, a head, arms, ears, more heads, hand, arms, and ears. A torso is thrown down the hill. She is possessed.

"Come on!" Melissa shouts. "We can't stand and watch. Push through!"

She urges everyone to keep moving and Elsbeth follows suit, pushing ahead, trying not to get hit by the rain of Z stuffs. We all try not to get hit by it, but I feel the splatter of something as it slips past my cheek. I glance at Tran's wife, knowing there is nothing I can do, but still feeling like a coward as we hurry by, using her as the distraction to occupy the Zs.

Tran is screaming at her in Vietnamese. I have no idea what he is actually saying, but I know what he's communicating. "They are dead! We have to go!"

She's screaming back at him and at the pile of Zs. Her refusal to leave without her children is obvious. It's even expected. I have thought a million times if I would have had the strength to go on in this world if I didn't have Stella and the kids. Probably not. I'm sure I would have eaten a bullet by now.

The group is ahead, following a split of the path away from the road, going up and deeper into the brush choked woods that cover the hillside. I look over my shoulder and I see Tran staring at us, watching us all go. I can see the fight in his eyes. I can see the resignation that it is all over. I can see the indecision of whether to stay or to go.

Then I watch him grab his wife by the waist and lift her up into his arms. His adrenaline has taken over as he seems to carry her like a pillow, barely an effort needed. She wails and cries, her fingernails biting into his forearms as she struggles to get free and get to her babies. But it is too late. Those Zs that she hasn't ripped to shreds are busy feasting.

When I see the tiny toddler arm being fought over, I turn away. There's only so much I can handle. Anymore of that and I know I'll hit my limit.

We hike for a good hour before Melissa calls a halt. Tran and his wife are still well behind us, just out of sight, it is hard to tell how far back because she went silent after twenty minutes or so.

"Bite check," Melissa says.

We strip and check each other. No bites. Everyone is good. We get dressed and wait. I can tell Melissa and the scavengers don't like staying put, but we have to wait for Tran and his wife. It is the least we can do. The very least.

"How long to the Farm?" Greta asks and she's shushed by several people.

Normally I'd be pissed at anyone shushing my little girl, but not today. Today she needs to shut the fuck up.

Then there is Tran. No wife. And we know no kids. But no wife?

He walks up to one of the scavengers and holds out his hand. It's West Bullock, a burly man with a barrel chest and these gnarled short fingers like blunt sausages. He's holding a wicked machete and keeps looking from Melissa to Tran and back. Melissa nods and he hands the machete to Tran.

We all watch as Tran walks back down the path and around the hill. We wait, our ears straining for some idea of what is happening. Then we hear the whacks and thunks. In a minute, Tran comes back up the path to us, fresh blood splattering his chest, neck and face. He wipes the dripping machete on his pants and hands it back to West. The man shoves it into its sheath on his belt and hands Tran a bandana. Tran nods and wipes his face and neck and hands the bandana back. West shakes his head and Tran looks at it then stuffs it into his back pocket.

He walks past us all without a word and keeps hiking. Melissa sighs, looks back from where we came, then up at Tran. She nods and waves us all forward. We follow Tran, trailing in the wake of his grief and despair. You can almost taste it on the air like a bitter wind.

Everyone knows not to say anything, even Elsbeth.

Another hour of shell-shocked hiking and Melissa calls a halt. She sends Andrew, Lanny, and Steven up the hill to the road. We wait a few minutes and they are back, quickly huddling with Melissa in quiet conversation. After a few nods, she turns to gather us all in close. Except for Tran. He's crouched on the trail a few feet away, his eyes staring at his dirt and blood covered sneakers.

"The road is clear for now," Melissa says, "and will get us to the Farm faster."

"But?" Carl asks.

"But there's a higher likelihood of running into Zs up there," Melissa says. "Andy's gut is telling him we haven't seen the last horde."

"Maybe your gut just didn't like the egg salad," Landon sneers.

"Not the road," Elsbeth says then glares at Landon. "Not the egg salad." He wilts under her look.

"So we stay on the path," Melissa states.

"Shouldn't we vote?" Stubben asks. "You ain't in charge, Melissa."

"Fine," Melissa says. "Anyone want to waste time voting or are you fine with me keeping you alive?"

"Alive," Charlie says.

"Alive," Greta pipes up.

The rest of us nod.

"Not what I meant, but whatever," Stubben mumbles.

"The other problem is daylight," Melissa says. "It was going to be cutting it close before, but with this detour, we aren't going to get to the Farm by sunset."

"Let's not decide yet," Stella says, knowing what Melissa is about to say. "Keep pushing on. If we see a place to hold up on the way, then we take it. If we don't, then we don't stop."

"We'll have to stop once it gets dark," Andrew says. "Too many drop offs along the way. We could all end up falling down the hill and crashing the Z party down there."

"Then our first priority is shelter before it gets dark," Melissa says. "I'm sorry we can't get there tonight, folks. We'll get there tomorrow, I promise."

"Promises are like assholes," Elsbeth pipes up. "They stink when you put your nose in them."

None of us have a response to that.

"Okay then," Melissa says. "We keep going until we find shelter. West and Alison know this area best, so we'll let them lead."

"There's an old tobacco farm a few miles up," Alison says. "That will work if we need it."

We nod to each other and push forward. Tran gets up and lets us pass before he follows. He keeps his distance, not wanting to be a part of the group, but not letting us leave him behind. I can feel the internal debate he's having: keep going on, or just give up. It's not an unfamiliar debate for any of us. I don't know if the kids have had to deal with it, but every adult on this path has looked that choice square in the face. My instincts tell me that we'll know his answer by the morning.

It's not quite 6pm when Alison steers us off the path and up a short incline. We come out of the trees and into a field, overgrown and unkempt, but still obviously part of a small tobacco farm. We stumble over the ups and downs of the long gone dirt rows of tobacco plants, now just wild weeds and grass. At the far end of the field is a dilapidated two-story structure. It had probably seen better days well before the apocalypse hit this part of the mountains, but now it looks like it is held up by the whims of fate.

"Yeah," Charlie scoffs, "that looks safe."

"You want to sleep in this field?" West asks, playfully grabbing Charlie by the back of the neck. "I think we just found our volunteer for first watch."

"No, no, I was serious," Charlie says, twisting away and out of West's reach. "I think it looks safe. That's what I was saying. Why? Did I sound sarcastic? Sorry, my bad."

"Exactly," West grins.

"Come on," Alison says. "It's fine inside. This tobacco barn is probably a hundred years old, but men that knew how to build shit to last, built it. Just watch out for spiders."

"Oh, no," Greta says, shaking her head. "Not going in there. No spiders, thank you."

That's my girl. She can hold her own with a horde of Zs, but mention spiders and she's done, thank you.

"Taking second watch?" West asks.

"Screw you," Greta says. "I. Don't. Do. Spiders."

"Tonight you do whatever you are told," Stella says. "And the first thing is to be quiet."

"Good plan," Melissa says as she motions for her team to split and each take a side of the barn.

We wait in the field, watching, the late summer sun beating down on us as it burns a little more before dipping behind the trees. It takes a few minutes, but soon all of the scavengers are back, giving the thumbs up. Melissa waves us in and we step into the musty darkness of the tobacco barn.

The architecture has always fascinated me. Tobacco barns aren't like regular barns. They aren't these huge buildings with one double-door entry on each end. They aren't designed to hold livestock and horses, or bales of hay. They are long and flat. Usually two stories with each story only about twelve or fifteen feet high. Thick beams crisscross the ceiling, with spikes and hooks every foot or so. The sides aren't boxed in like a barn either, but open to let the air get inside. Tobacco barns are for hanging and drying the harvested leaves of tobacco- huge, yellow brown things that can be a foot wide and more than a couple feet long. The tobacco is long gone, but the earthy smell has been left behind from decades of use.

"Upstairs," Melissa says and we all follow to the second floor.

The scavengers space themselves out evenly along each side of the barn, their line of sight broken only by the occasional frame post of the barn, otherwise they can see in every direction clearly.

"It'll keep the weather off us," Melissa says, "and give us a defensible place to sleep."

"Where are we going to cook?" Landon asks. "This place'll go up in flames if we start a fire."

"That's why we won't start a fire," Alison says. "We eat what we have, cold."

"Cold?" Landon asks. "What about in the morning? I brought green tea."

"Oooh, I want some green tea," Greta says, then sees her mother's look. "When we get to the Farm. Let's save it for the Farm."

"This blows," Landon says. "Stuck in some fucking barn like a yokel and can't even have my green tea."

None of us see it coming. We'd been so used to giving him space and letting him be, that I think we forgot about Tran. It just was easier to push it all out of our minds and let Tran keep to himself. So when he pounces on Landon, I think it takes even Melissa and her scavengers a few moments to realize what is happening.

"Jesus fuck," Andrew says as he dives for the two men.

Tran is on top of Landon, having tackled him and knocked him to the barn floor, his fists slamming again and again into Landon's head. When Landon gets his arms up to protect himself, Tran starts in on his gut, landing gut crushing blow after blow. The distinct smell of shit hits our noses. Tran is literally beating the shit out of Landon.

"Enough!" Andrew hisses as he yanks at Tran.

The man shoves him away and starts back in on Landon. It takes Andrew, Carl, West, Stubben, and Melissa to pull him off. Landon just lies there, whimpering, his arms covering his face. The rest of us stand around, looking at each other, waiting for someone to make the first move.

"You're a fucking douche," Brian says quietly to Landon and walks away to another part of the barn.

We all decide to do the same thing and leave Landon to his wounds and the shit in his pants. He eventually gets up and makes his way down to the field to get cleaned up. It'll take a lot of leaves and grass to get that shit off, but he's got nothing better to do.

Tran settles down and collapses against one of the support beams, his eyes closed, tears dripping down his cheeks. We share looks of empathy, but none of us know where this is going. Tran could pull out of it or he could spiral down until he gives up. Like I've said, it's a debate and choice we've all had to face. But facing it is the first step, and I don't know if Tran will go there. Nobody but Tran knows that.

The sun finally starts to set and we hand out some of the food. There isn't much left, just enough for a small breakfast, so we had better make it to the Farm tomorrow. You get used to hunger in the apocalypse, but it never gets easy. It slows you down, dulls your senses, and makes mistakes more likely. But we'll face that tomorrow.

No one is up for much conversation, so we pick our spots and bed down. I have Stella and the kids with me and we curl up into a tight ball, resting against each other for comfort and warmth. As the last rays of the purple and pink sunset fade, I watch the silhouettes of the scavengers against the open sides of the barn, their bodies rigid and alert. I wonder how many times they've been in this type of situation while out foraging. I'll have to remember to thank them in the morning. Not until recently did I really understand the shit they walk out into every time they leave the gate.

The Zs leave us alone during the night and I'm surprised to wake to the sun coming up over the field below us.

"Why didn't anyone wake me for watch?" I ask.

"You need your rest," Stella says. "It's easier on everyone if your leg is healthy than for you to stay up watching for Zs."

"But now that you're up," Melissa says. "Time to hike. We have to backtrack a little bit to get to the Farm. We still have a long day ahead of us."

It is a long day, made that much longer by Tran. He stays behind us, barely part of the group. His head is down; his eyes watching his feet take step after step. At times, each of us want to go to him, to give him useless comfort and speak useless words. But we don't. Not our place. Even still, I can't help looking over my shoulder every few minutes, hoping for eye contact, some way to tell him I get it. Which, of course, I don't. Useless words...

"Did they feel it?" Greta asks as we eat the last of our food for lunch. Water is scarce and I pass around what's left in our family canteen. "Or did they die quick?"

"I pray they died quick," Stella says, hugging Greta to her. "I prayed for that all night long."

"I don't even remember their names," Charlie whispers. "I only spoke to them a few times, you know."

"Josie, Jeremy, Laura," Tran says, suddenly standing by us.

"I'm sorry," Greta says and Tran looks at her.

"Thank you," he nods.

"We're all sorry, Tran," Stella says.

"Daniel," he replies.

"What?" I ask.

"Everyone calls me Tran," he says, "that is, uh, my end name"

"Last name?" Charlie asks. "Is that what you mean?"

"Yes, last name," Tran says. "But my name is Daniel. I took Daniel when we move to America."

"Oh," I say. "Sorry. I didn't know. I've always thought Tran was your first name."

"You didn't ask," Tran says. He looks at the group. "No one ask. Never."

He walks away and we watch him go, his shoulders slumped, his body looking to weigh a million tons, being crushed under the weight of his grief.

"We suck," Charlie says.

"You got that right," I reply. "We do."

There are only a few Zs to take care of the rest of the way. Just stragglers, no hordes or herds coming at us. Not that Andrew was wrong. We crested a hill at one point and looked off to the south, seeing a herd of a couple hundred way off in the distance. They were choking I-26, just south of I-240, a mass of putrid limbs swarmed about the abandoned cars and trucks. It was hard to tell from that distance which way they were going; we just knew they were moving. And then we descended the hill and they were gone, out of sight, out of mind.

Those were the last Zs we saw for a few hours. But not to worry, the next Zs we come upon make up for it. And explain why we hadn't seen even one for a long time.

They are all at the Farm. Waiting for us. Well, maybe not exactly waiting for us, but waiting. Just standing there, their grey eyes focused intently on what is beyond the several layers of fencing and booby traps that surround the acreage that is the Farm. I don't know what stuns me more, the amount of Zs between us and the Farm or the size of the Farm itself. Both are considerable.

"Okay, people," Melissa whispers, motioning for us to hunker down. "This is the hard part."

"Because the rest was so easy," Landon says through his split lips and bruised, puffy cheeks.

"You want to stay here?" Melissa asks and Landon looks down at his hands. "Didn't think so." She takes a deep breath and starts to draw a crude map in a patch of dirt. "We are here. The Farm is here. The Zs are between us and the Farm."

"I think we can see that," Stubben says.

"Can you?" Melissa asks. "Can you also see the way into the Farm?"

"Uh, well…no," Stubben says.

"Then care to shut the fuck up and let me show you?" Melissa snarls, her patience finally gone. I keep forgetting she just lost her husband. I want to keep forgetting that, but it slams into my brain like a wall of shit.

Melissa points to a spot off to the side of where we are and quite a ways away from the Farm. "We are going here. We have to do it quickly and quietly. Both of those are non-negotiable." She looks at me. "Can you move quickly?"

"If that's what I have to do," I say.

"It is."

"Then, yeah, I can."

She gives Landon a harsh look. "Can you move quietly?"

"Why are you asking me?" She just keeps looking at him. "Yes. Yes, I can move quietly. I don't want to die either. That's why I came with you guys. Whispering Pines is gonna be overrun pretty quick. I'll hold my own here, okay? Stop looking at me like that!"

"Way to be quiet," Charlie says.

"Hush, everyone," Melissa says. "When we get to where we are going, there's no turning back. Once inside, we are inside. You stay close, you keep your mouths shut, and you'll live. Break one of those steps and you'll die. And probably get the rest of us killed." She looks at each of us in turn. "Ready?"

We all nod, even Landon.

I have no idea how long it takes or how far we go before we get to our destination. It seems like all we did was double back on ourselves while walking in circles. But finally, we reach an overgrown rocky outcropping. There it is, just sticking out of the hill. Rocks.

"Uh...what now?" Carl asks.

"Now we knock," Melissa says. She walks up to the rocks and then she's gone.

"Nice trick," Brian says.

"Coming?" she asks as she peeks back out.

We all follow, except for half the scavengers, who are behind us, watching our backs. Between two large rocks is a narrow passageway. We all have to take our packs off and hold them against us as we scoot sideways forever. The light fades, fades, fades, and is gone. There are some murmurs and shushes as people bump into each other, but no one stops or complains.

And then we are in a wide open space. It's pitch black and I only know it's wide open from the echoes of water drops from above us. The drip, drip, drip, bounces around what must be quite a cavern.

"Can we get a light?" someone whispers.

"No," Melissa says. "Not until we are all the way inside."

"This isn't inside?" Landon asks. "Ow."

Someone close to him must have punched him. Good for them.

"Take hands," Melissa says.

We do and then we each feel a tug as we are pulled forward by the person in front of us. We leave the cavern and are in a tunnel for a long while. My leg is killing me and not being able to see the floor doesn't help. I stumble and just manage to stay upright several times. On and on we go until Melissa whispers for us to stop.

Then there's a quiet knock. Whatever she's knocking on is metal, that's easy to tell. From way ahead, I see a small slit of light.

"Hey," a man's voice says, "we saw you outside the fence. How many?"

"About eighteen," Melissa says. "Daddy gonna be okay with this?"

"Of course," the voice says. "As long as they can abide by the rules."

"They can and they will," Melissa says. "Or I'll walk them outside the fence myself."

"Good enough," the man laughs. "Then get your butt in here, big sis."

There's a clang of metal and the tunnel is illuminated in torch light as a huge door opens before us. Several men and women are standing there with rifles across their chests, watching us with indifference. We filter past and say a few hellos, but we're mainly ignored.

"Don't bother," Melissa says. "You're no better than livestock until Daddy says otherwise."

"So true," Elsbeth says. I try not to think what she means.

We follow a long, carved tunnel before we get to a wide set of stone steps. I make it up the steps although my leg is nearly ready to fall off, and we all step out of a small stone shed at the top of the stairs. Before us is the Farm and I want to cry. It is beautiful. I look at Stella and see the tears in her eyes. She hugs the kids to her and we just smile.

"Where's Tran?" Stubben asks.

I look about and don't see him. Melissa waits until we are all up the stairs and out of the shed before she calls down. "Tran? You down there?"

"Who you looking for?" a very large man, maybe in his late twenties, early thirties, with tree trunks for legs and arms bigger than my daughter. "That Asian guy?"

"Yeah, Pup, that Asian guy," Melissa says, frowning at the man. He ducks his head and looks away.

"I wasn't bein' racist or nothin', Mel, sheesh," the man says. "I just was wondering if that was who you was lookin' for. Cause he's outside the fence. We been watchin' him."

"What?" Melissa asks, more than alarmed.

She hurries past the man, past a row of sheds and a large red barn. We follow quickly until we are standing before a huge farmhouse and looking out across the fences at the swarm of Zs. Behind them all, up on the hill where we started before finding the rocks and the tunnel, stands Tran. It is really too far to see for sure if it's him, but we all know it is.

"Ah, fuck," Melissa says as Tran starts to walk right towards the Zs. "Dumb bastard."

"Melissa Helen Fitzpatrick Billings," a stern voice says from behind us. "You are mucking out the pig pens tomorrow for that. You watch your mouth, young lady."

CHAPTER SEVEN

"TRAN!" I scream.

"Quiet," Stella says.

"He can scream all he wants, ma'am," the stern voiced man says as he comes around in front of us. "Don't make no difference. This is a working farm. We're nothing but zombie bait. They keep coming and coming because our slice of Paradise just smells too good."

"TRAN! STOP!" I yell, cupping my hands to my mouth.

Tran doesn't stop. In fact, he starts to wave his arms and shout at the Zs. Despite my screaming attempt to divert their attention, the Zs lurch about, slowly realizing there is food right behind. Once they see him, they move as one, a swarm of undead, shuffle stepping to supper.

I keep screaming at him. For some reason I feel responsible. I don't know why. It makes no sense at all, but I just feel like my years as a shit neighbor have finally led to this point. If I'd invited him over for a beer or to watch a game. Or just to hang and play some pool. Maybe to one of my poker nights. Anything. But I did none of this and now, well...

"Don't look, kids," Stella says, steering the children away. "This is not to be seen."

"Good for the young ones to understand the way of life these days," stern voiced man says. "Hardens them to the daily truth our Lord has seen fit to bestow upon us. This is no accident, ma'am. This is God's will."

"Jesus, he sounds like Carrey," Landon says.

"You blaspheme again, young man," stern voice growls, "and I put you outside the fence."

"Daddy, calm down," Melissa says, turning to her father and placing a hand on his chest. "The past few days have not been easy." Melissa looks at us and tries to smile. "This is my daddy. You can call him Big Daddy Fitz. That's what he likes and what he goes by."

None of us introduce ourselves because the screaming has started. Tran's voice is high-pitched, a child's voice almost. Then it isn't. We can see the Zs swarming on him. A red mist fills the air as they tear at his body. One of them must have gotten his throat. Not another sound filters to us.

"How about we all go inside," Big Daddy suggests. "We'll let nature take its course then come back out later for refreshments."

"Refreshments?" I ask. "Refreshments! Are you fucking kidding me? A man just died!"

"There is no cursing here, sir," Big Daddy says. "And while yes, he did just die, he made that choice. That was an obvious suicide and that is an affront to God. That, sir, is a mortal sin. His soul is lost and cannot be redeemed."

"Daddy?" another horse-sized man says from the porch. "How many sweet teas do I need to pour?"

Big Daddy looks about and starts to count, then stops. He looks at Melissa and counts again, then stops. "Sweetie, Mel, where's your man?" Mel just shakes her head. "Oh, my poor girl, come here."

Melissa is enveloped in her father's arms. She instantly transforms from the tough woman in her late forties to a little girl sobbing against her father's chest. We all look away then up at the man on the porch.

"Hey, y'all," the man says, "I'm Gunga."

We stare.

"What?" he asks, looking startled. He wipes at his nose. "Do I got a booger or something?"

"Gunga," Carl says. "That's an interesting name."

"Oh, that?" Gunga laughs. "It is ain't it? Nah, it's because Toad couldn't say Howard when he was a baby so he kept calling me Gunga. Don't know why. My English teacher in high school made me memorize that poem by the Jungle Book guy. Not sure why. His name was Mathews and it's not like he ever had to memorize the Book of Matthew."

"Woulda been a good thing to do, though," Big Daddy says. "Gunga, don't worry none about the sweet tea. Go find your brothers. We need to have a family meeting and get this all sorted out." He looks down at Melissa and pushes her face from his chest, his thumb and forefinger wiggling her chin. "No need to go into it now, Sweetie Mel. We have plenty of time for that." He looks around at us. "But I think introductions are in order."

"Yes, sir," Melissa says, wiping her eyes. She turns and sweeps a hand at us. "These are my neighbors. We're having a bit of a problem back home."

"I can imagine," Big Daddy says. "How do you do, folks?"

Melissa makes the introductions, saving me for last. Not sure how I feel about that.

"So you're Mr. Smarty Pants, eh?" Big Daddy asks, smiling. I'm very glad he's smiling.

"I'm Jace, Mr. Fitzpatrick," I say. "Don't know about the smarty part, but I am wearing pants."

"Yep, that's him," Big Daddy grins. "You and I will be speaking further. Gotta run some ideas past you."

"I'm not really qualified to talk about farming," I say. "I could barely keep the kids' gerbils alive."

The wind shifts and the sounds beyond the fences drift to our ears. Smacking lips, slurping, crunching bones, bickering hisses and groans.

"How about we move this conversation like I said?" Big Daddy says, looking at Charlie and Greta. "Folks, you can all go around to the back of the house. We have a fine pavilion back there with picnic tables and such. Have a seat, take a load off. Rest those weary legs of yours and we'll have a right proper chat about what brings you to the Farm."

Melissa nods to the scavengers and they usher everyone towards the back of the grand farmhouse. I start to go with Stella and the kids, but a beefy hand stops me.

"How about you wait here?" Big Daddy looks at the others leaving. "I'd appreciate an unbiased account of what's been happening to y'all."

"Go ahead," Stella says, "I've got the kids."

"I'll be right there," I say as she walks off with the others.

In seconds, it's just Melissa and her father with me. I look about the Farm and nod.

"This is quite a place," I say. "Can't imagine the work it takes."

"We have plenty of help," Big Daddy says. "And we help plenty. Been waiting for this day. I've been telling Sweetie Mel here for a long time that that Whispering Pines place was bound for trouble. I do hate to be right on that."

"You love to be right," Melissa says. "I think it's the only thing you love more than biscuits and gravy."

"Now, don't blaspheme," Big Daddy laughs. "I'd rather be wrong with a plateful of biscuits and your country gravy in hand any day."

The sounds hit us again. Big Daddy's grin slides from his face.

"Fill me in," he says.

I do with help from Melissa when she can keep it together. I have to remember that she just lost her husband only a couple days ago. I've tried to push it from my mind, but maybe that's been the wrong way to handle it. With Bullhorn/Wall Street out there and Brenda going all dictator, I should probably be sharpening my senses, not dulling them with denial.

"You okay there, Hoss?" Big Daddy asks. "Looks like you tucked inside yourself for a spell."

Hoss… So that's where Jon got it from.

"I'm fine."

"How long you need to stay?" Bid Daddy asks.

"We don't know," I say. "This isn't permanent. We want to go home. We'll just need some help. We have two factions to deal with."

"One, the way I see it," Big Daddy says, "but let's get to the particulars later. And you and yours are welcome to stay as long as you need. We have the room and the food. Julio is coming back soon. You'll like him. He's a smarty pants like you, but with a Mexican accent."

"I'm pretty sure he's from Columbia, Daddy," Melissa says.

"Don't mean no offense," Big Daddy says to me. "I'm just a country boy that's been adjusting to the changing world well before this all happened."

Big Daddy looks out at the row upon row of fencing and the Zs beyond that. He sighs and leads us around the house.

Our group is seated and smiling –well, mostly smiling- as Gunga passes out glasses and pitchers of sweet tea.

"Sorry there ain't no lemons," Gunga says. "We just can't get them to grow right. Turn all nasty and shriveled."

"This will be fine, Gunga," Stella says, "thank you."

As I take a seat and plant a kiss on Stella's forehead, a group of men come around the other side of the house. They are dust covered and sweaty, with shotguns and rifles resting on their shoulders.

"There they are," Melissa says, getting up and going to them. She is swallowed in a group hug of muscles and perspiration. Finally, she gets free and looks at us. "These are the rest of my brothers." She points and they all line up. Tall, broad, built out of bricks, they look alike except for the first one that's bald as a cue ball. "This is Buzz, you know Gunga over there, and met Pup, this is Toad, Porky, and Scoot."

They all nod and say their hellos and howdys.

Buzz, the bald one, puts his fingers to his mouth and lets loose with an eardrum shattering whistle. We all look around, waiting for the other boot to drop, but instead, it's a stampede of boots and shoes that comes around behind the men. Children of all ages and sizes sprint to their fathers. Then come the adults. Men and women as diverse as I've ever seen a group. I always forget how homogenous suburban life can be.

A black couple and their three kids come over and introduce themselves as the Furtigs. Then several Hispanic couples come over with their kids- the Hernandezes, the Santiagos, the Rioses, and the Ortegas. They are followed by an Indian man named Patel that is surrounded by six daughters ranging in age from maybe six to sixteen. Behind him are three women of obvious Cherokee descent with their children.

Behind that are about ten single men of all races and colors. In front is a short Hispanic man, his torso bare, but covered in dark black and blue tattoos. They run all the way up his arms and up his neck. His head is shaved except for a thin, short Mohawk. On his belt, strapped to his right leg, is a nasty looking short sword. The sheath is only a few straps of leather, so I can see the various etchings on the blade. I can also see the deadly sharp looking edge it has.

"Smarty Pants, this is Julio," Big Daddy says. "Melissa says you're Columbian, but I say Mexican. Which is it now?"

I'm expecting a frown from the man over the ignorance of his home country, but instead he grins and gives a laugh almost as big as Big Daddy. "El Salvador," he says. "The Santiagos are Columbian." He looks me up and down and holds out his hand. "What's up, Smarty Pants?"

"It's Jace," I say, taking the strong grip. "Please don't call me Smarty Pants."

"You got it, Jace," Julio says. "And actually, I'm from Hendersonville, not El Salvador. That's where my parents came from. I was born in Park Ridge hospital."

"Then you have me beat," I say. "I was born in Oregon. Only been here in Asheville for about ten years before it all went to hell."

"This isn't Hell, Hoss," Big Daddy says. "This is where we are tested before the Lord decides where we go. Hell won't be so easy."

"Easy?" I laugh. "That's one way to say it."

A scream gets my attention and I reach for my belt, but stop my hand when I see that it's just all the kids, mine included, running around playing tag off away from the pavilion. Elsbeth is on the sidelines sitting cross-legged, watching them intently, her eyes darting from runner to runner.

"BD, we have a problem," Julio says, his hand on the hilt of his sword. "I know that girl."

"Elsbeth," I say. "She saved my life. Well, after having kidnapped me to cook for dinner. But I'm going with the saving of the life part as the character judgment."

"She's a cannibal," Julio says to Big Daddy. "I've had run-ins with her padre."

"She going to be a problem?" Big Daddy asks me.

"No, sir," I say. "I'll vouch for her."

"She looks at me like I'm a chicken leg and I slit her throat," Julio says. "You have no idea what you're dealing with there."

I think back to the sight of dozens of undead lying still around the dump truck and smile.

"I have a pretty good idea," I say, "but you have my word she'll be cool."

Of course, no sooner have I said that than here she comes, The Bitch in hand, her eyes locked on Julio.

"You ain't a nice man," Elsbeth says. "You broke Pa's hand one time. I remember. Oh, I remember that."

Everyone goes quiet, even the children, as Elsbeth closes on Julio. She eyes his sword and frowns.

"You should have pulled that already," she says. "You don't have time no more."

"Chill, Elsbeth," I say, stepping in front of her. "These are friends now. Just like us. Whatever happened before is done. You have to let it go."

"I should break his hand," Elsbeth says. "Only fair."

"If you want to talk fair, then I should toss you outside the fences," I say. "You know, for kidnapping me and prepping me for dinner."

"Your friends killed Pa," she says to me. "Maybe we should remember that."

"This is what you call cool?" Julio laughs and looks at Big Daddy. "This is the smart guy you've been talking about?" He pulls his sword and Elsbeth lunges.

I'm able to shove Elsbeth back, but she doesn't care, all her focus is on Julio. Then she stops, her face tense with violence, and looks down at her arm. And the hand that has grabbed it.

"Please don't," Greta says. "Don't kill him."

"Ha! You think this chica can take me?" Julio laughs. "You aint' right in the head, little girl."

Before I can get on Julio for that comment, Greta pushes past Elsbeth and gets right in front of him. Her face is stone cold blank except for her eyes. I know that look. Julio doesn't stand a chance.

"Not only will she kill you," Greta says. "She'll make you beg for it. You want to be the little girl that begs for his life? You want all these big, tough men to see you crying and wishing it could all be over? That what you want, doodles? You want me to stand over your steaming corpse and say I told you so?"

Julio is dumbfounded. His mouth opens and closes a few times before he licks his lips and says, "Doodles?"

She waves at his tats. "Doodles."

He looks past Greta at Elsbeth who is watching Greta with awe and great affection.

"She gets out of line and I come for you, little girl," Julio says. "Deal?"

"Deal," Greta says as she holds out her hand. Julio takes it and shakes. He tries to pull back, but Greta hangs on. "And it's Greta, not little girl. Call me that again and deal is off. You'll wake up with your cojones stuffed in your mouth."

"Greta!" Stella calls out. "Watch your mouth!"

"He better watch his," Greta says as she turns from Julio and walks back over to the other kids. They all stare at her, slack jawed, except for Charlie who is shaking his head, a hand covering his face, not surprised at all.

"Mr. Fitzpatrick," Stella says, "I apologize for her behavior."

He waves Stella off. "While I don't approve of anyone stuffing cojones in mouths, I do believe her point has been made." He looks at Julio and then at Elsbeth. "We going to be alright here?"

"Better be!" Greta shouts from the crowd of kids.

"Greta Stanford!" Stella says and marches over to her.

"I'm good," Julio says. "I like my cojones right where they are."

"I don't know what co-hoe-nees are," Elsbeth says, looking at me.

"Balls," I say. "Nuts."

Elsbeth smiles and looks over her shoulder at Greta. My daughter beams at her despite the hushed chewing out she's getting from her mother. Elsbeth looks at me, and then at Big Daddy and finally at Julio. She holds out her hand.

"I'm good too," she says.

Julio takes her hand and they shake quickly. Elsbeth hands me The Bitch, turns, and runs at the kids.

"I'm it!" she yells.

The tension is gone and the kids get back to playing. I can feel the collective sigh from the adults.

"How about we take a load off and get to know each other before we dive into the details of your visit?" Big Daddy suggests. "We'll eat some supper and then it'll be time for business."

"Works for me," I say as my stomach starts to growl.

The smell of wood smoke and cooking meat drifts across the backyard, which is pretty much the size of a football field, and I look over to see some of the brothers with Mr. Patel lifting a massive grill lid up by poles and setting it aside. Inside is two halves of a whole pig. A whole pig. At one point in our lives, we were vegetarians. That concept doesn't apply during the apocalypse, especially when barbecued pork is cooking right in front of you.

The Cherokee women, which I still haven't caught names for, get up and go into the house followed by Melissa and half her scavengers. They soon come outside with bowl after bowl of salads and side dishes: fried okra, mac and cheese, mashed potatoes, potato salad, devilled eggs (with paprika? Holy shit!), pickled beets, green beans, Brussels sprouts, berries and cream, and so, so much more.

For a brief second, the sight of so much food overwhelms me. We never had this kind of variety in Whispering Pines. It was all about what Stubben could get to grow and Tran could preserve and prepare. And then the wonder leaves me. Tran...

"I know," Stella says, her hand in mine, "I'm thinking about them too."

Big Daddy motions for everyone to take a seat and after a long, but uplifting, grace, we all dig in. Despite Big Daddy's earlier words, I'm pretty sure I just found Heaven on Earth.

Everybody eats until stuffed to bursting. The sun is about set when Big Daddy gets up. Without it having to be said, the tables go quiet.

"As much as I'd like to keep this joviality going, I think there is business," Big Daddy says. "I believe the front porch will be fine for our chat." He looks at Melissa and then me. "Bring your people you want present. We'll get a few things settled before calling it a night."

"Help clear the dishes," Stella says to Charlie and Greta, "and keep an eye on Elsbeth. I'm going with your father."

Soon we are seated in rocking chairs on the long, wide porch in front of the farmhouse. Big Daddy and Buzz, Melissa and Andy Crespo, Stella and me, and Julio. Everyone else is inside laughing and chatting as they clean the dishes by candle and lamp light. I notice then that there's no power in the house, but I could have sworn I saw wind turbines up on the hills.

"Where does the electricity go to?" I ask.

"Good catch," Julio says as he pulls a pouch from his pocket and opens it. He pulls a small piece of paper out and begins crumpling something in it. "We direct all power to the fences. Plus a few other things. Don't need electricity to farm, right BD?"

"Been farming for centuries without it," Big Daddy says as he pulls a corncob pipe from his pocket and loads it. "Why waste power on something that doesn't need it?"

Julio rolls a tight cigarette and lights it, drawing deep. I have always hated tobacco smoke, and get ready to tolerate it when the smell hits me.

"You have got to be kidding," I laugh. "Seriously?"

Julio smiles and hands me the joint. "Take it. I'll roll another."

He does and lights that as Stella takes the joint from my hand.

"What?" she smiles. "When's the next time I'll have a chance?"

Julio laughs hard and rolls a third.

"You folks all set with your wacky weed?" Big Daddy says, puffing on his pipe. "Ain't judging, just asking so we can get down to business."

"Actually, let's talk about this," I say, holding the joint out. "You grow this here? Hemp could be pretty useful."

"Nah," Big Daddy says. "I don't know nothing about growing hemp or marijuana. I leave that to the hippies."

"There's a commune two hollers over," Julio says. "Completely self-sufficient. Z-Day was long gone before they even knew something had gone wrong. They grow the killer bud and have acres and acres of hemp. We trade for cloth and biodiesel."

"Biodiesel?" Stella asks. "Can't you make that here?"

"We could," Buzz says, "but they have it down. Hemp oil into fuel. They even distill ethanol for us if we need something a little more high octane."

"Their corn hooch will knock you on your butt," Julio says. "Trust me. Some of the best around, and that's saying a lot since half the hollers have stills."

"So, twenty-four hours left?" Big Daddy asks, getting to the point.

"Less," Melissa says.

"Then it'll already happen before we get there," Big Daddy says. "What do you expect to find?"

"*We* get there?" I ask. "So you'll help?"

"Oh, I think that can be arranged," Big Daddy says. "But no more of your elitist nonsense. We are all in this world together now. Those that are right with the Lord need to stay together. We are here for a reason, Hoss. The Lord didn't put this nightmare before us to bicker and kill each other, now did He?"

"I don't know about the Lord," I say, "but I have two kids in there that I want to live to a ripe old age. That's enough for me."

"To get back to what you were asking," Melissa says. "I expect to find new neighbors."

"I don't," I say. "Brenda won't let that happen."

"Wall Street said that everyone had to leave," Stella says. "If Brenda takes a stand, then everyone will die."

"No, they won't," I say. "Brenda will cut a deal. I've been thinking it over and something has been bothering me. Why didn't she kill me?"

"What?" Melissa asks. "What do you mean?"

"I was alone in the jail all night," I say. "An accident could have happened, so why didn't it?"

"You mean besides the moral implications?" Big Daddy asks.

"That isn't an issue," I tell him. "Brenda's morals involve one person: herself. Everyone else can be damned."

"Good to know," Big Daddy says. "Mel has told me as much, but it's good to hear from others."

"Because she knew we'd come," Stella says, answering my first question. "She'd have a war on her hands."

"True," I say. "Or she knew we'd leave and where we'd go."

"You think Brenda is smart enough to have planned this?" Melissa laughs. "You have more faith in her than I do."

"I think Brenda knows when to cover her bases," I say. "Once she knew we were all leaving, I am sure she saw some benefit in it. There's no way she's giving up Whispering Pines without a fight."

"But that's what she's doing," Andrew says.

"No, she's not," I say. "But, like always, she isn't doing the fighting. She's leaving that to us. She has something up her sleeve, believe me."

Everyone is silent as they let that sink in.

"Damn," Julio laughs, breaking the silence. "You are smart."

"So you think she wanted us to come get help?" Melissa asks. "That this was her idea from the start?"

"No, no, not her idea," I say. "When it comes down to it, Brenda isn't that bright. But she saw an opportunity when it was presented. Any resistance she gave was all show. She plans on surrendering Whispering Pines and wanted to make sure that anyone that talked to Bullhorn told him that she got rid of the agitators."

"Bullhorn?" Big daddy asks.

"That's what he calls Wall Street," Stella says. "It's the wrong name."

"He shouts through a bullhorn," I say. "You agreed with me at one point."

"Whatever his name may be," Big Daddy says. "He'll be there with his people. That's who we have to worry about. All this talk about Brenda is just your theory, Hoss. We can cross that bridge when we get to it."

"Or she's collaborating with the guy," Melissa offers. "It could be that simple."

"Yeah," I admit, "it could be. Which means we have a serious problem on our hands."

"Not to be rude," Andrew says, looking at Big Daddy. "But the serious problem is there are only a few of you here. We don't have the numbers we need to take on those people."

"Don't worry about that," Buzz says. "We have plenty of people. They'll be here in the morning. Unless it's full harvest time, then most folks only come in for half a day to work. We make sure they get back home safe and sound well before dark."

"In about a month, this place will be nothing but tents as far as you can see," Julio adds. "We get the harvest in and everyone takes their share."

"They survive out there?" Stella asks. "Outside the fence?"

"Ma'am, not to be rude, folks have been surviving in conditions like this for centuries in these mountains," Big Daddy responds. "Now sure, they haven't had to deal with the Zs, but they have had to deal with hardships just as bad. Folk around here know how to survive." He spreads his arms wide. "This life is the life my daddy knew and his daddy knew before him. You can go back more than ten generations of Fitzpatrick's and know what you'd find? Hard workers, big eaters, and folk living with the land."

"You like this, don't you?" I say. "Not the killing, but the simplicity."

"Sure don't mind not having a government breathing down my neck," Big Daddy smiles as he tamps his pipe. "Or a bank doing the same. It may be a waking nightmare at times, but it's true living, that's for sure."

"Amen," Buzz says. Julio nods.

"So why risk it for a bunch of suburban losers like us?" I ask.

Big Daddy takes his pipe from his mouth and sets it aside.

"Where do you think they will come next?" Big Daddy asks. "You think all this Wall Street fella wants is a neighborhood where he can play hopscotch and ride his Big Wheel around? No. He wants to secure the entire area for himself. He doesn't care who dies. I've dealt with his lot before. When the bank tried to take my land; when the government tried to impose Imminent Domain so they could build an interstate throughway, just so tourists could have more road to drive their RVs on; environmentalists coming here to tell me that I'm raping the Earth." Big Daddy shakes his head sadly. "This fella ain't new. Just a new cover on an old story."

"When do we set out?" I ask.

"Soon," Big Daddy says. "We'll have to get our ducks in a row first. Plus, I want them to see us getting ready, make a show of it."

"Make a show of it?" I ask. "What does that mean?"

"You think they're watching us?" Stella asks.

"They've been eyeing the Farm for weeks now," Julio says. "And we let them. They're looking for the weak spots. They can go right ahead. There aren't any."

"Humility, please, Julio," Big Daddy says. "Let's not tempt the Lord."

"Right, of course," Julio says. "Either way, we are locked down tight. You'll see when everyone gets here in the morning."

"Speaking of," Big Daddy says as he stands up and stretches. "Dawn comes quick around here. Best we all get some rest."

"But soon when?" Stella asks. "What about Whispering Pines?"

"They'll still be there," Big Daddy says. "I'm leaning towards your man's theory. And if what Sweetie Mel has told me about this Brenda Kelly woman over the years, then I do not doubt that she has worked it out so your neighbors can stay and she is sitting pretty. Whether she's in cahoots or not with Wall Street. We have time."

"Not much," Julio adds.

"Why do you say that?" I ask.

"Because even if she is crafty, like you said, she ain't bright," Julio replies. "Eventually, she'll screw up and get herself and everyone else killed."

I can't argue with that.

We say our goodnights and go to find the kids. We gather them, and Elsbeth, and Melissa shows us to a guest room on the third floor of the farmhouse. We get settled in and I'm just about to whisper to Stella when I hear her snores. That's a good sign. If she's snoring, then she feels safe. And if she's feeling safe, then I'm doing my job.

"Daddy?" Greta whispers.

"What, sugar?"

"Are you going to have to fight?"

"Probably."

"Can I come?"

"Not a chance in hell."

"Charlie said he's going with you to fight."

"Charlie is full of shit and was probably just saying that to piss you off."

She's quiet for a while then, "Yeah, you're right." More quiet. "Is Elsbeth going?"

"Yes," Elsbeth says, "I am going."

"Will you guys be quiet, please?" Charlie asks. "Or is that request too full of shit."

"Sorry about that," I say.

"Make it up to me by shutting the hell up so I can sleep," Charlie says. "Jennifer says we have to get up with the roosters. That's going to hurt."

"Jennifer?" I ask.

"His new girlfriend," Greta giggles. "Mr. Patel's oldest daughter."

"She's not my girlfriend," Charlie says. "She's way older."

"You couldn't stop looking at her," Greta teases.

"Children," Stella says, sleepily. "Hush and sleep. You too, Daddy. Tired. Must sleep."

It takes a while for my mind to wind down, but eventually I crash out. Next thing I know, the roosters are at it and I can hear the farmhouse creaking and groaning as the household wakes and gets ready for the day. My eyelids part and I can just make out a dark purple stain outside the window. Morning comes early. Whoever Jennifer is, she's right.

But, to beat back the cruelty of the early hour, there are smells. Smells I haven't experienced in so, so long. Bacon and ham. Sausage and country gravy. I can smell grits, biscuits, and vanilla in something. Chicory coffee. My mouth starts to salivate. I thought dinner had been amazing last night, and now I will be treated to a breakfast that I didn't think existed outside my memories.

There's a knock on the door and a light brown face peeks in. "Charlie? Greta? Breakfast is ready in just a few minutes."

"What about us?" I say, stretching in bed as Stella gets up, trying to rouse the kids.

"Kids eat first," she says. I wonder if this is Jennifer. "That way they have full bellies in case."

She closes the door, leaving the "in case" behind.

"What does that mean?" Greta asks, all early morning growly and pissed. "In case of what?"

"I'm guessing in case we have to run for it," I say.

Charlie gets up quick and looks around. "Run for it? I thought we were safe? Aren't we safe?"

"We're safe," Stella says, "I'm sure it's just part of their safety protocol. This place may look wonderful, but it's only a few fences away from the Zs. You can't let your guard down."

"But you can stuff your bellies," I smile. "So get to it, you two. We'll be down in a second."

Elsbeth rubs her eyes and rolls over to look at us. She shoves the blankets off of her and gets up from the pallet on the floor.

"Good Morning," Stella says.

"Morning," Elsbeth nods. "It smells yum. Do we get to eat already?"

"When the kids are done," Stella says. "Maybe we can go find a shower to use?"

"You do that," I say. "I'm going to find the men folk and talk about men stuff."

"Good luck with that," Stella says. "Try not to sound too smart. Men folk don't like it when you get too smart for your britches."

"That only applies to women, not other men folk," I say. "So shut your mouth and go make me some grub, woman! And make sure those nethers are clean in case I feel like rutting later!"

Elsbeth's face is pure shock.

"We're just playing, honey," Stella says as she steers the young woman out of the room. "See you downstairs."

I smile and wave, then turn to the window and the line of pink/orange that is coming up over the horizon. The Farm begins to show itself in the morning glow and I look out at it from the third story. What I see is life, despite the shadows of the Zs along the fences. I may not know anything about farming, but I have to wonder if I could make a go of it. Maybe going back to

Whispering Pines isn't such a great idea. I wonder what everyone else would think?

"Are you kidding?" Landon says when I make this thought available to all as we stuff our faces with the amazing goodness that is before us on the long table. "I'm not staying in the sticks. I have a PS4 at home. A PS4."

"As much as I do not like your friend here," Big Daddy says, ignoring the look of anger and shock on Landon's face. "I have to agree. You folks need to go back to your homes. The key to our survival as a species is diversity. If we all hunker down together, then pretty soon we'll be more inbred than a Tennessee family reunion."

"I'm from Tennessee," Carl says.

"Yes, but you ain't exactly breeding now are ya?" Buzz says, smiling. The look he gets from Melissa wipes the smile off his face. "Didn't mean any offense. It was just a joke."

"Not funny," Melissa says.

"As I was saying," Big Daddy continues, ignoring his children, "we need diversity. We need more than just the Farm. Or the Commune. Or Critter's Holler. Or-"

"Wait, what?" I ask. "Critter's Holler?"

Big Daddy waves me off. "We'll get to that later. Back to my point, in order to rebuild we have to rebuild it all. Not just the life out here, but the life back in Asheville. Cities have their place. I admit I haven't been a fan of city folk or that way of living, but an urban center can provide a central place for trade, for security, for education, for society. I'm a man of the land, but not everyone is cut out for it."

"Amen to that," Landon says.

Big Daddy gestures at Landon and raises his eyebrows to prove his point.

"Wait, hold on," Stubben says, a rare enough thing. "You want us to rebuild the city?"

"Yes," Big Daddy says. "If it's done right, then there is a place for others to come. Security will be number one, since I'm sure plenty of folk from Georgia and South Carolina will want what we build, but it can be done."

"Georgia?" Stella asks.

"Like a Georgia peach," Elsbeth says. Everyone looks at her, but she just shoves a biscuit in her mouth and smiles, crumbs tumbling to the table.

"Okay," Stella says. "What do you mean folk from Georgia and South Carolina?"

"We run into them all the time," Julio says. "When out trading with the other folks. Stragglers escaping the herds that come pouring out of Atlanta or down by Columbia."

"Feel lucky we're up here in the Blue Ridge," Buzz says. "The Zs have a hard time getting up the mountains. Down by Charlotte?" He shakes his head. "It's a mess."

I'd never really thought about other survivors looking for homes other than locals. I just figured people stayed close to the familiar. Or that they all died. A stupid idea, but not out of the realm of possibility. I've never met a single person not from around here since Z-Day. Guess that shows me what I know. Then I think of all the bums. Jesus…

"We don't have the manpower to clear Asheville," I say. "Or we would have done it by now." I glance over at Elsbeth who is trying to see if she can simultaneously fit a forkful of eggs in her mouth, while her other hand tries to jam three pieces of bacon in there. "It's not just Zs, you know. Who are we to say who stays and who goes?"

"I think simple morality tells us that," Big Daddy says. "This young woman has come around, now hasn't she?"

Elsbeth finally looks up and sees that we're all watching her.

"Wuh?" she asks, bits of yellow flying from her lips.

"A little civilization may be in order, but she hasn't tried to eat any of us," Big Daddy smiles. "People do what they have to do to survive. We remove the 'have to' from that equation and we'll get civilization up on its feet in no time."

I rub my forehead, the million ramifications and variables rushing through my brain, and sigh.

"You've been thinking about this for a long time, haven't you?" I ask. "Us coming here just moved up your timetable."

"It did," Big Daddy nodded. "Got me to realizing that I may not be the only one thinking about this." He pushes his plate to the side and leans forward on his elbows, his hands clasped. "This

Wall Street fella, he's got the same plan, just not as inclusive. He doesn't want to rebuild. He wants to build over. And his way. We let that happen and we'll be at war for the rest of our lives. Not just with the Zs, but with people. And that scares me more than twenty acres of undead."

He lets that sink in for a bit.

He's right. People are the scary part of the apocalypse. Zs are like the landscape. A dangerous, bitey part of the landscape, but something that's just there to be wary of. Like rattlesnakes or a bad undertow at the beach. Okay, maybe a little more extreme than that. More like living with grizzly bears everywhere. But still, something you learn to deal with because they are now a part of nature. They are predictable, or as predictable as nature can be.

But people?

People are never predictable. And we can fortify Whispering Pines, or the Farm, as much as we want against Zs, but with the human element out there, we will never live with any semblance of security. Say we take out Wall Street (yes, I will give in and call him that) and all of his bikers and soldiers and whatever they are. Say that happens. Then what? We just go back to "normal" life in Whispering Pines? I figure shit out while Stella teaches the kids and douche nozzles like Landon sit around playing PS4?

Not sustainable. It only postpones the inevitable. It postpones the time when a new Wall Street comes along. Or all the cannibals hiding in dank basements run out of food in the city and come for us. Do I want to live in fear of the day the cannibals unite? Sweet Jesus, no, I have enough problems without worrying about becoming someone's long pork hoagie.

I realize everyone is looking at me.

"What?" I ask. "Did I miss something?"

"I asked if you thought we could establish a better form of communication," Big Daddy says. "The telephone poles are still up. I'm sure most of the lines are severed here and there from downed trees and whatnot, but with some work, we could have Ma Bell up and going again."

"I think that would be more for Carl and Landon to say," I reply.

"Oh, they can say all they want," Big Daddy responds. "I want your opinion. Otherwise, I wouldn't have asked."

"I, uh, I don't know," I say. This guy is really throwing a lot at me. Rebuild Asheville? Rebuild the telephone system? What's next? Get one of the hydroelectric dams running? There are like five or six in Western North Carolina. Just one could do the trick…

I can feel sweat breaking out on my forehead and suddenly my stomach is in knots.

"Where's the outhouse?" I blurt.

"Baby? Are you okay?" Stella asks as I stand up suddenly.

"Just need to use the facilities," I say.

"Uh, I'll show you," Stella says. "Just out back and to the side."

"I'm fine, I got it," I say, hurrying from the room. "Be right back. Talk amongst yourselves. Nothing to worry about."

But there's a lot to worry about. Too much, in fact. The variables. The millions of variables. The systems that would need to be brought back on line? Who knows how to do that? The miles of line to be checked. Miles of it! I just want to get home, sleep in my own bed, and worry about Zs at the fence and gate. I just want the simple life again, no matter how deadly or dangerous. I didn't come to the Farm to talk about city building and turning the infrastructure back on. I thought we'd get some help, maybe go back, kill some people, take back our suburban homes, and then deal with the usual shit that we deal with in the zombie apocalypse.

I barely get the outhouse door open before I spew my wonderful breakfast everywhere. I do mean everywhere. I completely miss the seat over the hole. There's puke on the seat, though, so I'm close at least. But there's also puke on the floor and the walls and pretty much all over me.

"Jace?" Stella asks quietly from behind me. "What's wrong? Are you sick?"

Her hand touches my shoulder as I brace myself against the doorframe to stay upright.

"Oh, baby, you are sick," she says. "Let's get you cleaned up and inside. You need to rest."

"I'm not sick," I say just as a loud gurgle from my guts tells her otherwise. "Well, not *sick* sick, just upset."

"Upset? Why? This is what we've talked about late at night when the kids are asleep," Stella says. "Building something."

"I meant Whispering Pines," I say. "Not Asheville as a whole. It's just too much. Who will be in charge? Who does what job? We'll need a ton more people just to make a dent in the damage and get things cleaned up. With more people comes more trouble. This isn't good, Stella. There's too much to deal with. Too much."

I'm close to hyperventilating and she can see this. She grabs me and pulls me away from the outhouse, doing a great job not to gag as she sees the puke on my shirt and jeans. She sits me down in the still moist grass and pushes me back so I'm laying out, my eyes looking up at the blue sky.

"Relax," she says softly. "You don't have to figure it all out. You'll be part of it, we all will, but it won't fall on your shoulders. There are other people in the world that are capable of making smart decisions, not just you."

"And we have the numbers," Big Daddy says from the back porch. "Sorry to eavesdrop. Just a little worried that our brain is cracking up."

"I'm not the brain," I say. "Carl is smarter than me. And as much as I hate to admit it, so is Landon."

"It's not about smarts," Big Daddy says as he comes into the yard. "It's about brains. You don't just think, you work out if that thinking is worth anything. You use common sense and life experience, Hoss. That's brains. I've met a ton of smart guys in my life. They could rattle off facts and figures until they were blue in the face. But they were dumb as paint. You get what I'm saying?"

"Yeah," I say. "But it doesn't make a difference." I push myself up onto my elbows. "I always thought the Farm was this vast place with people everywhere. When Melissa said we were coming here, I pictured dozens and dozens of workers hurrying about." I sigh. I can't help it. "But it's only a few families. A lot of kids. Wall Street will laugh his ass off when we show up."

"I'm about to laugh mine off, Hoss," Big Daddy says. "How about you clean the sick off yourself and come out front. I'd like you to meet some folks that have arrived while you've been sinning against the cooking."

I look at Stella. "What's he talking about?"

"I don't know," she shrugs, "I followed you out here."

I get up and see the puke. I go to a pump close to the house and wash myself as best I can, even drinking straight from the spigot and giving my mouth a good rinse. I run some water over my head and shake, feeling a little better.

"Presentable?" I ask Big Daddy.

He's smiling and nods. "That'll do, Hoss. Follow me."

I do. We walk through the kitchen, the dining room, and by the time we're in the living room, I can hear it: the buzz of people. A lot of them. How'd I not notice the noise before? Oh, right, the puking.

"What the...?" I ask as we step onto the front porch. "Where'd they all come from?"

"You know what the problem with Whispering Pines is?" Big Daddy asks as I scan the huge crowd. There must be at least fifty people, maybe even more. Men, women, teenagers. The only young kids I see, are the ones I've already met.

"I bet you're about to tell me," I say.

"I am at that," Big Daddy laughs. "Whispering Pines is exclusive. Even before Z-Day, it was exclusive. But not like now. You still shooting refugees that come knocking on your gate?"

"I don't," I say. "But, yeah, Brenda is big about that. They show any aggression and they get one between the eyes."

"You see, Hoss, a farm can't ever be exclusive," Big Daddy says. "It has to be inviting. Inviting to the sun, the rain, the wind, the day, the night. It has to be inviting to the right kind of insects. It has to be inviting to the people that work it. Otherwise, it shrivels up and dies. A farm is a living breathing creature. It may not always be perfect; it can have its predators, its blight, its disease. But there's always a solution to that. An inviting one."

I stare at everyone and they stare back.

"I think I get it," I say, "I really do."

"I hope so, Hoss," Big Daddy says. "Because I'm inviting you to be a part of the Farm. Whether you live here or not, you're a part of it. Can I count on you not to be a blight?"

"Yeah," I smile, "you can."

"Good." Big Daddy nods, clapping me on the shoulder. "Because your first job on the Farm is to be a friend and speak some words at my son-in-law's memorial. You have about fifteen minutes. Try to think of something nice, something that does Jon proud. And, Hoss? Now is the time you sell it. Now is when you invite them in. You have one shot. Don't waste it."

My smile fades. I think I'm gonna be sick again.

CHAPTER EIGHT

I look out at the crowd of unfamiliar faces, and the few familiar ones, and take a deep breath.

"I guess I was Jon's best friend," I say. "I know he was mine. He was a smart ass, which is one reason we got along; he was a fighter, another reason we got along; and he gave a shit."

There are some titters among the crowd, but I press on, Big Daddy standing in front watching me closely.

"Jon was there when I needed him," I say, trying not to choke up. "Even at the very end, he saved my butt. He played decoy and led the Zs away from that dump truck. He took off like a screaming mad man." I fail at the not choking up part. "Which he was. You'd have to be mad to want to save me."

I take another deep breath and look out at all the people I don't know. Now is my time to get to know them and for them to get to know me. Now is the time I invite them in.

"But at the very end, it wasn't the Zs that got him. They never could catch that ornery bastard. It was people," I say and watch for the reactions. There are the wide eyes of shock, the shaking of the heads in disbelief. But what I'm looking for are the nods of understanding. There are more of those. "People, man. People. Even in this time, where we have to come together as one in order to survive, there are still people out there that want to destroy. That want to tear down; that want to kill."

I'm so close. I have them. Not that this is a game. It's way more important than that.

"Jon hated those people. He didn't understand them. How could he? How can any of us? So, I ask you, in Jon's memory, what will you do?"

Silence. Which is good. They are on the hook.

"If you knew Jon at all, what do you think he'd do? Just wait here and see what happens? Or run like a mad man into the thick of danger to help whoever was in need?"

Nods. Many more nods. A whole group of nods.

"Jon taught me what to do and I will be forever grateful. If his death means anything to me, it's that while life may be important, saving life –that act of heroism- is even more important. That is what sets us above the Zs. That is what sets us above the people, those damn people, that don't understand, and probably never did, that without the sacrifice, without the willingness to say fuck it all and go screaming like a mad man, you can't really live at all. You're just waiting to die." I laugh a little and wipe my eyes. "Which is another reason Jon and I got along so well- neither of us have the patience just to wait around, especially not for something as boring as death."

I give the crowd a big smile, a smile filled with sorrow and hope, laughter and knowing.

"Thank you. Thank you, everyone."

"Well, can't say I approve of some of your language choices," Big Daddy says, coming up to me after I'm done. "But there were some fine words in there. Well done, Hoss."

"Thanks," I say.

"Have a seat and I'll wrap this up," Big Daddy says. "And stick close. I have some fine folks you're gonna want to meet."

Big Daddy does wrap it up, saying his piece and making sure everyone knows how much he did love his late son-in-law. By the time he's finished, the entire crowd is blubbering and sniffing. Melissa is a mess, but that is to be expected.

"That was nice," Stella says, taking my hand as we introduce ourselves to the many new faces. "Jon would have liked that."

"Yes, ma'am," Big Daddy says, "I believe he would have." He looks past us and waves someone over. "There's someone I'd like you to meet, Stella. She handles the education around these parts." He looks my wife square in the eye. "No point in saving the human race if the future generations are ignoramuses. Ah, here she is. Stella, meet-"

"Debbie? Debbie!" Stella nearly screams.

"Oh my Lord! Stella? I thought that was Jace up there speaking, but you know, I just couldn't believe it!"

The woman reaches out and embraces Stella in a huge bear hug. Huge because the woman is huge, not fat, but big. Six two, at least. Short black hair, long legs, long arms. I know quite a bit about Debbie Page, enough to know that she played basketball in college, which is pretty obvious. Stella holds onto her like she'll float away otherwise.

"Hey, Debbie," I smile from behind my wife.

"Hey there, Jace," Debbie grins, "it's good to see you."

Stella pushes away from her and looks her up and down. "I never thought…never thought…" She looks around and frowns. "Lisa?"

Debbie shakes her head. "She and the boys didn't make it out of Asheville. I was at WCU for a conference on Z-Day. I tried to get back, but never made it. I found a nice old couple hiding in their farmhouse and stayed with them for a long while before they died. I have their place now, about four hollers from here."

"What happened?" I ask. "To the couple?"

"Jace," Stella admonishes me, "you don't need to know that."

"Wandering Z got Mrs. Cleary. Pneumonia took Mr. Cleary a few months after," Debbie says. "It was rough." Her face stretches into a big smile. "But here we are! Oh, it's so good to see you!" Then it's her turn to frown. "Charlie? Greta?"

"Safe," Stella says, "they're around here somewhere."

"I thought you and Debbie could talk about the education initiative she's trying to get started," Big Daddy says. "But I have a feeling you have a lot more than that to chat about. I'm gonna steal your man away, if you don't mind?"

"Steal away," Stella says. "I'll find you in a bit. And try to check on the kids when you can."

"Will do," I say, kissing her. I give Debbie a big hug. "It's great to see you."

The two of them walk off and Big Daddy pulls me towards a group of men and women standing by the side of the house.

Someone announces that food is ready and half the crowd hurries around the other side towards the pavilion, leaving the front yard almost empty.

"Where do you want to do this?" a short, squat man with a round, tan face asks. "Ain't no place to sit out back now."

"How about the barn," Big Daddy says. "We got some stools and plenty of bales of hay in there to sit on."

We follow him to the barn and all get situated in a large circle.

"Folks, this is Jace Stanford," Big Daddy says. "A well spoken, if not a tad crude, gentleman that is going to help us get started what we all have been talking about for the past year."

"Emphasis on help," I say, "I'm not an expert in anything."

"Except for thinking things through," Big Daddy says, tapping his forehead. "Which is a pretty good skill to have these days."

I shrug.

They all introduce themselves and what they do. There's Stone Walton- apple and fruit farmer; Lydia DuPree- goats; Jessica Pickering- sheep and grass; Milton Scarborough- corn, squash, beans, tobacco, etc; Ed Chenewick- dairy cows; Ryan Craven and Alberta Jones- The Commune.

Each has their foremen/forewomen with them, but they stay back, letting their bosses do the talking. Everyone smiles and is pleasant, but there's a wariness in the air that tells me that Big Daddy has been the one really pushing things along. The rest of them are here to see what turns out.

Except for one man, sitting in the circle, but turned sideways, making sure he can get up and be gone in a hurry if he needs to.

"What, Critter? Don't want to introduce yourself?" Big Daddy asks the man.

He's long and wiry, his legs almost folded six ways underneath him so he can sit comfortably, and even still, he doesn't look comfortable. He has the look of a man that's never comfortable. His skin is deeply tanned and his face is sunken in and lined, leathery and weathered. His silver hair is shorn close to his scalp, which is just as tanned as the rest of him. Younger than Big Daddy is my guess, but hard to tell.

"I'm here out of respect," Critter says. "Not because I agree with what ya'll are talkin' 'bout."

"I know what everyone else does, Mr. Critter," I say. "But what is it you bring to the table?"

Critter looks about. "Don't see no table here, son. I think you be needin' your eyes checked."

"It's an expression," I say.

"I know that."

"Oh…"

"Critter here has a way of finding things," Big Daddy says. "Always has. When we were younger men, he sometimes found things right where they belonged, but decided they needed to be moved."

"I hijacked trucks, is what my brother is tryin' to say," Critter says. "Amongst other ways of procuring goods that may have had value." He shrugs, his bony shoulders going all the way up to his ears. "It was a livin'."

"Not exactly an honest living," Big Daddy says. "But we did what we could when our daddy died. I worked the land and Critter worked the highways."

"Brothers?" I ask.

"He's perceptive," Critter says. "You find him in a smart guy catalog, Hollis?"

"My Melissa vouches for him," Big Daddy says, "that's enough for me."

This seems to change Critter's attitude. He finally looks me in the eye then sizes me up completely. It's a few long, silent minutes before he nods.

"I'll trust Mel," Critter says. "But the second y'all start talkin' stupid, I'm gone, hear?"

"I hear," Big Daddy says. He looks about at the others. "Shall we then, folks?"

I listen as everyone describes their farms and land and what they can offer to the group. I'm amazed at the ingenuity I'm hearing. Ways of farming that go back hundreds of years that have been resurrected (no pun intended) for the zombie apocalypse. New innovations that take the tried and true, and add a level of automation and efficiency. These people don't need my help, they already know what they're doing.

"I still am not clear, BD," Alberta Jones says. "On why we should bother with some subdivision in Asheville? Why bring that kind of attention down on us?"

"You think there isn't any attention on us now?" Big Daddy asks. "I'm serious. That's no rhetorical question. I want to know what you all think."

Everyone agrees that with the few exceptions when it comes to wanderers, they've stayed pretty much hidden and unknown. No one has even heard or seen any evidence of Wall Street and his people.

"Suckers," Critter snorts. "This guy didn't get what he's got by strolling up driveways and knocking on doors." He points at me. "He was right under your nose and you didn't know about him, did ya?"

"It was a total surprise," I say.

"But he sure knew about you," Critter grins, his teeth crooked and tobacco stained. "He knew a lot about you, didn't he?"

"Seemed like it."

Critter spread his hands like the argument was made, but I could see no one was taking him seriously.

"What do you know?" I ask Critter. Big Daddy grins at this question. "You know exactly who I'm talking about, don't you?"

"Sure I do," Critter says. "I've come across him more than a few times, whether by myself or with a crew. My men know to steer clear of his like. Nothing but trouble there."

"Go ahead and tell them," I say to Critter. "You're just waiting to rub it in their faces."

Critter narrows his eyes at me. I can see the range of decisions that are going through his mind. I'm not expecting the smile.

He looks at Big Daddy and grins, "Okay, Hollis, you've got a smart one here."

"Thanks," I say. "I'm assuming that means I'm right. Tell them. Go on, Critter, tell them what you know."

"Edward Vance is the guy's name," Critter says. "He's a banker. Or was. Owned HomeSafe Banks. Biggest crook in Western North Carolina. The man did more money laundering than the Chinese mafia. Never afraid to get his hands dirty. Saw him put two bullets in the head of a fourteen-year-old boy once. Why? Because the kid had laughed at his daughter's braces."

He waits to let it all sink in.

"He was bad news before Z-Day. He's worse news now. Vance was worth millions. And I mean high millions. He didn't do things small. He wasn't a street corner gangster, he was big stuff; probably one of the biggest on the east coast. When Z-Day came, he lost his whole family. Watched them get attacked right before his eyes. He still has them locked up in his mansion down in Biltmore Forest. Feeds them himself with the bodies of his enemies. You think men like him go crazy in small ways? They don't. They take that crazy, and just like any type of capital; they invest it and make it grow. "

"Scary story," Stone says. "But it doesn't change anything."

"You think Vance leaves things to chance?" Critter snaps. "You think he doesn't know every little detail about y'all? You're a right bunch of idiots if that's what you think! He's had people watching all y'all for months now. Probably years. He knows your trade routes, he knows your routines. I bet he knows when it's time to harvest better than you do. This man is built like a Swiss watch. He's never wrong and he doesn't stop."

This hits home and everyone starts to talk at once. Big Daddy lets them get it all out before he puts up his hands to get order.

"Whispering Pines is just his starting point," Big Daddy says. "His Poland. We let him have it and pretty soon he'll roll over us all. He has the guns and the numbers to take us at any time."

"Then how do we stand a chance if we go after him?" Milton Scarborough asks. "At least we can take a stand on our lands. We know them better than he does."

"You aren't listening!" Critter shouts. "You don't know them better than he does! This guy does not believe in chance! I already said that, Milton, so keep up! He has every single working farm and ranch from here to the Tennessee border mapped out. He knows where y'all's bunkers are. He knows where you have supplies cached. He knows every way into and out of these hills. He's had nothing but time to study this while y'all have been busy playing farm, thinkin' the Zs were your problem."

"The Zs are our problem!" Ryan Craven shouts. "Just because some sociopath is out to get us, doesn't mean the Zs aren't still everywhere! We have been surviving day to day for what feels like forever, Critter! Cut us some fucking slack, man!" He looks at Big Daddy. "Sorry."

"Tempers and emotions are high," Big Daddy says. "It's to be expected. The one time."

"So what have you found?" I ask Critter. "Now that your highway robbery days are over. Big Daddy says you find things. What have you found?"

"Ah, that's the good part," Big Daddy says, "but I think what he's found has to be seen, not heard."

"And I ain't sayin' a word more about it around you'uns," Critter says. "No offense, but there's only a handful of people that I trust in this world and it sure as shit ain't a bunch of scared farmers."

"Are you saying one of us is a spy?" Jessica Pickering asks, her face nothing but shock and offense.

"I ain't sayin' that," Critter says. "Just like I ain't sayin' none of you *aren't* spies. I don't know. And until I do, I can't trust none of y'all."

"Then what's the point?" I ask. "Why are you even here if you aren't going to help?"

"Who said I ain't gonna help?" Critter asks me. "Boy, haven't you been listening? Vance knows everything, *almost* everything, about the area. Sooner or later, he'll know everything about me and my crew. When that happens, it's all over. I'm gonna protect what's mine. And I can't do that on my own."

"So you're in?"

Critter sighs and looks at his brother. "I take it back. The boy's an idiot."

"I'm just asking," I say. "I want to hear the words out of your mouth, Critter. I'm not a guy that leaves things to chance either."

"Yes, I am goin' to help," Critter says and stands up. "And if you want my help, you better get your ass up because we have some ground to cover."

Everyone looks confused and they all look to Big Daddy.

"Folks, you go ahead and mingle for a while," Big Daddy says. "Eat your fill, then get back home. Meet back here in the morning and be ready to go." Big Daddy looks at each of them. "If you choose to. No hard feelings if you don't. I think we all understand. But those of you that do show up, know that we are going to march our way to Whispering Pines and take that place back for my Melissa and all the other people that lost their homes. There are people still trapped in there, we believe. We may be their only hope."

They all stand and shake hands, talking about their fears and worries, but as far as I can tell, all are committed. Big Daddy keeps me back as the barn clears out. Critter just sits there, watching them all go. When the barn is empty, Buzz comes in and closes the barn doors.

"The twins are outside keeping watch," Buzz says, "you figure it out?"

"Ed Chenewick," Critter says. "He's one, I'm sure. There could be others, but I know it's Ed."

Buzz nods and leaves quickly. I can see the twins, Pup and Porky, standing outside, looking like they're having a casual conversation. The barn doors close and I turn on Big Daddy and Critter.

"Care to tell me what's really going on?"

"I've been acquainted with Vance for a long time," Critter says.

"I get that," I say.

"No, you don't," Critter insists. "I knew the man before Z-Day and knew what resources he had. When it all went to hell, I sought the guy out, thinking he'd have a plan, maybe. This was before I got my head on straight. I found him in his house, crazy as a loon. He was feeding his wife and kids bits of people. Had them chained in his basement home theater. I got the hell out of there quick as I could."

"I'm not following you," I say.

"I haven't let the man out of my sight," Critter says. "Once I couldn't keep my eye on him, I made sure someone loyal to me did. I have had Vance under surveillance since Z-Day. He went from lost his marbles crazy, to found his marbles in a pile of shit and put them back in his head without wiping them off crazy."

"This day has been coming for a while," Big Daddy says, "I'm just sorry it hit you first."

"Why didn't you say anything to us? Get a message to Melissa and warn her? You could have saved Jon's life?"

"Because Vance has spies everywhere!" Critter shouts. "Wake up, boy! You think all of these farms have survived because we've been holding hands and singing Kum Ba Yah? I'm the best scavenger there is and my crew is second to none. You think Melissa's good? Who the hell do you think taught her? But even being as good as I am, I can't find everything. Yet some of these farms have been replacing parts and equipment without me knowing how."

"And we'll know tomorrow morning who to trust?" I ask.

"Mostly," Big Daddy says. "That was just a smoke screen. Critter has men trailing each family. As soon as the traitors send out messengers, they'll be nabbed. I'm willing to bet that some of the back stabbers will still show up in the morning, playing their part. They'll think their messages got through to Vance and he knows we're on our way."

"But we'll have grabbed the messages and he won't? If he's as good as you think, then he'll know we're coming no matter what. Gonna be hard to hide a group our size."

"And we won't be hiding it," Big Daddy says. "We'll let Vance see us coming. It's you he won't see coming."

"Me?"

"And Critter," Big Daddy says. He suddenly looks very tired, his eyes shifting to his brother. "You sure they'll be on board?"

"I'm sure," Critter says, "they owe me."

"Who owes you?" I ask.

"You'll see," Critter says. "So let's get going."

"What? Now? Where?"

"Again, you'll see," Critter says as he goes to the back of the barn towards a small door. "Come on, boy. We ain't got all day."

I look at Big Daddy and shake my head. "What the hell is going on? I can't just leave. I have to tell Stella!"

"I'll make sure Stella and your kids are alright. You have my word on that," he says, "but Critter is right, you don't have all day. We played part of our hand by having this meeting. Everything is set in motion and can't be stopped. You go with Critter. He's got this part worked out. You'll see."

I stand there, frozen with indecision.

"Do I need to give you some countdown?" Critter asks. "Three, two, one. There, let's go."

I look back at Big Daddy and he answers before I can ask again. "They'll be safe. So will everyone else. Hurry along now. Daylight is burning."

I just go with it. I follow Critter out the back and he hands me a pack from the ground. He picks up one for himself and slings it over his shoulder.

"Food and water," Critter says. "Plus a Browning .45 and three extra magazines, if you need it. May want to get that out and keep it handy."

I do, slipping the slide on holster to my belt. I sling the pack over my own shoulder and we are off, hurrying into the tall grass and then slipping into the shadows of a grove of oaks and pines. I look back over my shoulder and my stomach clenches. God, I hope I'll see my family again.

My guess is, we have been hiking for about three hours, Critter not bothering to hide his disdain at the pace we have to keep because of my leg, before I notice we are going in circles.

"How many times are we going to pass that rock?" I ask.

"As many times as it takes," Critter says.

"Are you lost?"

"Am I what? Boy, don't make me smack you."

"I don't get it. Then why are we going in circles and doubling back on ourselves? You think we're being followed?"

"We're being watched. You're about to see what I found."

"By walking aimlessly?"

"Only aimless if there ain't a purpose to it," Critter replies.

"Care to let me in on the purpose?"

"Don't need to," he says.

"You are infuriating," I say as I shake my head.

That's when I see him, walking on my other side.

"Hey," the man says, "the water in your canteen filtered?"

I look at him for a second then down at the canteen hooked to my belt.

"Uh," is all I can say.

"It's filtered," Critter says, still hiking along like there isn't some guy that's made of muscle and armed to the teeth walking next to me.

Military. Not hard to tell. The way he walks, they way he's dressed all in black, the smears and smudges of mud across his face and forearms, how he holds his rifle, which is a funny looking thing.

"MP-5," the man says, reading my mind. "Quiet as all fuck. Unlike you."

"The boy's from suburbia," Critter says.

"Don't call me a boy," I say.

"I'll stop once I know you're a man," Critter replies. "How far we got, Stick?"

"Just over the ridge," the man (Stick?) says. "Captain is wondering why you brought a gimp with ya."

"You'll see," Critter says.

We get over said ridge and I see nothing, just a small clearing surrounded by maples. Critter just walks down to the center and takes a seat. He motions for me to do the same. I do and Stick relieves me of my Browning. In seconds, without a single leaf rustling or branch snapping, four men come walking into the clearing, all as in shape and equipped as Stick.

"Captain," Critter nods, "it's time."

The man Critter addresses looks at me and motions for me to stand up.

"Captain Walter Leeds," he says, holding out his hand.

I shake his hand and he points at the rest of the men.

"You met Weapons Sergeant Danny 'Stick' Kim," he says. "This is Master Sergeant Joshua Platt. Engineer Sergeant Dale 'Cob' Corning. Medical Sergeant Alex 'Reaper' Stillwater. And Weapons Sergeant, Sammy 'John' Baptiste is in one of the trees with crosshairs on the back of your head."

"Temple," I hear a voice call out. I have no idea where it is.

Captain Leeds rolls his eyes. "I don't give two standing fucks where your bead is, John. And don't give away your position like that again."

"Roger," the voice says. I'm pretty sure it has already moved.

"Smart ass," Leeds says and turns to Critter. "So Vance is making his play?"

"Tell him," Critter says as he lays back and rests his head on his pack. He closes his eyes and sighs. "And sell it good."

"Sell it?" I ask. "Sell what?"

"The job," Leeds says. "The reason we're here."

"Go on," Critter says, not bothering to open his eyes. "Just start from the beginning."

So I do. I tell the men everything I know while my mind tries to wrap around what I'm seeing. These guys are soldiers. Not just any soldiers, but like Special Forces or something. When I'm done talking, I wait for a response. And wait. And wait.

"Platt?" Leeds asks finally.

"We'll have to come in wet," he says. "Circle around and hit from the back."

"The cliff?" I say, shaking my head. "You won't get through the wire. Plus there's the cliff."

"Oh, a cliff," Cob says. "Well we better not go then. Cliffs are scary."

You'd think I'd be used to being mocked by now, but I'm not.

"Night cover," Platt continues. "We'll already be in when the main group hits."

"You think Vance will let them get to the gate before he strikes?" Leeds asks.

"Probably not," Cob answers. "He'll send out his bikes to start picking people off. Get them scared and harried before he hits them."

"So we have to get him harried first, or a lot of inexperienced people are going to die," Leeds says.

My mind is on fire. I'm looking from one speaker to the next like it's a fucking ping pong game. They are rattling off tactics and plans so fast I can barely keep up. Most of it is in abbreviations and soldier speak. I'm clueless.

"How close can we get before we have to be boots down?" Leeds asks Critter. "What gear can you provide?"

"Whatever you need," Critter says. "I'll take you shopping on the way back. We can Humvee it in for a good stretch. Take the old trails so we miss Vance's scouts. But we'll have to hoof it for at least a mile or two to the river. May be easier to go south and float down."

"And be sitting ducks?" Stick laughs. "Great plan, old man."

Critter shrugs, his eyes still closed. "Just spit ballin'."

"We'll go south and cross the river," Leeds says. "Then hike it in to the backside from Jonestown Rd. It'll be night and we'll have plenty of Zs to watch out for, but it's our best bet. I can guarantee that Vance has men all up and down the French Broad close to the subdivision. He'll be expecting something, just not from the direction we'll be coming."

"Wait," I say, my mind finally catching up. "The main group is all decoy? And we're the cavalry?"

"You aren't anything, civvie," Stick says. "You're a liability."

"That knows the layout of the neighborhood," I say smugly. They just stare at me. "What?"

"We've been in your neighborhood more than once," Leeds says. "You have the tan couches, right? And the pool table?"

I try to swallow, but my mouth has gone dry.

"We get bored," Reaper says, finally speaking. "Like really bored."

A low whistle has everyone crouching and backing into the underbrush.

"What the fuck?" I say.

Critter's eyes are open now.

"Company," he whispers. "Fuck me. How the hell were we followed? No one can track me."

"Should we hide?" I ask, spinning about. "Where the fuck did they all go?" I stop spinning and look at the top of the ridge. "Ah, shit."

Elsbeth.

She's standing there with The Bitch in her hand, her eyes darting from side to side. I see a tiny red dot light up on her chest. Then another one and another. She looks at me and frowns, and then looks down at herself. Her eyes go wide and she looks up at me in alarm.

"Don't shoot!" I shout. "She's friendly! I repeat! She's friendly!"

"You don't have to repeat," Stick says from right behind me.

I cry out and nearly piss myself as the others come out of the brush.

"It's that cannibal girl," Platt says. He looks over at me. "She's with you?"

"She is now," I say. "Long story."

"Make it a short one," Leeds says. They wait.

I fill them in.

"Anything else we should know?" Leeds asks. "Any other strays you brought home?"

"Nope," I say, "that's it."

"You any good with a rifle?" Stick asks Elsbeth. "I've seen you use that bat and blades, but can you shoot?"

"Don't need to," Elsbeth says.

"Fair enough," Stick nods.

"John. Bring it in," Leeds calls out. "John?"

"Fucking bitch knocked me down," John says as he comes staggering into the clearing, his hand rubbing his head. "Jumped me from one tree over."

The team all look at Elsbeth in awe, then start to laugh.

"You got taken by a canny!" Stick hoots. "Oh, you're never living that down!"

"She jumped me while I was in the damn tree," John says. "You ever had that happen before? Fucking spider monkey."

"Laugh it up on the trail," Leeds says. "We move out now."

Critter gets up, wiping the dirt and leaves from his ass, and smiles at me.

"Whatcha think of my find?" he asks. "Not what you were expecting, was it?"

"I'm pretty much done with expectations," I say. "No point in them."

"Took ya this long to figure that out?" Critter asks. "You must have been living a charmed life, boy."

"Don't call me boy, please."

"His name is Long Pork," Elsbeth says.

This, of course, leads to another round of laughter. Great.

I'd love nothing more than to rest, but Critter and the team all start hiking back the way we came. Or at least I think it's the way we came. Hard to tell with all the circling and doubling that happened. Luckily, just as I think my leg is going to fucking fall right off, we get to a rocky outcropping.

"Have a seat," Critter says, "I won't be long."

"Oh, thank God," I say and fall on my ass, my lungs heaving, my body feeling like it's one giant, throbbing, sore muscle.

"Don't get too comfortable, princess," Stick says. "We aren't done yet."

I laugh and look to see if Elsbeth is mad. Then realize he's calling me princess. God dammit. Like Long Pork isn't bad enough.

I sigh and sit up on my elbows as I hear a low rumbling. Is it an earthquake? Not unheard of in the Blue Ridge since the mountains are on a fault line, but pretty rare. Then half the hillside in front of me slides away and I scramble to my feet.

"Everyone in," Critter says as he pulls out of the hill in an Army Humvee. "We got miles to go before we sleep."

"You a poet now, Critter?" John asks as he climbs into the short bed in the back, his sniper rifle at the ready.

"You got this rig geared up?" Leeds asks.

"Everything we can possibly need," Critter says. "We're good to go."

We all load in. Leeds is up front with Critter driving. I'm crammed into the back seat with Elsbeth next to me, Cob to my right and Reaper to Elsbeth's left. Stick and Platt are in the bed behind us with John. Critter jumps out and scrambles away, leaving the Humvee idling. The hill closes behind us and then Critter is jumping back in.

"Can't leave the back door open, now can we?" he smiles.

Off we go, and despite being cramped, I am very glad I'm off my leg. I don't think I can walk another mile on it without crying. And it would suck to cry in front of these guys. That would just lead to another nickname.

"Now you can nap," Reaper says, "get some rest. It's going to be a long night."

I lean my head back and shuffle around, trying to get comfortable.

"Dude, stay still!" Cob snaps.

"Sorry," I say.

I close my eyes and try to take deep, even breaths to calm down. I'd really like to get some sleep, if I can. But there's no way I'm going to be able to sleep while Critter has us bouncing along the back trails. Half the time I think he's going to drive us right off a cliff before he takes a sharp turn and keeps us alive. I may be exhausted, but my mind is on full alert. It sucks, because I really do need the sleep.

"Wake up, sunshine," Stick says, poking me with the barrel of his gun. "Nap time is over. You're gonna miss graham crackers and milk if you don't hustle."

"Huh? Whu?" I mumble as I pull myself up from the backseat of the Humvee. I look past him and see the sun has gone down. "What time is it?"

"Does it matter anymore?" Stick muses. "Time is so relative. Do you have a doctor's appointment to get to? Are you going to miss your favorite TV show?"

"Stop fucking with him, Stick," Reaper says, shoving the man out of the way. "Here, let me have a look at your leg. Don't want you dying of infection before you can get shot by Vance's peeps."

"That's comforting," I say as I unbuckle my pants and gingerly push them down.

"I'm known for my bedside manner," Reaper says.

"That's why we call him Reaper," Stick says, "because Angel of Death was just a little too spot on, ya know?"

I wince as Reaper prods my wounds. "Not infected, but you need to keep it clean. And stay off of it if you can."

"Funny," I say. "Can I pull my pants up?"

"I've seen his penis," Elsbeth says from behind them.

The two men freeze and wait without looking back.

"Is she still there?" Stick asks.

"Yes," Elsbeth says, "it's bigger than Pa's was."

"Oh, that does it," Stick says, bolting.

"Yeah, I'm outta here too," Reaper says, leaving me alone with Elsbeth.

She wipes her nose with the back of her hand. "I've never been in a boat."

"You're quite the non sequitur generator tonight, aren't you?"

"I don't know," she says and turns around. "They say that's a boat. Or a raft. Which is a kind of boat. I asked why they don't just call it a boat all the time. They said because it's a raft. But it's also a boat. Which is dumb. These guys are soldiers and they're dumb."

"She's a real charmer," Critter says as I step out of the Humvee. "If she wasn't so attached to you, I'd snatch her up myself. But I value my life."

"He's old and mean," Elsbeth says, sticking close to me.

"I'm married," I say to Critter. A little too loudly as I get shushed by Leeds.

"I'd like not to alert Vance to our presence, please," he says, looking me up and down. "You going to be good for the next leg?"

"Funny," I say, "you guys are like the joke brigade."

"What did I say?" Leeds asks.

"You made a pun, Captain," John says from above us. I glance up, but can't see him through the leaves in the dark.

"Fuck," Leeds says, "I hate puns."

"Why, Captain?" John asks. "What'd they ever do to you?"

"Okay, I think we've let off enough steam," Platt says. "Game faces. We need to be at the river in fifteen. Any longer than that and we miss the window between biker patrols. We have two miles of river to float down before we can cross. Then we take the bank, work our way up Jonestown Rd, and back behind Whispering Pines. Even with guards watching, we should be able to stumble along like Zs and get through."

"What if the guards are my people?" I ask. "You aren't going to kill them, are you?"

"For a thinker, you don't do much thinking," Cob says. "There's no way Vance will put your people on guard. If he hasn't butchered them all, then he's got them locked down tight."

"Butchered them all?" I ask. "Do you think he has? I really think Brenda will talk him out of that."

"Right," Leeds says. "Brenda Kelly."

"What?"

"Let's just say that she's on our watch list," Leeds says. "Even without Vance's influence, she's a piece of work. The lady likes her secrets and special missions."

I think about the mission that got us into this mess. She had us thinking we were doing one thing when it turned out we were doing something completely different. Which we kinda fucked up. Hence the mess.

I'm left with my own thoughts as Platt orders strict silence while we hike it to the river bank, leaving the Humvee behind covered in brush and branches. It does only take us about fifteen minutes to get to the bank, but in that time, my leg is screaming. How the fuck will I make it up Jonestown Rd and then across the field, through the wires and down the cliff?

"You okay, Long Pork?" John asks, suddenly at my elbow. I hate the way these guys move. "You've got a hitch in your giddy up."

"Quiet," Platt says as I watch the men get the raft inflated and ready. He points at Elsbeth and me. "In."

I have to help Elsbeth and she almost dumps us into the river, but I keep my balance, and hers, and we plop down and wait. Critter is right behind us. Reaper, Cob, Platt, and Leeds, hop in too while Stick and John shove us away from the bank and then roll into the raft, guns on the sides, ready. We let the current pull us along, not wanting to paddle and make any more noise than we have to.

The two miles take forever, but soon we are at the opposite bank, right where the men want us. This time we get plenty wet as we get out. Stick pulls the plug and deflates the raft, rolling it up and setting it beneath some bushes, while the rest check their weapons and get ready for the hike to Jonestown Rd. If my bearings are right, then we are only around the corner. That is good, because my leg is killing me. Bad because that means I still have to get up Jonestown Rd.

"Lean on me," Elsbeth says as we get to the bottom of the road and start to leave Hwy 251 behind. "I can help."

My pride doesn't even blink as I let her take some of the weight off my leg. I'm slowing the men down and I can see from their body language that they are less than pleased, but not one says anything. It seems like eternity, but eventually we get to the top.

"Zs," John says, motioning for us to get down.

He slips forward in a crouch with Stick on his tail. I can barely see them as they come up on several shapes in the dark. It's over before I know it and we're moving again. Then we stop.

"More Zs," John hisses. "What the fuck?"

I don't know what he's used to, but I'm pretty used to Zs hanging around. They tend to do that in the zombie apocalypse. There are considerably more of them this time and Cob and Platt join in before they take them down.

One last yard and we're at the field above Whispering Pines.

"Son of a bitch," Leeds whispers, "that's one way to cover your six."

I peer into the dark and realize I can't see shit. Not because it's pitch black, it's not; there is plenty of light coming up from Whispering Pines. I can't see shit because of all the Zs. Hundreds of them. Those not caught in the rolls of razor wire are milling about, shambling and groaning, their arms dangling at their sides, legs shuffling through the dirt and dead grass.

"So we go back?" I ask, already turning in my crouch.

"No," Leeds says. "We push through. Goop up, people."

"Goop up?" I ask. "What does that mean?"

All I get for answers are quiet chuckles.

"Here," Elsbeth says, smearing something on my face.

"Oh, God, what is that?" I say, choking and gagging from the smell.

"Z," she says, "Z guts."

CHAPTER NINE

The mistake most people make when it comes to Zs, is that they think they are mindless. Not so true. Sure, they are stupid. Not going to ace any SATs even if SATs existed. But they aren't completely mindless. Just...singularly focused?

I only mention this because while Elsbeth and the Special Forces team whisper to me that smearing the insides of a Z all over my body will mask our scent and allow us to slip through the horde that is meandering around the field, I'm just not buying it.

"Fuck you," I whisper back. "There are too many. We may make it past three or four, but hundreds? Are you guys fucking insane?"

"Nut up, Long Pork," Stick says. The rest just stare at me.

"Critter?" I ask.

"Screw you, Long Pork," Critter says. "I have to wade in there, wait for y'all to get down, drop the ropes, then double back to meet up with my brother and the rest. Don't be whining to me like a little bitch. You only have to wade through these undead fucks once."

"Once too many," I say.

"Pussy," Critter replies.

"It works," Elsbeth says. "It stinks, but it works." She nods over and over until I nod with her.

"Fine," I say, taking a deep breath and doubling over from the stench. I get myself under control and look at Leeds, his gore smeared face only a shadow in the night. "How do we do this?"

"Just keep moving," Leeds says. "Meander. Don't go in a straight line or look like you have a direction in mind. It attracts attention, plus it could start a stampede. The others will think you've spotted food and then we'll be overrun."

"Act like a Z, dude," John says, "you can do it."

I can. I've done nothing but study the undead for a long while now. I know their patterns of movement, of attack. I know where the weak points are in the wires and ditches. I also know where the strong points are. If I work my way through the lines, following the hidden path, and time it right, I can tangle up most of them without anyone realizing.

"Okay," I say, "follow me."

Stick and Cob both laugh, and then stop.

"He's serious?" Cob asks. "You were just pissing yourself."

"And my bladder's empty," I say. "You want me to get you through here or not?"

"We can get through just fine," Leeds says. "We told you that-"

"You've been in Whispering Pines before, yeah, yeah, I know. But not with this many Zs in the field. Follow me."

I start to shuffle and stagger. I come up on the first few Zs and some of them turn to me, their blank eyes falling across my body, their noses lifted to the air. Then they turn away. I push and stumble deeper, moving to the left for a while then to the right. I hope that I know what I'm doing as I come up on a long line of razor wire.

I follow the wire for a few feet then push through, letting the unconnected metal part around my legs. A blade catches on my jeans, but slices through without snagging. I freeze for a second, waiting for the pain. There is none, which means there's no blood. Dear God, if any of us get nicked we are screwed.

Through wire, over ditches, around barricades of metal spikes, we all move haphazardly, looking like drunken frat boys after a party brawl. It takes forever to reach the edge of the field and the cliff, but we get there. There are two guards on duty, neither of which I recognize. They are staring right at us.

"Uh...hey...are those...?" one mutters as Stick and Cob jump at them.

They don't make another sound except for the snapping of their necks. The team secure their lines to the deck and toss them over. Critter stands behind us, his eyes scanning the ground and houses below.

"Why not just take the stairs?" I whisper.

Stick only smiles at me as he hooks in, throws his legs over and jumps. The sound of the rope whizzing through the carabineers on his belt echoes through the still night, but we don't see anyone stir below. Cob follows quickly.

"Everyone, now," Leeds says, strapping a belt around my waist and getting me hooked up to Stick's line. John does the same for Elsbeth and Cob's line. "Feet down and all eyes, got it?"

They nod and are gone from sight, leaving Elsbeth and me with Critter.

"It ain't hard," Critter says, "just hold on here and then push off with your legs. You control the speed by gripping the rope here and-"

Elsbeth jumps and is down in seconds.

"Not her first time, I reckon," Critter smiles as he undoes the other lines and lets them fall. "Damn confusing thing, that canny girl."

"My turn, I guess," I say. I get up on the rail and start to lean back, ready to jump. "One, two, three." I don't go anywhere. "Okay, I got this, I got this." I look up to say a quick prayer and see something troubling.

Zs. A lot of them. Just above the deck.

"Critter," I say.

"Stop pussing out, Long Pork," Critter says, "get your ass down there."

I can hear a hiss from below as the team grows impatient with me.

"No, look," I say, nodding my head. "Did anyone cut themselves on the wire?"

Critter freezes and glances over his shoulder. "Ah, fuck," he says. "I don't think so." He pats himself down then stops just at his calf. His hand comes away black, the color of blood in the night. "Fuck me."

The Zs are watching us, their senses confused by the smell of fresh blood and the smell of their own. Then one moans and they all start moaning.

"How'd they get through the wire and ditches?" Critter asks.

"Numbers," I say. "They must have clogged a point and just started climbing over their own. It's a weakness in the system, which is why we always have guards present to keep the numbers down."

"Could have mentioned that before," Critter says and looks at the rope and me. "Only one line. I'll take the stairs."

He shoves me just as the first few Zs fall onto the deck. The last thing I see before I'm flailing down to the ground, is Critter bolting for the stairs and a whole shit ton of Zs pouring over the cliff edge and onto the deck.

That's a lot of weight. Too much weight.

I can hear the groaning of the wooden structure as I try to slow myself down. Part of me doesn't want to put the brakes on my descent since most of me wants to get away from the swarm of undead hell that's about to rain down on us all.

Then the ground is there and I try not to scream as I slam against it. I try. I fail.

"Shut him up," Leeds hisses as Reaper clamps his hands over my mouth. "What the fuck, Long Pork?"

"Captain," John says, "the situation has changed."

The team all follow his gaze and look up. Zs are falling from the sky. I guess they think the stairs are too slow too. Great, kamikaze Zs, just what the world needs next.

Reaper pulls me to my feet and we scramble out of the way, as the first bodies explode on the ground in front of us. Zs that haven't had their brains splattered everywhere look at us, their broken jaws trying to chomp with hunger.

"Go, go, go!" Critter calls as he takes the steps three, four at a time. "Go!"

"Shit," Leeds says as he looks to his team. "Assume all are hostiles. We head for the gate."

"What?" I say. "My neighbors could still be here!"

"The operative word is 'could'," he replies and points at the Zs that are still plummeting down at us, and the ones that are falling down the stairs after Critter. "There's no 'could' about them! We shoot to kill and we head to the gate. Take that out and

Big Daddy and the rest can come streaming in when they get here."

"That won't be until tomorrow," I say.

"Or never," a loud voice says from the dark. "I have to say I am unbelievably disappointed with your performance, Captain Leeds. I have been dreaming of the day you and your team finally showed yourselves to me. I was thinking of an epic firefight, all Black Hawk Down, but what do you give me? A whimpering bicker fight like a couple of ten year olds. So sad."

The area is bathed in bright light as twenty spots shine on us.

"Did you really think I hadn't thought of which way you'd come in?" Vance says (yes, I'm calling him that now). "That's why I put my most useless men up there to guard. Expendable."

I have to shield my eyes against the glare of the lights and can only see an outline of a man. He stands there, surrounded by other outlines, many of which have matching outlines of rifles. How nice. Shadow puppets of the damned.

The groaning gets louder and I get close to Elsbeth. She looks at me and I nod back at the platform that is so very close to collapsing. She wraps my arm around her shoulders, and then takes me by the waist. I look around and see the team with their weapons to their shoulders. Leeds is standing there, his pistol up, pointing at the outline.

"Sir?" John asks.

"Equalize the environment," Leeds says.

"And what does that mean?" Vance asks. "Is that one of the many useful military euphemisms? Are you going to neutralize me?"

"No," Leeds says, "men?"

Gunfire erupts and the lights start to go out. Elsbeth grabs me and pulls me to the side as Vance's men return fire. I can hear screams of pain and the sound of bullets whizzing by my ears. Men and women are shouting, Vance is bellowing (does he have his bullhorn with him?); gunfire and the smell of cordite fill the air.

But all of that is drowned out by the explosive snaps and cracks of the support struts on the platform. The weight of the Z swarm has finally outdone the engineering that took us so long to complete. Eight by eight beams of hardwood splinter, metal braces buckle, boards crumple. The whole thing comes down like an unwanted Las Vegas casino. I risk a look and see it collapse on itself, folding and falling.

"Come on!" Stick yells. "This way!"

I'm pretty used to these guys just appearing and I'm pretty thankful to see Stick on one side and Cob on the other.

"Where's the rest?" I shout over the chaos.

"Not with us," Cob says. "So fucking move your gimp ass, Long Pork!"

I do. I dig deep and push the pain from my mind. I give Elsbeth a small shove, telling her I got it, but she doesn't let go. She moves us, steers us, like we are one being. I have to wonder how many wounded she's saved from hordes of Zs, just to surprise them with dinner later. They being the dinner, of course.

Stick and Cob spin about, changing directions like they are on poles, moving from side to side with fluid ease, shooting and reloading, each in perfect sync with the other. We pass house after house and I have to wonder why we aren't stopping to seek shelter. We can't stay exposed forever.

But the sounds behind me tell me why. I risk a glance and see so many Zs on our asses that I wonder if they've been doing pilates all this time to get in shape for the great Whispering Pines mad-dash marathon. These are not slow Zs. Don't get me wrong, they aren't exactly sprinting hurdles here, but they aren't just stumbling along. They have a goal and they are going for it, pushing their putrid, undead legs to the max. I can sort of sympathize.

"Fuck! Fence!" Stick says as we follow the curving landscape and run right into six feet of pine boards. "This way!"

He directs us down the fence to the front of the house. We hurry out into the front yard and are instantly exposed. Lights are coming on everywhere- searchlights, house lights, vehicle lights, flashlights. From every direction, the street is being illuminated. Which doesn't make things easier. The chaos of illumination blinds everyone equally and random gunfire quickly follows in the confusion.

"Side," Cob says and directs us between two houses. "In here."

He kicks in a side door and we stumble into a garage. Cob slams the door closed and looks about for anything to block it with. He grabs a large trashcan while Stick wheels over a lawnmower. Elsbeth flips over a folding table in the corner and Stick takes it from her, adding to the barricade.

"Inside or make a stand here?" Stick asks Cob.

The man is about to answer when the large garage door is punctured by gunfire. One of Vance's men must have seen us. Stick cries out and clutches his leg, then crumples to the ground. We all hit the concrete and flatten ourselves out.

"How bad?" Cob asks.

"Kneecapped," Stick says, "I'm done."

"Fuck," Cob shouts and returns fire at the garage door, making his own holes in the aluminum. "FUCK!"

"Get inside," Stick says through gritted teeth. "I got this."

"We can get you in too," Cob says. "You aren't done-"

"Get. Inside," Stick says. "I. Got. This."

Cob doesn't argue and crawls on his belly to the door that leads into the kitchen. Elsbeth and I follow, looking back only as we get to the threshold and Cob gets the door open. Stick is pulling grenades from his vest. He catches my eye and smiles, and then waves.

"Nice to meet ya, Long Pork," Stick says. "Don't make it all a waste, okay?"

"Yeah, okay," I say as Elsbeth pulls me inside and kicks the door closed.

"Out back," Cob says. "We can't stay here."

Then I see the two women crouched by the island in the kitchen. They stare back at me, their eyes wide with terror. It's Cheryl Best, one of the HOA Board members and her partner, Lacy.

"Come on," I say. "You need to get up and get out now!"

"Go!" Cob shouts at the women as they just huddle there in the dark. "Ah, fuck it!" He shoots out the glass doors and shoves Elsbeth and me through.

I look past him when we hit the concrete patio just as the kitchen wall explodes. I'm blinded by the flash, but not before I see the fridge rocket into the two women, crushing them against the counter. A geyser of blood spurts up into the flames and then I'm flying back as the air is sucked from my lungs.

My ears are ringing and I can barely breathe as I roll over, coughing and struggling to get my bearings. I see Elsbeth on her hands and knees, Cob pulling at her to get up. Beyond that, I see legs. Lots of legs.

"Zs," I croak, then get my voice back. "Zs!"

Cob, spins, his M-4 to his shoulder instantly, and fires in short, controlled bursts. I stagger upright and Elsbeth pulls at me, her face a striated mess of cuts and slashes. We back up, Cob with us, his rifle firing, firing, firing, click. He lets it fall to his side on the strap and pulls his M9 Berretta, opening fire on the Zs with the semi-automatic pistol, taking careful shot after careful shot.

Head shots each time, killing every Z he hits. But it's not enough. There are too many coming for us. We can't back up fast enough and Cob's pistol clicks empty. In the time it takes him to let the magazine drop and slap a fresh one home, the Zs have covered the ground, shuffling over the burning debris from Cheryl's kitchen.

Cob keeps firing until the last second when they overwhelm him, then he pulls two grenades from his chest and yanks the pins free.

"GO!" he screams at us.

We do, as fast as our wounded bodies can take us. Elsbeth and I, limping, staggering, falling, half-running away. We get to the next yard (no fence, yay!) and I trip, hitting the ground hard. Cob goes up in a burst of fire and flesh behind us. The Zs around him become charred mist. All I can do is look at the sprinkler I tripped over, sitting there in the lawn, set against the backdrop of flame and death.

Who keeps a sprinkler out in their lawn? You aren't allowed to water lawns in Whispering Pines. Not anymore, at least. Total waste of water. Brenda is going to have a shit fit when she finds out about-

"JACE!" Elsbeth screams. "GET UP!"

I realize she's been pulling at me and pulling at me and I've just been sprawled there, my eyes and mind on the sprinkler.

"GET UP! GETUPGETUPGETUPGETUP!"

"I'm up!" I shout as I grab her and yank myself to my feet. "This way!"

I have an idea. And I hope it's the right one.

Zs are still after us. No, let me rephrase that- *flaming* Zs are still after us. Those that survived Cob's sacrifice burn as they moan and hiss, ever on the hunt for flesh, flesh, flesh. But they've been slowed. So have Elsbeth and I. Exposure to back to back explosions can do that to a body, but we have some space. It should be enough to get us to where we need to be.

"This way," I croak, my throat raw from the smoke and from yelling. "That house. There."

Elsbeth helps me to the front door and I kick over a potted plant, looking for a spare key. There isn't one. Of course not, he's too fucking smart for that. Any man that locks his door during the zombie apocalypse isn't just going to leave a key out front. That's crazy talk.

No worries. Elsbeth puts her boot through the side window next to the front door, reaches in and unlocks the bolt and handle. We hurry inside and slam the door behind us, both resting our back against it. I don't have any fantasies that we are safe, but I need a quick breather. From the harsh gasps coming from Elsbeth, I can see she does too.

"Okay, this way," I say and take her by the hand, pulling her up the stairs.

"Where are we?" Elsbeth asks. Then, "Isn't this the house we were just in?"

"You have no idea how right you are," I laugh, surprising Elsbeth and myself with the sound.

Upstairs is a bathroom and two bedrooms. One is the master bedroom and the other is usually used as a guest room if the house isn't occupied by a family. Which this house isn't. But instead of a guest room, there is something else.

"Oh...," is all Elsbeth can say as I shove the door open and she gazes at the walls of weapons before her. "Is this Santa's house?"

"Is it...what?" I shake my head. "Never mind. Grab what you can and let's get going."

"Why don't we stay here?" Elsbeth asks.

I go to the window and point at the flames and smoke just down the street. "Because this block is going up soon. We have to get to Phase Two. The fire won't be able to spread because there's nothing to burn between here and there, just asphalt and dirt. Plus, there's a back way out by my house."

Elsbeth is confused, I can see it as the firelight flickers across her face. She shakes her head.

"No," she says, "we go to your house, but we don't leave. We stay." Her eyes are almost manic and I wonder what is going on in her head. "No more running."

She scoops up a courier bag from the floor and starts filling it with pistols, extra magazines, and ammo. Her hands are flying, seeming to know exactly what to grab. There is way more to this young woman than I know. She hands me the bag and I sling it over my shoulder, taking out one of the pistols and slapping in a magazine.

She fills another bag then slings that over her shoulder. She goes to the walls and ignores the row upon row of rifles, instead focusing on the rack of blades. She grabs up a sword of some kind. A tactical short sword? Fuck if I know what it's called, but it has a blade about twenty inches long, curved and wider at the end than at the hilt. The hilt itself is black with knuckle guards protecting the grip. There's a second one and she takes that.

I realize she doesn't have The Bitch anymore. When did she lose that? Did she have it when we rappelled down from the field? It's all such a blur.

"Here," she says, tossing me a modified pickaxe. The thing is bigger than a normal hatchet with a wide blade on one side and a rounded spike on the other. It's surprisingly light, but still feels solid and sturdy. "Now we go."

"I don't exactly take kindly to looters," Stuart says as we step into the hall and almost run right into him. He's shirtless and the lower half of his torso is wrapped in dirty, bloody bandages, tightly wound around his belly and back. His face is gashed and his arms are covered in cuts, but he stands there strong, his jeans covered, legs not seeming to be a problem.

"Jesus, man," I say, "it's good to see you."

"Likewise," he nods. "Hello, Elsbeth. Ready to kill some Zs then?"

She nods.

"Give me five seconds," he says and ducks into his armory. He comes out quickly with a Kevlar vest on and several bandoliers of shotgun shells across it. A black Mossberg 500 rests against his shoulder (Stuart has shown me that one a few times. It's a favorite of his).

"Where to then?" he asks.

"His house," Elsbeth says and starts for the stairs.

"Then this way," Stuart says, motioning to his bedroom.

We get to his back window and I see a rope ladder dangling from the sill.

"As soon as it all went to shit, I made my move," Stuart says. "Been under armed guard at Dr. McCormick's since Wall Street got here."

"Vance," I say, "his name is Edward Vance."

"Yeah, I know," Stuart says. "He made that clear. I just keep calling him Wall Street. It pisses him off."

We climb down into his backyard and crouch low. He takes the lead and motions for us to follow. I have a clear look at his wrappings and see a nice, fresh stain where his wound is. The bastard just never calls it quits.

We dash from house to house, checking our rear constantly to see if we are being followed, but we stay Z free until we get to the hillside that leads down away from Phase One and to the entrance of Whispering Pines and the gate. Stuart holds up his hand and we stop.

Vance's people are everywhere. Bikers ride this way and that, people are shouting at each other in the chaos as trucks drive up the road, their beds filled with either armed men or what looks like barrels of water.

"Why not just turn on the hoses?" I whisper. "Each house has garden hoses on both sides. That's part of the fire plan."

"One of the first things Wall Street did, was to shut off the main water supply," Stuart says. "Water is life and it's hard to fight and argue when you are dying of thirst. He's been rationing it out. Whispering Pines is a prison camp, Jace. He never wanted it for himself. He wanted it to keep people he finds locked up."

"Fuck," I say.

"You got that right," Stuart nods, "follow me."

He leads us away from the hillside and to a thicket of trees by the last house on the ridge. He doesn't even pause and slips into the trees, his body melding with the shadows. Elsbeth follows without hesitation and I do too, but I'm lost as soon as I'm past three trees. I feel a hand take mine and Elsbeth pulls me along behind her. The ground begins to slope and soon I'm struggling not to slip and slide my way down.

Then we stop and I see we are at one of the rock walls that line this part of Hwy 251, making it unnecessary to put up any fencing or razor wire.

"Now what," I ask. But Stuart answers me quickly with a length of rope he pulls from underneath a clump of blackberry bushes. One end is already tied to the trunk of a pine tree, the other end he tosses over the edge and down to the road.

"We're going outside?" I ask.

"We'll skirt the perimeter and come in via your escape route," Stuart says. He sees the look on my face. "What? You thought that was a secret? Please, Jace, I've had plenty of time on my hands to map every single way in or out of Whispering Pines. You did a piss poor job of hiding that path. It's protected, I'll give you that, so I never mentioned it since it was secure, but hidden?" He just shakes his head, grabs the rope and starts to climb down.

I follow and Elsbeth is right behind. We go a few yards then flatten ourselves against the rock and peek around at the gate. No one is manning the watchtower; they're all a little busy with the fire, and from the sounds of gunfire, busy with Leeds and his men.

"Go," Stuart whispers and shoves me forward.

I crouch/run/flail my way past the gate and over to some thorny bushes that are almost as deadly as the Zs. At least they give us cover as Stuart and Elsbeth join me. We stay low, but move as fast as we can up the road and around to Sixth Avenue.

Before Z-Day we always joked about Sixth Avenue. It's not much of an avenue; more like a potholed street with single wide trailers lining each side. We move past trailer after trailer until we come to number 14.

Stuart certainly wasn't lying about knowing my escape path. He expertly finds the "hidden" head of it and scrambles down the large rocks and boulders, into the ravine behind my house. He just as easily navigates the "randomly" strewn razor wire and is up the other side of the ravine before I'm even down the first part. I know I'm holding up Elsbeth, but she waits patiently, watching our backs, as I painfully clamber up the other side and lean my back against my fence.

Sounds echo around us, caught in, and amplified by the rocks of the ravine. I try not to flinch, but with each gunshot, it gets harder and harder. I know what's happening to me: shock. I feel my jeans and my hand is sticky wet with blood.

"What now?" I ask.

"Get inside," Stuart says, "wait and watch."

"Then?"

Stuart shrugs. "You're the thinker. I'm just the soldier." He pushes the tops of three boards and the bottoms swing out. "After you."

I crawl underneath into my backyard and keep crawling until I'm at my patio door. I slowly turn the knob, knowing I'm being overly cautious since there's no way anyone can hear it with the noise going on. We all get inside and stay low.

Elsbeth crawls to the water dispenser in the corner of the kitchen and puts her mouth right up against the spigot. She drinks deep and then nods at us. We each take a turn and I sigh at the soothing wetness against the desert my throat had become. Sitting there, water dripping from our chins, we look at each other in the gloom. I know they are looking to me for a plan, but I don't have one. I was relying on Leeds and his men. I was relying on Big Daddy and the force coming from the Farm. I was relying on something other than myself.

Not the best idea in the zombie apocalypse and I realize my mistake, as I look around my house, the familiar shapes of furniture just hanging out, like they were waiting for me to come home.

"Phase One is going to be a lost cause," I say finally. "That means they'll be heading this way soon."

Stuart nods in the dark. "So not much time then."

"What you thinking, Long Pork?" Elsbeth asks. She taps my head gently. "You have some good thinks in there?"

I sit there, trying to sort through my thoughts when several large explosions rattle them free. The explosions also rattle the house and pictures fall from the walls, shattering on the carpet and vinyl.

"That," I say, "is a great idea."

"Not following you," Stuart says as another explosion rocks Phase One, the blast felt all the way over here.

"What do you think is causing that?" I ask.

"Could be the small store of C4 in my pantry," Stuart says.

"Oh," I reply. "Yeah, well, maybe, but I'm thinking a bit more mundane." I look over at the stove and smile. "For everything we've lost since Z-Day, what has been a constant that's never let us down?"

Stuart follows my gaze and nods. "Take it all down?" he asks. "Leave them nothing but ash?"

"Might as well," I say, "it's all gone to shit anyway. Whispering Pines is over, right? All signs point to yes. Rebuilding Asheville will need to wait. We have to burn it to the ground first." I look about the place I have called home for so long, even pre-Z. "Time to start over."

"Time's wasting," Stuart says, "we have to hurry."

Elsbeth looks back and forth. "What is happening? What are we burning to the ground?"

"Everything," I say. "Thomas Wolfe was right. You can never go home."

CHAPTER TEN

It takes us longer than we'd like, as we go from house to house, turning on the gas stoves. Those that don't have gas ranges do have gas hot water heaters. I let Stuart sever those lines, since I don't think my skills are up to it. Would suck to blow myself up prematurely.

Elsbeth's job is to take the small amount of liquid fuel we can scavenge from the houses (gasoline, kerosene, fucking citronella lamp oil, etc) and pour lines going from the front doors of each house to a central spot at the end of my cul de sac. We're breathing heavy by the time we meet back at my house.

"Yours too then?" Stuart asks.

"No," I shake my head, "it'll cut off our escape route."

"Lucky you," Stuart replies.

"Hey," I snap, "you think this place will last long when everything else goes up? Do you? You're a fucking idiot if you do!"

"Don't fight," Elsbeth says quietly.

"I get ya," Stuart says. "I do. No problem. You're right. It'll catch as soon as Tran's house goes up anyway."

"Right," I say, "Tran."

Stuart looks at me, his brow furrowed. "Tran didn't make it then?"

I shake my head, realizing he doesn't really know anything. He's been dealing with Vance this whole time, in his own hell.

"He killed himself," I say. "He couldn't take it."

"Couldn't take it?" Stuart asks. "Oh…was it his wife? Or the kids?"

"All of them," I say. "We got swarmed."

"Shit," Stuart says, shaking his head. "Poor guy."

"Listen," Elsbeth says. "I hear people? Do you hear people?"

We go silent and then can hear it.

"Jason Stanford!" Vance shouts. "I know you're here somewhere! Come on out, Jason!"

"Why the fuck would I do that?" I say. "He's an idiot."

"Time to get back to work," Stuart says. He looks at Elsbeth. "You know what to do then?"

"Kill," she says, "and don't stop killing. Then run."

"Save yourself," Stuart says. "Find the others if you can. Warn them."

"You will come too?" Elsbeth asks, looking from me to Stuart. "You will run with me? After the killing, right? Save yourselves too?"

"Sure," I say.

"You bet," Stuart nods.

We are such liars.

"JASON! PLEASE!" a woman screams.

"That's not Vance," I say and crawl to the front window for a look. "Holy shit…"

Stuart looks past me to the street. "Doesn't change anything," he says, "we're all fucked anyway, Jace. Stick with the plan. This ends tonight. Hear me?"

"But look, man," I say. "Look at them all."

Standing down the street is Vance and his people. Many have Zs on catch poles, while others have our neighbors tied to lengths of rope, their hands behind their backs, their feet only loose enough so they can walk. Bikers are riding every which way, swirling in and out of the groups, kicking out and laughing at the neighbors, staying well clear of the Zs.

"Do I have to explain what happens if you don't come out, Jason?" Vance shouts. "Was what happened to your friend not preview enough?"

He nods to one of the men with Zs and the guy walks it over to the first person in line: Edna Strom, the Head of Z Cleanup. She and her team handle all the bodies of Zs that get caught in the razor wire and fencing. The irony is not lost on me.

Without hesitation, the man sics the Z on her and the thing takes a huge chunk out of her shoulder before it is yanked back. Edna falls to the road, screaming and screaming, unable to grab at the wound as her instincts want her to. Another man walks over and kicks her in the gut, doubling her over. As she bends, he brings a bat down against her skull. The crack echoes everywhere and she is still, a pool of blood filling the cracks in the pavement.

I look over my shoulder, but Stuart is gone. So is Elsbeth. They've stuck to the plan so I guess I have to also.

"Jason!" Vance yells. "You see how this is going to go, don't you? Maybe not exactly like that. Some I'll keep alive until they turn. Maybe the children? Nothing makes me laugh like watching a bunch of kiddie Zs scampering about."

He chuckles to himself.

"I came across a whole playground of them in West Asheville after Z-Day. They couldn't get out of the chain link fence that surrounded the playground. I just sat there and watched them for hours. I'd go back every once in a while when I was bored. Even thought of bringing my own kids down to play. Like a dog park for Zs! A Z park!" He turns to one of his men. "Write that down. That's happening."

He sighs and looks around.

"Fine. I'm done waiting."

He studies the line of prisoners then starts to point at them. I can hear him singing "Eeenie-Meenie-Miny-Mo" before his finger lands on a victim. I don't know the guy well, Herbert or Gordon or Stan or something, but that doesn't matter. Vance'll get to the ones I do know well soon enough.

"Hey!" I yell as I go to my front door and peek out. "No shootsies, okay?"

"You have my word," Vance smiles. "I'd have killed you by now if I wanted to. I just want to have a conversation."

"About what?" I ask as I walk out into the street, a good thirty yards away, facing him. "What the fuck could we possibly have to talk about?"

"Your friend, Jon, the one your fearless leader, Brenda Kelly, let die? He had a lot of nice things to say about you."

I look about. Brenda isn't one of the prisoners. Vance catches this.

"Oh, I have plans for her too," Vance says. "She plays along and she'll live to a ripe old age. You too, Jason."

"And what am I playing along to?" I ask. "You already started Eenie-Meenie-Miny-Mo without me. That's my favorite. Maybe some hopscotch? Kickball? Jacks? What's you poison, Eddie?"

"Mr. Vance," Vance says. "That's how you'll address me. No one calls me Eddie." His voice catches a little. "Not anymore."

"Is that so?" I ask, watching him closely. I'm counting in my head at the same time, which is as hard as it sounds. I have to skip some numbers and it's more an approximation of counting, but I'm pretty sure I'm sticking to the timing of the plan. "Who used to call you Eddie? Your wife? What's she call you now? From what I've heard, it probably sounds something like 'gggguuuuuhhhhhh blubblubblub'. That about right?"

Even in the dark of night, I can see his face turn red with anger. He grabs one of my neighbors and shoves her at the Zs. Two of them lunge and her arms are flayed open. The handlers yank the Zs back and Vance kicks the woman to the ground. Then he keeps kicking her. And kicking her. Then stomping on her. On her head. Over and over and over and over. His eyes watch me the entire time. He doesn't even so much as glance down at what he's done.

I start shaking, trying to keep it together. I can hear Stuart in my head telling me the same thing. "Keep it together." My hands tremble and I push the pickaxe against my leg, desperate to stop. I shove hard against my wound, hoping the burst of pain will clear my mind, chase the fear away. It doesn't; it just hurts really bad.

"Look at you!" Vance laughs. "Jesus, man, you are a mess. How long did you think you'd actually live in this world? Did you think Whispering Pines was untouchable and you'd grow old with your wife and kids? Maybe have some grandchildren to play with?"

"Yeah," I say, being honest with him and myself. "For a second there, I actually did. Then you came along and shit all over it."

"I shit all over it? I did?" Vance looks at me, his head cocked. "Denial much, Jason? How did you think I learned of this place? A human interest piece in the newspaper? No, sir. I learned from some of the survivors. Those that didn't get blown away at your gate. I did not intend to work my way this far north to the river. I was concentrating on downtown and south. But hearing the stories of men and women and even children that were shot without mercy just for looking for some security, some safe place to call home, well, Jason, that had to be investigated."

He raises his arms and spins around. "And look what I found! Paradise? A new utopia? A true democracy? Hardly. I found a corrupt bitch lording over a bunch of scared and frightened neighbors. It wasn't exactly hard to figure Brenda Kelly out. Well, that's not true, exactly. I thought I had her figured out, we did have a deal and plan in place, but she sent you and your friend Jon to spy on me. That wasn't part of the deal, so I had to up my timeframe a little. Go off book and improvise."

Pacing back and forth, his eyes never leaving mine, he continues, "Didn't work out as well as I would have liked. I had hopes for this place. Oh, well, this part is still good, right? We'll rebuild Phase One at some point. Might be easier just to start with one section anyway."

"Might be," I say, my stomach in knots. My internal clock tells me I have seconds. Just seconds. "Might not."

Vance eyes me then looks about. "You had another friend with you when you went a spying, didn't you? James Stuart? Ex-marine? Where is he now, Jason? I thought he was still laid up in your pitiful excuse for a hospital, but my men say he was missing when they checked. Left a couple corpses behind."

"He could be anywhere," I shrug, "fuck if I know."

I'm usually so good at timing. What's taking so long?

"Fuck if you know?" Vance muses. "Oh, I think you know a lot. That's what I was able to get out of Jon. The man was strong, but not a professional. He only could take so much pain before he started talking. How much pain can you handle, Jason? It'll be easier for both of us if we don't have to find out." He sighs big and shakes his hands, flexing his fingers. "Oh, to fuck with this. Just somebody go grab him, will you? I'm tired of this shit."

With bikers speeding everywhere around me, I have nowhere to run, even if I wanted to, as half a dozen men walk towards me.

KRACKBOOM!

That's the sound that envelopes us all as the first house goes up. It's quickly followed by a second and a third and a fourth. One after the other, the cookie cutter houses in Phase Two explode. I hit the ground as shards of vinyl siding and brick fill the air. Several bikers go down hard from the concussive force of the explosions. The prisoners, my fellow neighbors, all start screaming and duck down, unable to cover their heads because their hands are tied behind them.

Then she comes. Like a vision from a spaghetti western, blades held out from her sides, the glow of Phase One behind her. If she'd had a long duster on, she'd be Clint Eastwood in drag. But she isn't, she's just Elsbeth. And that's quite enough, thank you.

Two bikers go down as they whiz by her, their heads tumbling in the air like stray dodge balls. One of the bikes rams into two men coming at her, they crumple under it, arms and legs flailing about. Elsbeth rolls and comes up, impaling one of the men, eviscerating the other with a swipe. The impaled man's eyes go wide as she brings the blade up through his torso and out his shoulder, splitting him in half, his blood spraying like a geyser.

It is complete chaos as Elsbeth gets up and leaps at two men and two women that are charging her. She hits the first man feet first and he goes down like he's a sheet on a clothesline, just folding around her legs. His back hits the asphalt and the sound of each and every one of his ribs cracking can actually be heard over the continuing explosions. She digs her heels in before she tucks her shoulder and rolls forward off him, both blades swiping at the women before her. Their legs separate from their bodies and they fall, their screams added to the chorus.

The last man looks at her and runs. Smart guy.

The pavement next to her is pocked with gunfire and she rolls backwards over and over until she's able to leap to her feet and sprint towards the next group of Vance's people. They fire well before she gets to them, but their aim is hindered by the absolute fear their faces show. They've watched what she can do.

Elsbeth ducks and dodges, bouncing from foot to foot, never leaving a still target to get a bead on. By the time she reaches them, half have given up, their empty rifles just hanging from their hands. She slices, she dices, and she turns them into chopped shit. The last man, wild with terror, his finger clicking uselessly over and over on the trigger of his empty AK-47, just screams at her and then spits.

Elsbeth stands there for a brief moment; the rare time of stillness, she shows all night. Then she jams her hand into his mouth, yanks out his tongue, and lops it off. The man grabs at his bleeding mouth and runs screaming, as she bounces the tongue in her hand once, twice, then pops it into her mouth. She chews and chews, then her eye catches mine and she stops. She spits the tongue out apologetically and continues her slaughter.

Biker after biker, gunman and gunwoman after gunman and gunwoman, fall under her blades. She shows no mercy, no remorse, and no signs of stopping. From one to the next she rips them apart, sending steaming piles of guts to the ground, more heads rolling, limbs flying. She even does some spin move where she leaves a man intact until piece after piece slowly slides from him, leaving a pile of bloody parts.

All the while Vance is screaming at everyone, shouting for his people to, "FIGHT HER! YOU COWARDS! KILL THE CUNT!"

Then he sees me, still hunched over in the middle of the street and he stalks forward, his eyes filled with rage and madness. I assume it's madness; it could be something he ate earlier. No, no, it's madness.

I get to my feet, my body protesting every movement. I still have the pickaxe in my hand, but it is so heavy, like an anchor connected to my arm. I'd just drop it if I could, but I don't think my hand will comply.

"Jason," Vance hisses, "we could have done great things. Your abilities to work through problems married to my vision of the future? Great things, Jason. Great things."

I can see what's in his hand, but my mind just isn't tracking.

"Why'd you have to spoil it? Everyone has spoken so highly of you. Brenda especially. I will say, in her defense, that she warned me you could be headstrong and a bit difficult at times. But I'm used to personalities like that."

He's closer now, his hand rising, the gleam of metal rising with it.

"You get used to stubborn people when you work in finance. No one wants to be wrong, everyone wants the credit. But you work through that. Don't get me started on the criminal element! Hoo boy! They can be like little children."

It's in my face now, the hole so black, so dark, right at eye level. It's like looking into a bottomless pit, but sideways. And a little smaller than a pit. A bottomless hole? Fissure? Puncture?

"Hello! Jason! I'm talking to you!" Vance shouts. "Jesus, man, I'm holding a fucking Desert Eagle to your eyeball and you space out? What the fuck is wrong with you?"

"Chicken shit," I say. Not sure why. Didn't mean to. Oh, wait, yeah, I know why. "You think you have what it takes to rule in this world? You think your years as a big banker and then crime boss make you destined to lord over us all? You're nothing but a chicken shit."

His face loses some of the confidence; the bottomless hole/fissure/puncture dips a fraction of an inch.

"You think because you were a rich fucking bully you can just take over?" I lean in, pressing my eye right against the barrel of the gun. "Bullshit. Pig shit. Chicken shit. You. Are. Chicken. Shit. Want to know why?" He doesn't answer, but then he doesn't shoot either, so I keep talking. "Because a real man would have put his family down, not keep them locked in a basement like animals. A real man would have done the right thing, the hard thing, the only thing. But not you. You're nothing but a chicken shit."

He takes a step back, his hand now shaking worse than mine. He lowers the giant pistol then raises it again. Lowers then raises. Over and over.

"Oh, fuck you," I say as I bring the end of the pickaxe up into the soft flesh under his chin. "Chicken shit."

His eyes glaze over and he drops to his knees. The Desert Eagle falls from his grasp and the inexplicable happens: it goes off. He slumps to his side, his body still and I look down as a searing pain explodes in my left side. Bright red blood spreads across my shirt just under my ribs. I wonder what organs are right there. Probably ones I need.

"Are you fucking kidding me?" I say as I fall to my knees, my palms pressed to the wound. "A fucking misfire? The bastard drops the fucking gun and THEN it goes off? Fuck me."

I slump to my side, my soon to be dead eyes staring right into Vance's already dead eyes. This is not the last image I want in my head.

"Long Pork? Long Pork! Jace! JASON!" Elsbeth screams as she slides to me. Her hands pat my body and I scream.

"Stop that," I say. "Jesus…"

"We have to get you up," Elsbeth says. "It's not safe. Can you walk?"

"Can I live, is the question," I say, feeling the warmth leaking from my side.

Elsbeth rips my shirt away and looks at the wound. She nods. "I'll be right back."

"What? Don't leave me, god dammit! Elsbeth!"

What the fuck? She'll be right back? Where the fuck did she need to go? I'm fucking dying here!

"Hold still," she says, suddenly right at my side again. Did I pass out a little? Probably.

"Hold still?" I ask. "What the fuck f-AAAAAAAAAAAAAAAAAAAAAAAAAAA! FUUUUUUUUUUUUUUUUUUUUUUUCK!"

I had a vasectomy a few years after Greta was born. Stella and I had decided that we were good with only two kids; a replacement for each of us, is how we saw it. Why am I saying this? Because when the doctor tried to inject the anesthetic, he slipped and ended up piercing the other side of my scrotum. That was the worst pain I had ever felt. Ever.

Until Elsbeth shoves two hunks of red hot metal against the front and back of my side, cauterizing the gunshot wound. That one wins. Not even a contest there. I'll take a hundred more needles to the scrote before I'll go through the old cauterize the wound trick. I mean, she doesn't even offer me anything to fucking bite down on. What the fuck? In all the westerns I've watched, you always offer the wounded guy something to bite down on. A piece of wood, a leather belt, a bullet. Does she? Noooooooo, she does not.

"That'll stop the bleeding," she says. "I'll help you up."

"Up? Why?" I ask even as she's yanking me to my feet. Scrote pain is now third on the list. Standing up after having your side cauterized is second on the list. Not liking this list. Not at all. "Why can't I just rest and we wait for Big Daddy to swoop down and save us? It's a little smoky, sure, but you get used to it."

"Zs," she says, pointing down the hill at the herd coming at us.

"Oh, right, we're still in that world," I say. "Fuck."

"Can he move then?" Stuart asks, his face covered in soot and blood. "Can you move? We have to move."

"I'm seeing that," I say. "But where? I don't think I can get down and back up the ravine."

"You'll have to try," Stuart says. "Come on. Somebody help here."

Stuart's untied our neighbors and several hurry forward to help me through my house and out the back. Good thing we didn't blow it up, eh? That's why they pay me the big bucks.

Stuart doesn't bother swiveling the fence boards and just kicks right through. I can see the stain has pretty much taken over the bandages, yet the guy is still going. Remind me to thank the Marines.

"Hey, Stuart, you're hurt," I say as I'm helped/carried through the fence. "Elsbeth has this really great treatment she knows. We should take a break and let her fix you up."

"Nice try," Stuart says. "Ah, shit."

We all stand at the top of the ravine and you can just feel the despair wash over the group.

"That's a lot of Zs," someone says then I realize it's me as everyone glares. "What? It is."

The ravine is filled with Zs and more are tumbling down to the bottom from the other side. All the noise must have drawn them to us. I'll bet every Z just hanging out down by the river is now trying to clamber up the rocks and boulders to get at us.

Even if we fight our hearts out we can't take them all. Not even with Elsbeth's help.

"Other way?" I say. "Cross the street and go down that ravine?"

"No way through the wire," Stuart says. "This is your path. Only way out."

The groans and moans of the Z herd echo back to us from the street. Doesn't look like we can go the other way even if we try.

"I'll go out fighting," Elsbeth says. "Pa always said never give up. Fight until you can't fight."

"Sorry," Stuart says, looking at Elsbeth. "For killing your pa. Don't get me wrong, I'd do it again to save my friends, but I am sorry he had to die."

Elsbeth watches him; we all watch Elsbeth. She is still holding one of her blades, after all. Then she lets that go and hugs Stuart, her face buried in his shoulder. That's a stunner.

The groans are louder and I look over my shoulder and see a couple dozen Zs shuffling towards us. A few of them catch fire as they get too close to Tran's burning house. Everyone else turns and watches them come. Elsbeth lets go of Stuart and picks up her blade.

"I don't know where my other one is," she says, wiping her eyes. "Poop."

"You can say that again," I say.

"Poop."

"So, down there and fight, or make this a backyard brawl?" Stuart asks.

"Backyard brawl," I say, "I'm too tired to climb down."

He nods. "Backyard brawl it is. Everyone grab something to fight with. A board, a rock, a small stick you can jab in an eye, whatever. Just grab it and keep fighting until you can't."

"Keep fighting until you can't," Elsbeth repeats.

So we grab up what we can and walk through the fence, ready for our last stand in Whispering Pines.

There's no signal given, no war cry, no drums beating as we march to our deaths. It's really more like a bunch of people on Black Friday running to whatever sale merchandise they can get. Kinda makes me nostalgic for the past.

I come at the first Z, one hand clutching a knife Stuart tosses me, while the other hand is pressed up against my side. I'm probably hurting myself more by pressing so hard, but the pain gives me drive, it gives me focus. I jam the blade of the knife right into the eye of the Z and it falls. Taking the knife with it, of course.

"Shit," I say.

I stumble around, looking for another weapon, but I don't have time as a Z reaches for me. Its hands are nothing but bone and sinew and I grab them, snapping its fingers right off. The thing pauses for a brief second and I do have to wonder what's going through its rotten mind. But I don't wonder long as I sweep its legs out from under it and go all romper stomper on it, smashing its head into pulp.

Hands grab me from behind and I jam my elbow up and back, smashing it into a Zs chin, snapping its jaw right off. Did you know the elbow is the hardest part of the human body? It's a good thing to know.

I turn and kick out, sending the jawless Z falling into a group of six more that are hungering for my tasty (yet terrified) flesh. All around me there are screams of rage and pain; screams of violence and despair. Weaponless, I lower my shoulder and charge, plowing right into the Zs. Bet they didn't see that coming!

Of course, being Zs, they are less than stable and we all go down in a pile of flailing limbs. I push up, my hands going through the Z's chest I'm on like fucking cream cheese. Shaking the goo from my hands, I make two fists and start going to town. I rain down some serious beatings on these mother fuckers!

Every wound that's been inflicted on me, every single death I've witnessed, all the bullshit of this fucking world, not to mention the fucking bullshit of the GOD DAMN Whispering Pines HOA, all of that fuels my wrath. I land blow after blow, my knuckles cracking open, my living, red blood mixing with the undead, black blood of the Zs. I don't stop until I'm straddling nothing but pulp then I get to my feet, raise my hands, and scream into the night!

"I FUCKING WIN!"

Then I'm tackled around the waist by two Zs and I go down hard.

Fuck.

They claw at me, fighting each other for first taste. Oh, but they won't be getting it, not this night, no fucking way. I reach up and grab one of the Zs by its head and twist until its head cracks right off its spine. I slam the Z head into the face of the other Z, over and over, again and again, until all I see is a pulpy crater of putrid flesh. I bring my knee up and flip the thing over my head, rolling to my side and shoving up off the ground.

Faceless, but not dead, the Z staggers to its feet, its arms reaching for me. It can't see since its eyeballs are just jelly, but damn if it doesn't hone right in. Fuck it, let it come. As it gets closer I grab its forearms and yank down, ripping its arms right off. Back and forth I slam the thing's own arms against its skull until it cracks open like a rancid melon.

Pop!

Z arms in hand, I close on the next ones. I use them like clubs, bludgeoning the Zs to their final deaths until the arms are shattered and useless. Tossing the shards of bone and flesh away, I try to find new weapons. There are plenty, but they are clutched in the lifeless hands of my fallen neighbors. I finally see what is going on: we are losing.

"Fuck," I say. "Fuck, fuck, FUCK!"

Several Zs, and by several I mean like ten or so, turn about and look at me. I shake my head, ready for them, ready to take my turn at the Z buffet. What was I thinking? That we'd really survive the night? Dealing with Vance and his band of shitheads was hard enough. Pile on one serious herd of Zs? Yeah, good luck with that.

Have I said fuck lately? Yes? Well, let me say it again.

Fuck!

They come at me and I look around, but there is nowhere to go. I have the ravine at my back (Z filled, thank you), houses on fire to my right and left, choking any escape route with flames and smoke, and a fuck ton of Zs just finishing up the appetizer course and ready for the main dish. Which is me.

I can see Elsbeth hacking and slashing, holding her own, but she's surrounded, no way she'll make it to me to save my butt this time. Stuart is bellowing like a Viking berserker, his hands chest deep in a Z as he rips the thing apart bit by bit. So he's occupied. My neighbors are succeeding and failing at varying degrees ranging from "DIE, MOTHER FUCKERS, DIE!" to "OH, GOD! WHY IS IT EATING MY ASS FIRST?" Overall, not a favorable outlook.

But no one likes a tragedy, especially me. And the surest way to turn tragedy into triumph?

"EVERYONE HIT THE FUCKING DECK!" Leeds screams as he, Reaper, John, and Platt kick through the boards of my fence, their M-4s up and ready. "DOWN NOW, YOU STUPID FUCKS!"

Don't have to tell me twice. I dive for the dirt as burst after burst of rifle fire explodes over me. A couple people cry out, not having listened (you should always listen to the guys with the guns), and I hope there's no friendly fatalities. I turn my head and watch as Z head after Z head is pierced by expertly placed bullets. I don't see a single body shot as Leeds and his team clear the yard.

"Get up, Long Pork," John says as he grabs my elbow and yanks me to my feet. "There's more coming, we gotta go."

He's right, I can hear the Zs and see their shadows through the flames and smoke.

"People! If you want to live you will follow us now!" Leeds shouts.

Those not seriously wounded help those that are and we stagger our way to the ravine, following Leeds and his men. It takes them all of five seconds to put the Zs in the ravine down. As soon as the last one falls, the back of its head splattering against the rocks, we all scamper down the rocks and up the other side. Well, I don't really "scamper" as much as cry like a baby with each agonizing step.

John and Platt take lead and clear us a path, making sure every single shot counts, as we come up out of the ravine and into the path of yet another horde of Zs. They are really coming out of the woodwork tonight. Z after Z drop as the team mows them down. Leeds and Reaper step up when John and Platt have to reload, keeping a constant stream of lead pouring into Z heads. The rest of us play back up, smashing and bashing skulls as hidden Zs come at us from the sides.

Neighbors fall, their wounds too much for them, but we get them up, holding them by the waists, by the arms, slinging them over our shoulders. Okay, by we I mean Stuart and Elsbeth and a few others that aren't all fucked to shit like me. I kinda just stumble in a daze, yelling, "There's one!" and "Over there! Look out!" I do my part.

Straight down the middle of Sixth Avenue we go, a swath of undead corpses left in our wake, until we hit Hwy 251. We all look around. Not a Z in sight. Oh, wait, there's one. John takes it down. Now there's not a one in sight.

"I'd like to rest now, please," I say, my head spinning. A black fuzz has encroached on my vision, constricting my sight. The world around me is inside a dark tunnel and I can hear people talking to me. Hell, I can see their mouths move, but fuck if I know what they are saying.

"I'm just gonna sit down," I say to the faces in front of me. "Just take a load off. I'm tired."

Then the tunnel closes and the darkness takes me.

CHAPTER ELEVEN

The black becomes grey becomes light that filters between my eyelids. I squint and blink, bringing the world into focus as soft fingers stroke my cheek.

"I hope this isn't Heaven," I say, my throat scratchy and raw, "because that means you died too."

"Maybe it's Hell and I'm here to kick your ass forever for going off on some stupid suicide mission?" Stella says as her face comes into focus. "Did you think of that?"

"Anywhere you are, no matter the amount of nagging, is Heaven to me," I smile. Ow, smiling hurts.

"Good answer," she says and leans in and kisses me lightly on the lips.

Again with the ow.

"Can I sit up?" I ask, honestly not knowing the answer.

"No," Stella says. "Dr. McCormick says you need to be still for a few more days."

"A few more?" I ask. "How long have I been out?"

"Six days," Stella says. "But I don't know if 'out' is the right word for it. You were raving for a couple days as you burned off a fever. Then there was the day you kept insisting you were fine and fell out of bed at least, oh, I don't know how many times."

"Eight," Greta says from a chair in the corner of the room. "Hey, Daddy."

"Hey, Baby Girl," I smile. More ow. "I'd give you a hug, but I don't think my arms work."

"Mr. Stillwater finally sedated you so you could sleep and stop being stupid," Stella says.

"Mr. Stillwater? Who's that?" I ask.

"Reaper," Charlie says from the doorway. A pretty girl is standing right behind him. I know her. What's her name? Oh, Jennifer, right.

"Those guys are so cool," Charlie says. "John showed me how to take out a Z from two hundred yards!"

"He showed him," Greta laughs, "but he didn't hit anything."

"I was close," Charlie frowns. "With some more practice, I'll be all snipery snipe like. Plink, plink, plink. Down go the Zs, from a very safe distance."

"And what have you been up to, my love?" I ask Stella.

Her face clouds over and she looks out the window at the gorgeous day. I follow her gaze and see we are at the Farm. I'd know that view anywhere. She turns back to me and purses her lips.

"I've been sitting in on the tribunals," Stella says. "Which have turned out to be completely worthless."

"Tribunals?"

"For Brenda Kelly and her cronies," she answers. "We've been deciding if they deserve to be punished for colluding with Vance."

"And I hope the answer was yes," I say, "because she was in league with him for sure."

"Unfortunately, there's no way to prove that," Stella says. "Vance is dead. His people are either dead or scattered to the wind. There is no actual evidence of her collusion."

"What about Stuart? He said he knows she had this all planned with Vance. That they were going to turn Whispering Pines into a prison camp."

"Yes, he was very clear on that when he spoke," Stella says, her eyes locking with mine. "But it's he said, she said. Literally. No one could provide hard evidence."

"Okay, so there's no evidence that she colluded," I say. "I hope, at the very least, she's being tossed out on her ass. She deserves a bullet to the head, but a walk out there with the Zs is fine by me."

Stella doesn't say anything.

"Okay, what is happening to her?"

"You won't like this," Stella says.

"Oh, I'm sure, but tell me anyway."

"She was re-elected as HOA Board Chair."

I try to swallow, but my throat is closing up. I look about and see a glass of water, I reach for it, but Stella gets there first and puts the glass to my lips. The water is sweet, but not sweet enough to wash the sour, bitter taste from my mouth.

"I'll kill her myself then," I say when I can speak again. "I won't even make it clean. I'll gut her and toss her outside the fences. Let the Zs have their way."

"Jace," Stella says, her eyes going to the kids. "The HOA voted. Stuart is raging pissed, but even he understands that. We are nothing if we just toss the rules and laws to the side. She was tried, she was found not guilty, and the HOA voted. It's done."

"I didn't vote," I say.

"I did," Stella says. "For us. I voted against, and it was close, but people are scared and don't know what the future holds."

"Better an evil you know than an evil you don't, is that it?"

"That about sums it up."

"Fuck me," I whisper. I rub my forehead and close my eyes. "This is fucking great."

I can feel sleep pulling at me again and I yawn. Then my eyes open and it's suddenly night. A small candle is lit on the bedside table and I can see someone sitting in the shadows in the corner.

"Hey," I say, just to be polite.

"Hey," Stuart replies. "It was my turn to watch you."

"I need watching?"

"Yeah, you do," Stuart laughs. "You are a shitty patient. Did you used to sleepwalk before then?"

"Before then what?"

"Before the Great Burning of Whispering Pines."

"Not that I know of."

"Then you'll have to watch yourself from now on," Stuart says. "Because your subconscious has taken up a new hobby and it involves random wanderings. Not the best thing in a world overrun by Zs."

"Yeah, I can see the downside," I say. "How are you feeling?"

"Like an old man that's had the hell beaten out of him," Stuart says. "But I'll survive. It's what I do."

"Thanks for letting me in the club," I say. "Surviving is right up there on the list of good shit."

"Amen," Stuart says. "You want me to get Stella then? It's like 2am, but she told me to fetch her if you wake up."

"No, no, let her sleep," I say, trying to push up on my elbows. Ow, ow, ow. Everywhere on my body. Ow.

"Don't bother," Stuart says. "Your nocturnal travels have pretty much put your recovery back a few days. Stay still. That's Dr. McCormick's orders. Reaper's too. I'd listen to him more, he can kill you with his pinky."

"Don't fear the Reaper," I chuckle.

"She told you about Brenda then?"

"Unfortunately."

"What are we going to do about that?"

"What can we do?"

Stuart shrugs. "That's the 64 million dollar question. I don't think anything can be done. We just wait and watch. She'll show her true colors again. She only won the Board Chair again because there are more mindless sheep than thinkers in our bunch."

"Why was there even a vote?" I ask. "Whispering Pines is gone. Burned to the ground."

"The houses, yes, but the neighborhood is still there. Everyone plans to rebuild. It'll be different, but still home. Oh, and the Church of Jesus of the Light is still standing. Preacher Carrey refuses to leave. He's still there, waiting to yell at us for our sins when we get back. So, it'll feel just like home when we rebuild."

"I'm guessing Big Daddy had a say in that," I say. "He still wants to rebuild Asheville, doesn't he?"

"Not sure," Stuart says. "You'll have to ask him. I'm an outsider right now. He's friendly, but not saying a word to anyone. I have a feeling he's waiting for you to be up on your feet before he makes any announcement."

"Okay. Whatever," I sigh. Then the yawns come again. "Fuck. How can I be so tired?"

"You got your ass turned inside out," Stuart says. "Elsbeth saved your life by cauterizing that gunshot. It kept you from bleeding out. But whatever she used was less than sanitary, even if it was red hot. Dr. McCormick and Reaper spent a few days cleaning that wound, just to keep gangrene from setting in. I think it was a lot closer than Stella wants to admit."

"Yeah, this is about as close as I'll get to knowing how a Z feels," I say. "Ugh."

"Just go back to sleep," Stuart says. "I'll tackle you and toss you back to bed if you try to go for a hike."

"Thanks."

It's just a matter of seconds and I'm out again.

This pattern goes on for a few more days before I start to sleep normally. My first day out of bed I spend on the front porch of the big farmhouse, the sun warm on my face. I sit there in one of the rocking chairs and watch the kids running about, playing tag and make believe. Except for Charlie. He's busy off to the side sitting with Jennifer. I know we've had the "Talk" already, but it may be a good time for a refresher course. The zombie apocalypse is no place for accidents of the teenage libido kind.

"First team is going back today," Big Daddy says as he takes a seat next to me. "Julio's leading, with Master Sergeant Platt and Sergeant Baptiste as escorts."

"First team?" I ask.

"To see what can and can't be salvaged at Whispering Pines," Big Daddy says. "Gonna need a full inventory before the rebuild starts. It'll take Melissa and her team a long time to scavenge what's needed as it is, no point in wasting that time by not having a comprehensive materials list."

"Why are you pushing this so hard?" I ask. "I know you can't have everyone stay here on the Farm permanently. There's too many of us. But we could spread out to the other farms and ranches. I say let Whispering Pines go."

Big Daddy shakes his head. "That Brenda Kelly won't let it go. She's like a pitbull, that one. As soon as I saw how resolved she was, I decided to back her." Big Daddy smiles. "Keep your enemies closer and all that bunk. Pardon my French."

"I'll let bunk slide," I smile. "So you aren't really supporting her?"

"I'm supporting you, Hoss," Big Daddy says. "What I said before, the plan to make Asheville something again, is still a good plan. Whispering Pines is part of that, even more so now."

"How do you mean?"

"What we learn from rebuilding Whispering Pines we can apply to Asheville," Big Daddy says. "And with that Special Forces team around, we'll have a better chance at salvaging things. They'll lessen the loss of life."

"But not stop that loss."

Big Daddy shrugs. "It's the world we live in. People are going to die. Big herds of Zs will come at us, up from Atlanta, over from Charlotte, down from Virginia. It'll take them a while with the terrain, but we'd be fools to think those Zs won't eventually make it up into our mountains. They have all the time in the world."

"Okay, so we rebuild with Leeds and the boys watching our backs," I say. "Critter never said where they came from."

"Fort Bragg," Big Daddy says. "They were up here for training when it all went down. They didn't even bother to try to go back. They hunkered down and have stayed off the radar until now."

"Lucky for us," I say. "Hey, where is Critter? I'd like to have a word with him."

"He's off doing Critter things," Big Daddy says. "Which I sometimes try not to think about. He's my brother and all, but I'd say we are two sides of the coin when it comes to morals. What's this word you'd like to have?"

"Why the hell he took off, leaving us to fend for ourselves," I say bitterly. "The guy just ran."

"That he did," Big Daddy nods. "Ran to the river, swam across it, ran all the way to that Humvee then drove his butt right here. Then he drove me and the boys to his 'garage.' It took us all four of the Humvees he had, plus the three pickups and six cars, to get everyone back here safe and sound. So when you have that word, make sure it's thanks."

"Damn," I say, "I will."

I watch him and can see he has more.

"What?"

"Critter and I had us a long talk before he took off to his place," Big Daddy says. "And Julio and Leeds confirm it."

"Again, what?"

"They don't think Vance is alone," Big Daddy says. "I'm not 100% sold on it, but they have a theory that Vance was part of something bigger. That maybe Asheville was his territory and there are others like him out there, staking claim to theirs."

He lets that sink in. I don't like the sinking it does in me.

"What? Some type of cabal?" I ask.

"Maybe. Maybe not," Big Daddy says. "Critter thinks more than a few of the crime bosses may have survived. Makes sense. If Vance can carve out a place, then why can't others?"

"What does that mean for us?"

"It means we watch closely. Not just for Zs, but for signs of other organizations. Maybe from Atlanta or Charlotte. Maybe from over in Knoxville. Or as close as Greenville and Spartanburg. Critter is convinced. I'm leaving that element up to him. We have rebuilding to do. That's our worry right now. If there are other mad men out there, then Critter will let us know."

"Great," I say. "Just great."

Big Daddy nods then gets up. "Yep. Listen, we'll talk more later for sure." He looks past me to the end of the porch. "I think someone has been waiting to see you."

I follow his gaze and see Elsbeth sitting on the railing. She is watching me intensely.

"Yeah, I think you're right," I say. "Thanks for the sunny info."

"Oh, that's just a fraction," Big Daddy says. "But I'll wait until you're better so I don't break that brain of yours."

"Too late."

Elsbeth doesn't come over right away after Big Daddy leaves. She sits there, her eyes boring holes into my skull, until I throw up my hands.

"What?" I say. "Are you going to spend all day staring at me?"

She hops down from the railing and walks slowly over to me. When she gets to my side she looks down on me. I have no idea what the expression on her face means until I see the tears welling up. Then she throws herself against me and hugs me until I cry out. Some of the kids stop playing and spin about, their eyes on me, worried.

"All good," I gasp. "Keep playing."

They do; they're kids.

"Elsbeth?" I say. "Hard to breathe. Crushing bones. Ow."

"Oh, stupid me," she says and lets go quickly. She starts to smack herself in the head then freezes, forcing her hands to her side. "I was scared."

"You didn't look scared," I say. "You looked pretty fucking impressive."

"Not fighting," she replies, shaking her head back and forth quickly. "When you were dying. I almost killed you."

"You saved me," I say. "You stopped the bleeding. That was a Desert Eagle. It took out a good amount of my side." I've had a chance to look at the wound; I'm not exaggerating. There's a lot less of me on my left side than my right. "You were my hero."

Elsbeth keeps shaking her head.

"The doctor lady said that you were 'fected. She wasn't nice to me about it."

"That's just Dr. McCormick. Not exactly a huggy kind of lady. What did Reaper say?"

A small smile creeps onto Elsbeth's face and I'm glad to see it. "He says I could be a medic person. If I want. John says he wants me to be a snipper person."

"Sniper," I correct, "not snipper."

"Yes, sniper person," Elsbeth continues. "Platt says I'm scary enough to be whatever I want. Is that a mean thing? I can't tell with Platt. He frowns so much."

"What does Leeds say?" I ask.

"He says he'd be happy to have me," she smiles. "After some training. He calls me rough around the edges."

"You are that," I say. "So Special Forces, huh? You're suited for it."

The smile fades from her face. "But I have to pay for it."

"You what? Pay for it? What does that mean?"

"Leeds and Big Daddy say the training comes with a price."

"Oh. And what's the price?"

"I have to show them where the rest of the cannies are," she answers. "The ones I know about. They say cannies are too dangerous to keep around." Her eyes tear up again. "Does that mean they'll kill them? They ain't all bad people. Just hungry people. Can I just tell them where the bad ones are? The sick ones?"

I shudder at the thought of what she defines as "sick."

"You tell them what your conscience feels is right," I say. She's puzzled by this. "You know that feeling you get when you do something you know is bad?"

"You mean when Pa would hit me for being stupid?"

My heart nearly breaks. "No, that feeling inside you. You also get a feeling when you do something good. Like when you saved me. Do you remember what feeling you had then?"

"Yeah," she nods, "it felt right. I had to save you."

"Or what?"

"Or my guts would turn squishy and I'd feel all- Oh! That's my cons-, that's my cunsh-, that's what you mean?"

"Yes, your conscience," I say. "It helps you know right from wrong. Good people, like you, have a strong one. At any time you could have left me and Stuart to die. But you stayed."

"You're my friend," Elsbeth says. "Stuart is my friend now too. I didn't want you to die."

"Well, there you have it," I say. "Follow those feelings and you'll do what's right. We'll help the cannies we can, and let Leeds handle the ones we can't."

She nods. "Okay." She looks out at the front yard. I can see her focus go past the kids to the rows of fences and wires. And the ever present Zs beyond. "They keep coming because the life is here. The people and the animals. They won't ever stop coming."

"No, they won't," I say, "but we'll manage them. We'll fight them."

"Until we can't."

"Yep. Until we can't."

She turns and hugs me again then runs down to the kids, joining in the game. She is instantly "It", a role I can see she loves as she runs about, chasing the other kids, the sun shining down on her.

"I think she's adopted us," Stella says as she takes the seat next to me where Big Daddy had sat just minutes before.

"Have we adopted her?" I ask, looking at my beautiful wife.

"As long as she doesn't try to eat us," Stella smiles at me. "Yes. We have."

"Good, because she needs us," I say.

"And we need her, if you're going to get yourself fucked up like this again," Stella says. "Which I expressly forbid to happen."

"Fine by me," I say and reach for her hand. She takes it instantly.

We sit there for a long while, watching the kids play, watching our son fail at flirting, watching life keep going. People come by now and again to see how I'm doing. People I know and don't know. There is hope and expectation in their eyes. I hope I can live up to both.

Life will never be easy. But when was it ever, really?

Just another day on the Farm. One day we'll have to go back, but until then, Z-Burbia can wait. I'm cool right where I am for the moment.

THE END

About The Author:

A professional writer since 2009, Jake Bible has a proven record of innovation, invention and creativity. Novelist, short story writer, independent screenwriter, podcaster, and inventor of the Drabble Novel, Jake is able to switch between or mash-up genres with ease to create new and exciting storyscapes that have captivated and built an audience of thousands. He is the author of the horror/military scifi series the Apex Trilogy (DEAD MECH, The Americans, Metal and Ash) available from Severed Press. He is also the author of Bethany and the Zombie Jesus, Stark- An Illustrated Novella and the YA horror novel Little Dead. Jake Bible lives in Asheville, NC with his family. Find him at www.jakebible.com.

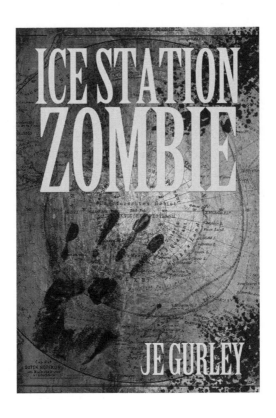

ICE STATION ZOMBIE
JE GURLEY

For most of the long, cold winter, Antarctica is a frozen wasteland. Now, the ice is melting and the zombies are thawing. Arctic explorers Val Marino and Elliot Anson race against time and death to reach Australia, but the Demise has preceded them and zombies stalk the streets of Adelaide and Coober Pedy.

www.severedpress.com

The Coalition

When the dead rose to destroy the living, Ron Cutter learned to survive. While so many others died, he thrived. His life is a constant battle against the living dead. As he casts his own bullets and packs his shotgun shells, his humanity slowly melts away.

Then he encounters a lost boy and a woman searching for a place of refuge. Can they help him recover the emotions he set aside to live? And if he does recover them, will those feelings be an asset in his struggles, or a danger to him?

THE STATE OF EXTINCTION: the first installment in the **COALITON OF THE LIVING** trilogy of Mankind's battle against the plague of the Living Dead. As recounted by author **Robert Mathis Kurtz.**

www.severedpress.com

RANCID

Nothing ever happens in the middle of nowhere or in Virginia for that matter. This is why Noel and her friends found themselves on cloud nine when one of their favorite hardcore bands happened to be playing a show in their small hometown. Between the meteor shower and the short trip to the cemetery outside of town after the show, this crazy group of friends instantly plummet from those clouds into a frenzied nightmare of putrefied horror.

Is this sudden nightmare related to the showering meteors or does this small town hold even darker secrets than the rotting corpses that are surfacing?

"Zombies in small town America, a corporate conspiracy, fast paced action and a satisfying body count- what's not to like? Just don't get too attached to any character; they may die or turn zombie soon enough!" - Mainak Dhar, bestselling author of Alice in Deadland and Zombiestan

www.severedpress.com

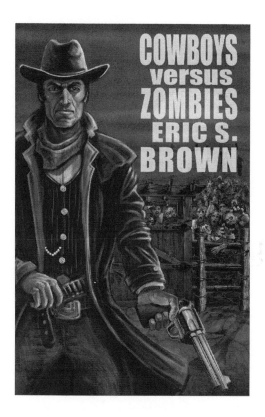

COWBOYS VS ZOMBIES

Dilouie is a killer. He's always made his way in life by the speed of his gun hand and the coldness of his remorseless heart. Life never meant much to him until the world fell apart and they awoke. Overnight, the dead stopped being dead. Hungry corpses rose from blood splattered streets and graves. Their numbers were unimaginable and their need for the flesh of the living insatiable.

The United States is no more. Washed away in a tide of gnashing teeth and rotting, clawing hands. Dilouie no longer kills for money and pleasure but to simply keep breathing and to see the sunrise of the next dawn. . . And he is beginning to wonder if even men like him can survive in a world that now belongs to the dead?

www.severedpress.com

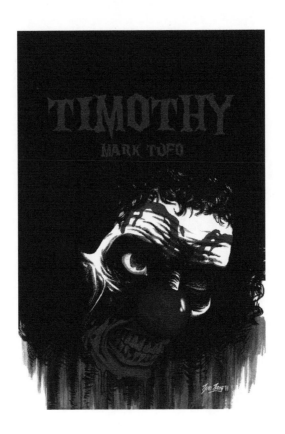

TIMOTHY
MARK TUFO

Timothy was not a good man in life and being undead did little to improve his disposition. Find out what a man trapped in his own mind will do to survive when he wakes up to find himself a zombie controlled by a self-aware virus.

Printed in Great Britain
by Amazon